He stopped beneath a large tree outside the hotel and turned her to face him. "I don't want to waste another minute. One thing I learned over the past few days is the error of putting something off until tomorrow because tomorrow might not come. The way I see it, marrying and loving you is the single most important thing I will do with my life. With Delgato headed for the noose, I don't want to put it off any longer. I can't risk it. I knew it today when I found you unconscious back at the cantina. I want you in my bed tonight."

Rose bit her lip. "What about our wedding and the family waiting for us in Chicago? Giles has been making plans for months now." Her magical wedding hovered on the horizon.

"I'll marry you anywhere and everywhere in every language and religion there is to make sure you're mine, darlin'. We have a few things to work out between us before we go to Chicago and let Giles have free rein. Tonight is for us. I know how I feel about you, and you know how you feel about me. All I've thought about is you for the last few days. I burn for you in ways I didn't think possible."

Her stomach hitched as she gazed into his whiskey-colored eyes and nodded her head. "I don't think I can wait much longer, either. You're all I've dreamed of for months."

He stared into her soul. "Then, let's continue this conversation in your room."

Catching Rose

by

Virginia Barlow

Calhan Brides Series

Catching Rose

Contact Information: info@thewildrosepress.com

Cover Art by *Jennifer Greeff*

The Wild Rose Press, Inc.
PO Box 708
Adams Basin, NY 14410-0708
Visit us at www.thewildrosepress.com

Publishing History
First Edition, 2024
Trade Paperback ISBN 978-1-5092-5264-0
Digital ISBN 978-1-5092-5265-7

Calhan Brides Series
Published in the United States of America

Dedication

For Nellie. You’re one of the strongest women I know.

Chapter One

Chicago, Illinois

May 1, 1872

He left her standing at the altar.

Rose Shayna Tanner had dreamed of a magical wedding and her own prince charming since she sat starry-eyed at Mama's knee listening to fairytales as a child. When Chase Calhan proposed, she thought all her dreams had come true. For weeks she counted down the days with so much excitement she couldn't eat or sleep.

Until today.

A tear dropped onto her cheek and rolled unheeded down her face. Swiping at her face to remove the tell-tale evidence, she gazed out at the remnants of her happy ever after with unseeing eyes.

This part of her fairytale romance should end with her knight in chaps and spurs carrying her away on his dappled charger to his ranch house far away.

And not this.

Another tear followed the first.

The grandfather clock in the corner ticked the seconds away with the sensitivity of a gong, and she winced with every beat.

Clutching the much-read telegram in her hand, she stared at the blurry words swimming before her eyes.

Rose Tanner, Delaney Estates Chicago, Illinois-Stop

See you in church-Stop
Can't wait-Stop
Ranger Chase Calhan, Houston, Texas -Stop
April 22, 1872-Stop

Three hours elapsed past the time for the ceremony to begin while she lingered in the drawing room waiting for her absent Texas Ranger.

Sitting on a satin armchair in her lace gown while her magnolia bouquet drooped in her hands, she peeked through the window at the elaborate canopy covering a large portion of the back lawn. An elegant seating area lay beneath, facing a white archway adorned with red roses and a waiting preacher.

The guests no longer reclined in the comfortable chairs arranged for their benefit and wandered the grass beneath the canopy, sipping wine and asking discreet questions.

Her best friend, Shanna, and her husband, Reese, who happened to be a U.S. Marshal and her absent groom's brother, dealt with the guests offering apologies. They invited the throng to partake of the delicate finger sandwiches and fruit hastily arranged on a long linen-covered table after the groom failed to make his appearance.

Menservants kept their glasses filled while an orchestra played soft music in the background.

Giles, Shanna's butler, directed the proceeding with his usual expert finesse, seeing to the guests' needs before they were aware they had any.

The heavy perfume of her bouquet thickened the air around her and made her nose twitch. She hadn't eaten any breakfast, and her stomach resented the cloying scent.

A crack of thunder split the air, frightening the life out of her, and she jumped in reaction. Glancing out the window, she sighed as rain splattered her perfect wedding, sending the guests scurrying for cover.

Of course. Why wouldn't it rain today of all days?

Rose wilted in her seat and took another swipe at her cheeks. She re-read the telegram, staring down at the cream-colored parchment while she grappled with reality. Every insecurity she entertained during their courtship ran through her mind and tightened her chest.

What if he never came? What if he changed his mind or found someone more exciting? Of average height with brown hair and brown eyes, she possessed none of the beauty fairytale princesses did. Chase didn't seem to mind, and she thought him the perfect man to make her dreams a reality.

What if she were wrong?

How could her enchanted romance come to this?

Clutching her shaking hands tighter around her bouquet, she sucked in a breath and thought hard about what she wanted to do next.

Her fiancé's image flashed across her mind. Standing six foot four inches in his stocking feet, with silky blond hair, warm whiskey-colored eyes, and a killer smile that could melt the skin off a rattlesnake in the middle of January; he had a straight nose, a square jaw, and a mouth-watering body. Although noteworthy, none of his other attributes drew her like the wicked seductive glint in his eye.

As a top officer of the Texas Rangers' "A" company, he had a success rate for catching criminals equal to none, and he knew it. No one got away from Chase Calhan. Lean and muscular, he preferred to do his fighting with a knife and had a talent for getting into trouble. Dangerous, funny, and handsome as hell, he stole her heart the second their gazes met.

Their courtship spanned the last year with sporadic visits whenever he could break from his current case. Every time he took her in his arms, he whispered lustful things into her ear with his smooth Texas drawl. The man could talk her into anything and everything with his sexy knowing eyes, hot kisses, and gorgeous body. And as soon as they were married, she'd let him.

Lost in her daydream, she jumped when her mother opened the door to the sitting room.

"It started raining a moment ago. Reese and Shanna have taken care of the guests, and many of them are leaving. Thank God your ranger didn't come, or we'd all be out standing in the storm. Let's get you into your room and out of this dress. There's no sense sitting here fussing over something we don't know the answer to. I'm sure Chase has a reasonable explanation for his absence."

Only her mother could look past a situation like this and find a rainbow. A sad smile twisted her mouth as she ticked off the number of times Chase said he loved her and stared down at her three fingers. Whispering lustful things in her ear and declaring his love were two different horses. And the discovery made her pause. "If he didn't want to marry me, he should've called the whole thing off and not left me standing here wondering about his sincerity."

Shanna followed her mother into the room, and Rose glanced up.

"Are you worried Chase changed his mind?" Shanna's brow wrinkled with concern.

"Not really." Rose shrugged and ducked her head. "I'm worried about *me*. I'm the problem. He could have anybody he wants. Why me? I mean, look at me." She waved her arms to include her brown curly hair, white gown, and sparkling shoes. "There's nothing special here. I'm *normal*, while he's handsome, smart, funny, and wicked. His kisses make me weak in the knees, and when he's close, I can't think or breathe…" Her voice trailed off while she twisted her engagement ring around on her finger.

Shanna smiled and sank into the overstuffed chair beside her. "There's nothing *normal* about you, Rose. You're the most sensible person I know. You're smart, pretty, and caring. Your heart is bigger than all the oceans put together. You're beautiful, and Chase knows it too. He'd be a fool to let you get away."

"See?" Rose wailed. "I'm pretty, not beautiful. Smart but not clever or intelligent. And who wants to be sensible? You can throw a knife, fight, *and* shoot. I can't do any of them."

Shanna searched her face, waving her hand toward the near-empty lawn. "No doubt, this situation is embarrassing and makes you ask questions you wouldn't otherwise, but I know Chase has a good reason for not being to his own wedding. You are the love of his life, and he would be here if possible. You must know that." The silence stretched between them. "Are *you* having second thoughts about him?"

She dropped her chin, shaking her head. "I know how he makes me feel when he touches me, but I don't know if he experiences the same thing. What if he runs into a beautiful woman who can shoot like Reese? Or throw a knife like you? I'll be dropped like a flapjack when a platter of bacon is served. Maybe he ran into someone more exciting, and she's the reason he isn't here."

Her friend's warm hand covered hers. "First of all, Chase would do no such thing. When Calhans fall in love, it's for life. Second, he has had many opportunities to find someone different, and he hasn't. He wants you, Rose. You're the most loving, giving person I know. You need to believe in yourself before the doubts will go away. I know who you are, and so does Chase. Everyone who came today attended because they love you and you've touched their lives in some way. I would be dead twice over if you hadn't stepped in to save me. And I certainly wouldn't be married to Reese and have the life I do without you. Your generosity and warm, loving heart make you one-of-a-kind."

"Then why isn't he here? If he cared as much as you say, he would be here no matter what he had to do to accomplish it." The bitter words slipped past before she could stop them, and she flushed when her mother shot her a disapproving glance.

Shanna patted her hand, smiling when Rose met her gaze. "Everyone knows your value, but you." Taking her by the hand, she drew her to her feet and toward the door. "Come on. Let's get you upstairs and comfortable. Chase deserves a chance to explain, and we'll give him one. I know something important kept him away, or he'd be here. And judging from his impatience to get a ring on your finger, I suspect he will turn up in the next week or so. And once he does, he'll convince you of his sincerity."

"As my best friend, shouldn't you be threatening to kill him instead of taking his side?" Rose tucked her arm in Shanna's as they strolled through the empty corridor to the staircase.

"And I will if I discover anything less than a life-or-death situation kept him away. At this point, even Reese will help with his demise." Giving her a hug, Shanna left her alone in her own chamber.

Her friend's threat soothed the broken fragments of Rose's pride as she took off her exquisite lace gown and donned a simple day dress. She should be leaving on her honeymoon to experience all the delightful things her new husband promised, not staring with unseeing eyes into the empty fireplace as she fought back tears of frustration and anger. After an hour of soul-searching, she left the emptiness of her chamber for the cozy drawing room and the distraction the family provided.

At one point during the long evening, Chase's two older brothers stood on either side of her, sipping whisky. Dwarfed by their tall, muscular bodies, she experienced a warm glow from their show of support. Max lived in the far north, patrolling the Yukon for the Northwest Territory Mounted Police, while Connor lived in New York and ran the family shipping business. Both stood six foot, possessed blond hair and blue eyes like their siblings, were powerful, dangerous men, and were single. A fact their mother planned to change soon, as she often commented.

"He'll be back. One thing our baby brother isn't is dumb. And he'd be asinine to let a fine-looking woman like you get away. There's a reason he isn't here, and if it's not a damn good one, I'll hunt him down and kick his ass." Max's deep voice covered her in a blanket of warm acceptance, which would have given her the tingles if she weren't so heartbroken.

"Thank you." She sniffed and took a sip of her wine to cover the lump in her throat. Chase had a hell of a family.

"He hasn't been the same since he took you out to the garden after Reese's wedding. He used to have a mind sharp as a razor until he fell in love with you. I'm hoping he gets his ass back here, marries you, and honeymoons until he can't stand up straight." Connor shot her an amused glance. "Once he gets all the lovin' he plans on, he'll be back to normal, and we'll have our brother back. Until then, we hold on as best we can."

Rose ignored the heat flooding her cheeks and nodded, unsure of how to answer.

Connor put his hand on her shoulder. "Keep your chin up, Rose. He'll be back, or I'll help Max track him down. You became part of us the day you accepted his proposal, whether the preacher performed the ceremony or not. If you need anything in the meantime, don't hesitate to ask. You have my address in New York. I'm here anytime, day or night. Send me a wire, and I'll hop on the first train out."

"You are both very kind, and I appreciate the offer." She managed the words past the lump in her throat. As an only child, she never experienced this kind of loyalty and support. The acceptance and love surrounding her made her shake her head in amazement.

"There's nothing kind about it. We take care of our own." Connor gave her a warm smile before he and Max strolled away to speak to Reese.

Madelaine, the oldest of the bunch, widowed four years previous in Santa Fe, had a son named Jeremy and now lived with their mother. Five feet four inches, with a figure as delicate as a China doll, she sported dark brown curly hair, blue eyes, and took after their father. Motherly and sensitive, she kept the conversation light and positive as she bustled around her siblings at dinner.

Maggie, Chase's mother, a lithe figure with graying hair and wise blue eyes, took a seat beside her afterward and told stories about the brothers' growing up years, keeping them entertained until well past bedtime.

When Rose settled into her lavender and cream bedroom, tugging the intricate coverlet to her chin, she stared at the elegant silk-covered wall and gave in to the demons of self-doubt she kept at bay all day. The words of his family floated above the uncertainty like a rainbow above storm clouds. They all believed Chase loved her and would be back, but the cold empty spot beside spoke volumes for the opposition.

Her self-pity lasted all of five minutes until reason won. If his family believed in him, she would too, until something or someone proved her trust in error.

Tossing and turning with anxiety and frustration, the clock struck midnight before she drifted off out of pure exhaustion.

Morning arrived, and her troubled heart burned with a million questions as she dressed in black satin, heralding her mood. The family greeted her with sympathetic smiles as she took her seat and accepted a plate of food. Nothing provided relief for the uncertainty nagging at her, and her breakfast tasted like sawdust in her mouth. Swirling her uneaten food on her plate, she glanced up when Giles entered the dining room and presented Reese with a telegram.

Casting a quick glance her way, the butler lowered his voice for the marshal's ears alone.

The telegram had something to do with her absent

groom. She could feel it in her bones.

Taking the parchment from Giles, Reese gave the missive a quick scan. A glint entered his eye as he folded the telegram up and tucked the paper into his pocket. "Chase is in Houston on an assignment and plans to return in a week or two." His gaze swept over Rose's face. "We will reschedule the wedding when we know more. Giles will make all the arrangements." Shooting a glance at his two brothers, he rose to his feet. "I feel like a smoke. Care to join me?"

All three of them left the dining room without a backward glance.

Shanna stared after them with a frown while Rose leaned back in her chair.

"I didn't think they smoked." The glint in Reese's eye made her want to run after him and shake him until he told her the truth.

"They don't." Her friend gave her a quick smile. "I'm sure everything will be fine. Chase let us know where he is and when he will return. Things are looking up."

"Then why do I get the feeling there's more to the message?" Rose gave up pretending to eat as the knot in her stomach grew. She stared at the closed door and then at Shanna. "If Chase is fine, why did they all leave?"

Shanna glanced from the door to her friend's face. "Reese will tell me if anything is going on. Don't worry. Calhan's have nine lives, and they're hard to kill. Everything will work out. You'll see."

Rose didn't, and the knot in her stomach grew with each passing minute. When her friend rose to go find her twin daughters in the nursery, she followed, but thoughts of the telegram kept her occupied until she gave into temptation.

One hour later, she stood in Reese's empty office and stared down at the folded parchment on the desk. She took a chance he would leave the missive here when he left to go to the station, and her assumption proved correct. Whatever the message contained worried the marshal enough he roped his brothers into a private conversation, and she wondered why.

Max and Connor left for New York following their talk mentioning something about a French sea captain who required an interpreter. Living and working in the Yukon around French trappers for the last few years, Max spoke the language well and agreed to assist.

When Reese left following his secret talk with his brothers, he tugged Shanna to him and kissed her. The pair clung together for several minutes, whispering, and the love they shared permeated the air around them. Shanna flushed and nodded when Reese gave her a wicked grin and disappeared through the open door.

Rose witnessed the scene with a twinge of envy. The love and respect they had for each other shone bright with every glance and gesture, and she wished she could find the same joy with Chase, but first, she had to find him. And marry him.

Until then, here she stood in Reese's office, contemplating the worst sin she'd ever committed. Reading another person's mail. Her sensible mind argued she should trust the brothers' words, but the devil in her wanted to know what they knew and what they didn't tell her. With shaking fingers, she picked the parchment up and unfolded the telegram. Chase's name jumped off the page at her, and she sucked in a breath as she perpetrated the sin.

U S Marshal Reese Calhan, Delaney Estates, Chicago, Illinois-Stop
In Houston- Stop
Saving Grace-Stop
Tell Mama I love her-Stop
Chase Calhan, Houston, Texas-Stop
May 2, 1872, 9:00 a.m.

Chapter Two

Saving Grace.

Rose's gaze riveted on the name and then dropped to the date and time. Her fiancé wired *his brother* at nine this morning, the day *after* their supposed wedding, to inform him he planned to save a woman named Grace. He made no mention of Rose or the important event he missed! An event he wired to say he couldn't wait for. And instead, sent his love to his *mother*. Biting her lip, she agreed with the logical part of her mind. A man should love his mother, *but still!* Sinking into the large leather armchair behind the desk with the telegram still in her hands, she swallowed the lump in her throat.

Tell Mama I love her-Stop

What about her? Shouldn't he mention his almost *wife* somewhere and his supposed love? Placing a hand over her stomach to quell her queasiness, she shook her head in denial. If her fiancé fancied her like he claimed, there would be some mention somewhere.

And who the hell is Grace? The intact portion of her heart cracked as she considered the ramifications. What a fool she turned out to be. The sensible girl who double-checked the facts before jumping into any situation just got fooled by a smooth-talking handsome-as-hell ranger who could kiss like the very devil.

Anger and hurt waltzed through her veins, and Rose's chin rose to the occasion. If Chase Arthur Calhan thought he could get away with breaking her heart and leaving her standing alone before the priest while he saved some female named Grace, he had another thought coming. Four weeks ago, and so in love she couldn't sleep, she kissed her man goodbye before he left to finish up his last case. The sight of his handsome face smiling back at her as he cantered away, leaving her standing on the wooden steps of Tanner's Mercantile in Rock Creek, Wyoming, would be emblazoned on her heart forever more.

"I've dealt with some nasty characters in my time with the rangers, and there is a situation I must take care of before I can make you mine." His deep voice sent shivers down her spine as she envisioned being his in every sense of the word.

Clinging to him, she protested. She worked too dang hard to get Chase Calhan into her life and bed to let him go without a fuss.

"I don't want to spend the rest of my life wondering if today my past catches up to me. I'd rather take care of the situation beforehand. But don't you worry none, darlin'. I've turned in the paperwork stating my resignation from the rangers. I'll be back. And when I do, we'll get married and go honeymooning so we can make my mom a grandma for the fourth time. Now, come give me a good-bye kiss so I have something to remember until I get back." His deep voice sent shivers down her spine as she walked toward him. The wicked grin on his face and the heat in his gaze told her they'd be doing a lot more than kissing in the very near future.

He grinned before kissing her senseless again. "In the meantime, don't let some smooth-talking cowboy steal your heart. You belong to me, and I don't take kindly to rustlers."

"Fine, but if you're not there when the priest is ready to begin, I'll marry the first attractive man I see, raise a half dozen kids, and forget all about you." She teased to lighten the heavy feeling she got when he rode away.

"No. You won't." He growled. "I'm the man you love, and I'll never let you go." And with one more heated kiss, he got on his horse and rode away. This happened the first of April at her parents' mercantile.

Rose's lips twisted as she recalled the scene noting his lack of declaration for her. Belonging to a man and possessing his heart were two different things.

Thinking of the first time she laid eyes on the youngest Calhan, she sighed. He stood next to his brothers at Reese and Shanna's wedding, laughing about something they said. When he glanced her way, their gazes met, and Rose stumbled. A slow smile spread over his face, and a wicked glint shone from his eye as he bowed from clear across the room. When he stood upright, he did a heated inspection of her body, starting from the top of her head and ending at the toes of her kid-skin shoes. His grin widened as his lids dropped over his eyes, and he studied her like a lion gazing at a gazelle he planned to eat for lunch. Her heart did double time, and her breath came fast.

Then he stood in front of her and asked her to dance with such a wicked intense stare she wondered if he read her mind. Rose glanced up and had not been the same woman since.

Brought back to the present by someone's footsteps down the corridor, she folded the telegram and placed it back where she found it. If anyone knew her plans, they'd stop her, and she wanted to gaze into Chase's whiskey-colored eyes when she asked him why he missed the most important day of her life, their wedding. If he intended to break her heart, he could damn well do it to her face.

She jumped in alarm when the door opened, and Shanna stepped into view.

"I thought I'd find you here. What does the telegram say?" Her friend's clear blue eyes met hers. "Don't worry. I'd do the same thing in your situation. So, no judgment."

Rose passed the folded parchment to her and leaned back against the desk.

"Who the hell is Grace?" Her friend's tone sharpened when she said the name. "I don't understand what's happening."

"Me either." Rose frowned. If Shanna didn't know about Grace, who did? "Did Reese say anything more?"

Shanna shook her head and covered Rose's hand with her own. "What do you plan to do?"

She shrugged. "Go to Texas and get an answer. I want to know why he didn't come for the wedding, and I want to know about Grace."

Her friend nodded in agreement. "There won't be another train to Houston until early morning. I'll loan you whatever money you require. And don't tell me 'no.' " She shook her head when Rose opened her mouth. "I want answers, too. And I want you to be happy. What good does inheriting all my family's money do me if I can't use it to help the people I love?"

After arguing for a few minutes, Rose relented. "Fine. But I'll pay you back one way or another."

"Not until you're happily married and all this is behind you. Then we'll discuss the matter." Her friend wore her stubborn expression and folded her arms over her chest for effect. “We’ll figure this out together.”

Rose hugged her. “I don’t want anyone to know my plans in case they try to stop me.”

“I won’t say a word unless I don’t hear from you, and then I’ll send Reese after you.” She meant every word, and her threat wrapped around Rose’s heart like a safety net.

“I have no idea what I’d do without you.” She turned away before her friend could see the effect her words had and hurried to the door.

Determination rang with every step as she made her way to her room. Her logical mind wanted answers, and now she’d get them.

She wanted to believe she possessed some special characteristic, as Shanna suggested yesterday in the drawing room, but deep down, she knew she didn’t. Gazing into a gilt-edged mirror above the porcelain wash basin as she splashed cold water in her face, she paused and stared at her reflection. Brown curly hair, brown eyes, and a turned-up nose didn’t amount to anything more than a normal girl wishing to be a princess, and now reality demanded an accounting. She may be plain. She may be simple and normal, but her tarnished knight on a dappled gray charger would not get away with walking out on her. She would have his explanation for tampering with her heart or die trying.

****

Rose left in the wee hours of the next morning, taking precautions to not wake the family.

Packing her traveling case with her older clothes, she called for a carriage and rode to the train station. Once she purchased a ticket for Houston, she sat down to wait, and her mind returned to Chase, like always, keeping her busy as the train chugged toward her destination. Listening to the clack of the train wheels as they sped along, she fought her imagination as pictures of her fiancé danced in her head. Remembering the feel of his hot mouth moving over hers, the possessive way he held her and touched her, she sighed. Marrying him won first place as the most exciting thing to happen to her. And waiting for him on the day of the wedding, her worst. She could call the whole thing off and go home to Wyoming, but life in Rock Creek bored her to tears without Shanna there. Chase carried her away to a land of love and adventure, too magical to be real. Without him, her future loomed like a waterless walk in the Sahara with no shade and no hope of rescue.

Rose sighed over the pitiful image and shook her head. No one could change her future but her.

Studying the other passengers, a wistful sigh escaped when a young couple whispered together on the seat in front of her. An older couple two rows ahead on the other side of the train car held hands while his wife napped on his thin shoulder.

Rose shook her head. Marriage, romance, knights, love, and happy ever after. Did she notice because hers eluded her?

Assessing her fellow passengers for individuals traveling alone, her gaze fell on a single man four rows ahead of her, frowning at a dark-haired woman and her busy four-year-old son who sat across the aisle.

She knew the child's age because he told everyone his name, Tommy, and held up four fingers announcing his time on earth. His mom shushed him and apologized to the single man, who settled back for a nap with an annoyed sigh.

She would be a good mother if she had the chance depending on what she discovered in Texas. And if her fears proved correct, and Chase found another? Her heart thudded with loneliness as she swallowed the lump in her throat. Then she would hold her head high, tuck her heart out of harm's way and get on the first train out of Texas, no matter the destination.

The clack of the train wheels along the track mocked her with their song. *Saving Grace. Saving Grace. Saving Grace.*

In desperation, she lifted the collar of her jacket over both ears and pretended to sleep. An event which eluded her more and more with each passing mile.

Arriving in Houston an exhausting two days later, Rose stepped from the train onto the covered wooden platform and wilted. The heat and humidity weighed her down, making her pink calico dress stick to her in a matter of minutes. The air smelled of the sea, oil from the locomotive, and the scent of leather.

Finding her sunshade, she snapped it open and lifted the pink ruffled affair over her head. The same color as her dress, Chase bought it for her the day before he left the last time. She brought the object to Houston to protect her delicate complexion. Although, on second thought, the article would come in handy if he warranted a smack over the head.

Gripping the handle of her traveling case with her other hand, Rose gazed around with interest. Houston train station bustled with activity. Not as busy as Chicago but busier than she expected. In Chicago, she had Shanna and the menservants. Here, she had no one.

People swarmed around her as they rushed about

their business, like ants gathering stores for the coming winter. Standing alone in the middle of the platform, someone bumped into her, knocking her sideways, before rushing away.

"Hey!" She tightened her hold on her traveling case and lifted the sunshade back over her head. A moment's hesitation took hold as she considered the hordes of people around her and her vulnerability. Things were different without her six-foot-two hero in chaps and boots.

The brown-haired woman and Tommy hurried past in the opposite direction.

Shaking the worry from her head, she lifted her chin and squared her shoulders. She came for a reason, and anyone who got in her way better watch out. Blowing a wisp of hair out of her eyes, she surveyed her surroundings. Hot, sticky, and tired, she wiped the perspiration from her brow with her forearm, still clutching her case. As soon as she got a little space, she planned to remove the jacket she wore. Night lingered over the city when she left Chicago, and she wore the jacket for warmth. Her seat on the train had been drafty and uncomfortable. So, she kept her jacket on as a layer of security between her and the other passengers. Now, it added to her discomfort.

Standing on tiptoes and weaving side to side to see past the milling crowd, she caught sight of a line of hackney carriages waiting for passengers out on the street.

Perfect.

Clutching her valise in one hand and her parasol in the other, she hurried in their direction.

Signaling one of the carriages, she told the driver to

take her to Texas Ranger Headquarters and sank onto the leather seat with a sigh as the driver closed the door. The empty interior of the carriage quieted her nerves as they rolled away from the depot. Queasy with anxiety over what she would find, she hadn't been able to eat or sleep. And wouldn't until she gazed into Chase's eyes and asked her questions. Rose set her case on the floor of the carriage and snapped her sunshade closed, ignoring her rumbling stomach. Once she knew the truth, she would adjust her circumstances as befitting the situation. Marry Chase or dump his body in the Rio Grande.

Placing her sunshade beside her case, she folded her arms and gazed out the little window at the city. The carriage rumbled over the cobblestone streets and turned a corner. She should be wrapped in her new husband's arms in a romantic hotel in France, not bouncing along the arid streets of Houston, Texas, searching for her missing groom.

Closing her eyes as the hackney traveled across the city, she wilted against the seat and gave in to the rumbling of the cobblestone street. Lord, her body ached from all the jostling, but she knew when she lay down later tonight, she wouldn't sleep. She couldn't. Not until she knew the reason he left her standing at the altar.

Frowning, she stared at the opposite wall of the coach. Chase would do anything for anyone. His easy-going nature and wicked smile were two of the many reasons she loved him. Loyal and honest to the marrow of his bones, he kept his word no matter what and would give his last piece of bread to help another. So why now and why her? Nothing of her current situation made any sense.

Rubbing the weariness from her eyes, she withdrew

a kerchief to dab at the perspiration on her brow and froze. The cloth smelled of Chase's cologne, and a knot rose in her throat as she remembered walks in the moonlight and his sexy drawl when he called her darlin'. She wanted children and grandchildren, picnics, birthdays, anniversaries, and Christmas', walks on summer evenings, ice skating on the lake, and cuddles in front of the fire. Hell, she wanted a lifetime with him, but most of all, she wanted his heart and the fairytale wedding she dreamed of. She would get none of those things if she didn't get the answer she hoped for.

The hackney carriage drew to a stop in front of a large building, and she sighed.

"Here you are, miss. Headquarters of the Texas Rangers." The driver helped Rose from the carriage and set her valise at her feet.

"Thank you." She paid the man and turned to face the large brown building, her gaze wandering from the flat roof down the stucco front to the street at her feet.

This is it. Closing her eyes, she focused on taking deep breaths to calm the nervous flutters in her belly. For the first time since she set eyes on Chase Calhan, she did not imagine them naked in bed together but envisioned wringing his neck. Squaring her shoulders for the meeting ahead, she marched in the front door.

****

Chief Walter M. Tafford, head of "A" division in Houston, crossed his hands over his ample belly, leaned back in his chair, and propped his boots on his desk. His dark gaze wandered over Miss Rose Tanner with interest. She wore her brown, curly hair plaited and tied behind her back with a pink bow. Clear brown eyes sparkled up at him when she dipped a little curtsy. Chief

Tafford guessed Miss Tanner to be around five feet three inches tall, weighing approximately a hundred pounds. Her pink calico dress clung in all the right places revealing a slender well-formed body, the kind a man dreamed about. Not too big and not too little, she would fit inside a man's arms just right. Looking her over from her head to toe, he whistled inwardly. A real beauty. No wonder Ranger Calhan blew into town anxious to wrap things up and head back to Chicago. If *he* had a girl like Miss Tanner waiting on him, *he'd* be in a hurry too. He saw the flash of annoyance in her eyes when he didn't answer her question and figured she could be a handful when she got riled. Better and better. A woman had to have a little fire to be interesting. And she had his attention. The chief shook his head. Ranger Calhan was one lucky son of a bitch.

Rose cleared her throat and folded her arms, waiting for his answer. Her foot tapped against the wooden floor while she faked a nonchalant attitude.

Chief Tafford spit tobacco into the spittoon beside his desk and wiped his mouth with the back of his hand. He received a telegram from Ranger Calhan's brother earlier in the day and couldn't tell her any more than he told the marshal.

"Ranger Calhan left for San Antonio to catch a man he's been hunting. He assured me he would take care of the situation within the week."

She stared at him. "Chase left for San Antonio to find someone a week ago, and you haven't heard from him? Not even a telegram?" Her soft melodious voice belied the flash of fire in her eyes.

Chief Tafford nodded. "My men go out on assignment for weeks at a time with no word. It's not unusual to hear nothing for months. Ranger Calhan can handle this."

The lady clutched her bonnet in front of her with white hands and shifted her feet. Her traveling case sat beside the door. She must have come here straight from the train station. Her expression ran rampant with emotion.

"Fine. I have one more question. Who is Grace?" Her voice shook, and her gaze narrowed.

The chief uncrossed his boots and dropped them to the floor. "I have no idea. Never heard of the woman."

Miss Tanner's jaw tensed, and she stared at him as if assessing the truth of his statement. Poor little thing must be having a hard time dealing with the ranger's absence.

Rising to his feet, he walked around in front of his wooden desk and leaned back with his arms folded. "There's nothing to worry about, Miss Tanner. Why don't you go on back to Chicago and wait for Ranger Calhan there? I've been in contact with Marshal Calhan in case something goes wrong, but this is no business for a woman to get caught up in." Taking her arm, he steered her toward the door. "I assume you need a hotel since it's too late to take the train tonight. Why don't we get you a nice room at the Depot Hotel so you can catch the early train back to Chicago? I will have one of my men escort you. A pretty girl like you shouldn't be out on her own."

The lady dug her heels in. "And if I refuse? I want answers, not a pat on the head and an escort to the train depot."

Chief Tafford frowned and scratched his whiskers. A lady this enticing had no business running around without a man to keep her safe. "My men will handle this." As the chief opened his office door, a sudden thought struck him. "Do either of the Calhan brothers know you're in Houston?" A familiar man would come in handy if Miss Tanner planned to be difficult.

She straightened, her chin lifting as she met his gaze. "No, they do not." Tugging her arm from his grasp, her chin lifted another notch. "Thank you for seeing me and giving me information about my fiancé." Picking up her traveling case, she speared him with her gaze. "I will see my own self out."

She walked away without a backward glance.

Chief Tafford shook his head as his gaze followed her out. Spunky, beautiful, and full of passion. Ranger Calhan had all the luck. What he'd give to be twenty years younger with a woman like her on the market.

He hadn't gone two feet before Ranger Kaplan stepped to his side.

"There's a telegram for you, sir. I set it on your desk." He stared after Miss Tanner with a frown. "Who is she?"

Chief Tafford studied the man beside him. Dark, brooding, and possessing a penchant for intrigue, Kaplan seemed to know more about his communications with his rangers than he did.

"A visitor who requires a ride to the Depot Hotel." Calhan requested information about his family be kept minimal, and the chief agreed.

"I'd be more than happy to escort her, sir."

Ranger Kaplan didn't like being sent on errands, and the fact he volunteered surprised the chief. Staring after the ranger as he escorted his visitor out, Chief Tafford shook his head. There's no telling what a beautiful woman could get a man to do, and he figured Miss

Tanner could get whatever she had a mind to. Sighing, he strolled back to his office and sat down to read his telegram, putting the matter from his mind.

Chapter Three

Rose stalked toward the door. Nice, but delusional. If the chief thought she planned to sit in a hotel room and wait for the men to handle things, he had another thought coming. And she wouldn't be returning to Chicago until she had answers.

"So you're Miss Tanner. I am Ranger Kaplan. Chief Tafford sent me to see you to the Depot Hotel. If you will follow me, I'll get us a carriage." A tall man with dark hair and brown eyes approached. His gaze wandered over her face and body with interest before returning to her eyes.

"Thank you." A carriage ride she didn't have to pay for would be welcomed to preserve her funds. After her meeting with Chief Tafford, she relaxed a little of her anger against Chase. He claimed he didn't now Grace, and the possibility existed her errant fiancé had a valid excuse for not being at the wedding. Either way, she would know the truth before the week expired.

Stepping out onto the street, she took a minute to get her bearing as Ranger Kaplan ordered a carriage. Her mind traveled over various scenarios as she waited. The obvious one being the chief didn't know about the other woman if Chase kept her existence a secret. Twenty minutes later, she sat back on the leather seat facing the ranger.

Something in his face made the hair on her arms

stand on end. His gaze flickered over her, and a smile turned his lips up. "You are engaged to Ranger Calhan, are you not?"

"I am." She wore his ring for now. "Why do you ask?" Chase told her none of his fellow Rangers knew about her or their wedding except Sam, his partner, and the chief. Her suspicions about the man multiplied. He knew her name without being introduced, and her gut said the chief didn't enlighten him.

The ranger shrugged. "Calhan talks about you all the time, and now I have a face for the name."

He was lying, and the way he said the words made her wonder if knowing her face was a good thing. Turning away to discourage further conversation, she gazed out the little window until the carriage drew to a stop.

Disembarking, Kaplan helped her down and took her case. Inside the lobby, he gave the desk clerk her name and waited until she paid and acquired her key before motioning her aside.

"I plan to keep an eye on you until Ranger Calhan returns. I will meet you in the hotel dining room in an hour. Let me see what room the clerk gave you." Taking the key from her surprised fingers, he flipped the tag over and read the number. With a smile, he handed her the key and touched his hat. "See you soon."

Later, she could never decide if the fact the ranger demanded to see what room she stayed in made her change her mind or his high-handed manner. No one *kept an eye* on her without permission. Not even Chase.

As soon as his carriage disappeared down the street, Rose demanded her money back and walked away, holding her case tight against her side. Halfway down the next block, the hotel Excelsior stood across the street, facing her. The two-story, white-washed building with a black metal railing on the top floor sported a flat roof like every other building in Texas and looked like a nice place.

Rose tugged her traveling case higher. The Excelsior would have to do, because she didn't have the energy to walk much farther and didn't want to spend more money on a hackney. Glancing both ways before crossing the busy road, she strolled inside the hotel, asked for a single room, and paid the man. Ignoring the curious stares of the men sitting around the bar, she took the key, and gripping her case against her, marched up the stairs to find room twenty-five.

The room smelled like stale cigar smoke and cheap whiskey, making her want to gag. Rose shut the door and bolted it before setting her valise on the bed. Crossing the room, she lifted the bottom pane of the window for some fresh air. Drawing the pale-yellow curtains aside, she leaned out to gaze at the city. She sucked in a deep breath, closed her eyes, and pictured Chase's handsome face smiling back at her. Several minutes passed by while she focused on her breathing and wished happy endings happened in real life.

When her eyes opened again, she jerked back in panic.

Ranger Kaplan stood across the street with his hands on his hips, gazing up and down the road! How the hell did he know she changed hotels or what direction she took? She didn't agree to his command to meet him. Something about his interest and the way he lied made her nervous.

Rose bonked her head on the window pulling it back

inside and shoved the curtains closed, putting her back to the wall. Her breath came fast between her parted lips. Did he see her?

Peeking through the drapes, she discovered another man beside Ranger Kaplan deep in conversation, and the knot in her stomach grew. They pointed at several more hotels lining the street and walked away.

She blew out a breath of relief. She checked into this hotel under her mother's maiden name, so if they asked the desk clerk, they wouldn't find her. If she were sensible, she'd jump on the first train back to Chicago, but right now, finding the truth about Chase's defection took precedence. That and finding out about Grace.

Until then, she made no promises.

Taking a seat at the little table next to the window, she gazed at the cheap hotel room. A narrow wooden bed stood against one wall covered with a patchwork quilt, and yellow calico curtains hung from the window opposite the door. Opposite the bed, several hooks were mounted on the clapboard wall to hang clothing on. The table where she sat held a small porcelain pitcher and bowl with a round mirror above it on the wall next to the window. A chamber pot peeked from beneath the bed, and she sighed. Either it or the outhouse out back. Neither one offered much of a choice as far as personal needs, but then she'd grown used to Delaney Estates and the luxurious room Shanna kept for her.

Her room there boasted a wide luxurious bed with a lavender and rose floral coverlet complimenting white gilded furniture. A sprawling marble fireplace stood on one wall keeping the room toasty warm on cold winter nights, and she had her own indoor bathroom where she could bathe and take care of her personal needs. Her bedroom window overlooked the flower gardens in the back of the two-story house, and when she opened the pane in the spring, the scent of the blooms filled her room with their delightful fragrance. The entire area at Delaney Estates had to be three times bigger than this little cubby hole.

Rose's mind returned to the problem at hand. Something about the whole situation with Ranger Kaplan gave her the creeps. Did Chief Tafford order him to make sure she got on the train to Chicago as he suggested? Rose frowned. No man controlled her destiny or her destination, least of all Ranger Kaplan, and she would have to be extra careful he did not interfere.

Chewing on her bottom lip as she thought the situation over, her stomach rumbled, reminding her she hadn't eaten much breakfast. With the possibility Chase might have a valid excuse for breaking her heart, her appetite had returned, until she remembered Grace.

The grumbling in her stomach grew louder by the second, so she rose to her feet, hoping the hotel served lunch this late in the afternoon. Patting her hair into place and splashing cold water on her face, she situated her traveling case and locked the window. Grabbing her reticule, Rose left the safety of her room and ventured downstairs. One glance at the bar area convinced her she should find food elsewhere for men, tobacco smoke, and the smell of liquor permeated the room.

Lifting her chin as she stepped out on to the wooden boardwalk, she risked a quick glance up and down the street before heaving a sigh of relief. Neither man could be seen, which suited her fine. Opening her parasol, she crossed the street and walked halfway down the next block in the opposite direction to a restaurant she spotted earlier. The checkered curtains covering the windows beckoned her, as did the smell of freshly baked bread.

One hour later, she left the establishment with a full stomach and a smile. The homemade soup and thick scones did the trick, and she could think again. The waitress told her the stagecoach office stood near the train tracks, so Rose hailed a hackney carriage and asked the driver to wait when she arrived at her destination. Inside she purchased a one-way ticket to San Antonio. The only stage left at six in the morning and cost her fifteen dollars. Frowning over the amount, she paid the man and did a quick calculation. If the rest of her journey continued to be this expensive, she'd be out of money before the end of the week.

Tucking the rest of her bills inside her reticule along with her ticket, she returned to the hotel and hurried to her room. Turning the key in the lock as soon as she closed the door, she pushed the small table against the door and added the chair for good measure. Rose didn't like how the men stared at her when she walked past and knew she had taken a chance traveling alone. She hadn't considered the danger important until one of the cowboys by the bar asked her if she'd join him as she sailed past. Chase would be furious if he found out. Or not, depending on the true nature of his feelings.

Opening her reticule, she retrieved her pistol and placed it on the nightstand next to the bed. As she removed her night rail from the case, she thanked the stars Reese taught her to shoot after Shanna informed him she didn't know how. Her friend gave her the pistol as a present afterward, saying friends made sure friends knew how to shoot.

Undressing behind the small screen, she folded her

pink gingham dress and placed the item back in her traveling case. Twisting her engagement ring on her finger, she wondered for the hundredth time what Chase's answer would be when she demanded to know whether or not he loved her. She wished he were here to hold her in his arms and tell her everything would be okay like he used to before he broke her heart.

Tugging the patchwork quilt back, she slid beneath the cool sheet with a sigh. She didn't blow the lantern out beside her bed because the darkness and noise of the hotel scared her more than she thought it would. Lying awake for hours, Rose jumped at every sound, and the unfamiliar smells of cheap whiskey and cigar smoke didn't help.

Boots walked up and down the hall. Women laughed. Doors opened and closed. Rose sighed. She vowed to get the truth at any cost, and the universe tested her resolve.

The people in the room next to hers were jumping on the bed. The headboard thumped against the wall next to her head, making it difficult to sleep. When the thumping got louder and faster, she sat up, clutching the quilt to her chest. She considered hitting the wall and telling them to quiet down when the man moaned and the woman screamed.

Dragging her pistol onto her lap, she glanced at the wall. What in the world was he doing to her? Should she go for help? Glancing at the door, she bit her lip, unsure if she dared leave the safety of her room unless it was a matter of life or death.

Then, the woman screamed "yes" over and over while the man moaned.

Rose didn't know what to do. First, the woman

sounded like she could be in pain. Now, she didn't know for sure because the woman yelled "Oh God" again and again. Glancing at the door as the headboard thumped faster, she wondered how someone could jump on the bed so fast they took the Lord's name in vain. She never wanted to scream "Oh God" when she did it. The thumping grew so loud; she clapped a hand over both ears, and right when she thought the bed would come through the wall, the couple gave a loud scream, and all grew quiet.

She stared at the wall and waited. The deep voice of the man said something, and laughter erupted from the woman. Rose shook her head. City folks were difficult to understand. Making a mental note to ask Shanna about the strange behavior, she replaced the pistol on the nightstand and lay down with a sigh. She would be happy when this was over, and she could move on with her life. Whatever that might be.

Rolling to her side, she tucked her hands beneath her cheek and thought of something pleasant to keep her mind from overthinking. She must get some rest so she could face whatever tomorrow brought. The problem with pleasant thoughts is they involved Chase and what she supposed her life would be like with him. Turning to her other side, she hit her pillow and closed her eyes. She thought about the most boring thing in the world, Rock Creek, and her plan worked. For the next thing Rose knew, a rooster crowed in the distance.

Jumping up, she dressed and packed her traveling case, glancing out the window while she brushed and plaited her hair. The sun had not risen yet, and pink lit the distant horizon behind the line of stucco buildings. Replacing her pistol inside her reticule, she snapped her traveling case closed, ready for whatever came next.

Hurrying downstairs, she called a hackney carriage. Twenty minutes later, she handed her traveling case to the stagecoach driver and took her seat inside.

Three men sat inside the coach, staring when she climbed in. Sliding to the far corner, she gripped her reticule in her lap. The weight of her pistol calmed her. They should be in San Antonio six days from now, and unless other passengers arrived soon, the journey would be a long, awkward ride.

A woman and a small child climbed in a few minutes later, to her satisfaction. She had never been so glad to see another woman in her life and smiled wide with welcome. The woman shook her hand and settled her son on the seat next to her.

Rose hugged the small victory to her chest. Things were looking up.

The humidity damn near killed her. The coach proved stuffy, and whatever breeze wafted in the windows made her hot and sticky.

She shifted in her seat.

The little boy fell asleep, thank God, after spending the first three hours crying. Dust rolled in and settled on their perspiring bodies, making an uncomfortable situation worse.

Removing her kerchief from her reticule, she wiped her face and grimaced at the dark, dirty smudges. She didn't mind the heat or the screaming child. She didn't mind being scrunched up inside the stagecoach or the hot stickiness of her body. But she did mind not knowing where she stood in Chase's life and heart. Once upon a time, she would have followed him into hell but not now.

They arrived in San Antonio without incident a

week later. The clock struck noon when Rose stepped from the stagecoach onto wobbling legs and stiffened her knees for balance. She hadn't been able to straighten them for hours, and the blood flowing to her feet pricked her like pins. Accepting her traveling case from the driver, she gazed around. Where to now? She had no plan other than to find Chase.

And Grace.

Her gaze fell on an eating establishment farther down the street, and her stomach grumbled. The stagecoach stopped for fresh horses daily, and the passengers were fed. The greasy beans, cornbread, and gruel the stage stop offered turned her stomach. She hadn't eaten much of anything for days, and her stomach let her know about it.

Stepping across the street lugging her traveling case, she stared at the long boardwalks disappearing in both directions. Weary from her long ride and hungry, she sighed with frustration.

"May I be of assistance? You look lost." A man standing nearby smiled and offered a hand up onto the boardwalk.

"Thank you." Setting her case down by her feet, she adjusted her hat and peeked at the man beneath her lashes. Good looking with dark hair, piercing blue eyes, and a wide smile, he sported a handlebar mustache and dressed like a gentleman in a tailored suit, hat, and leather shoes.

The man bowed from the waist. "I am Jonathon Matthews, at your service."

Rose smiled and dipped a curtsy. "Miss Rose Tanner."

The warmth of his hand holding hers made her

shiver. If she were not in love with Chase, this man would give her goosebumps.

Mr. Matthews gazed around. “I notice you arrived with the stagecoach just now. Do you have family or friends coming to pick you up?”

She shook her head. “They don’t know I’m here. I traveled alone because I’m looking for someone.”

“Ahhhh.” His gaze sharpened on her face. “It is not safe for a beautiful woman to travel alone. Especially in a strange city. Let me help you get settled into a hotel so you can conduct this search.” Glancing down the street, he whistled for a carriage. “I’m staying at the Menger Hotel. It is a well-known respectable hotel and one of the best in the city.”

Rose bit her lip, too tired from the long drive and lack of sleep to care much about where she ended up as long as the room contained a bed. “Thank you, but I don’t have much money. I need something less respectable if the price is too high.” She planned to keep the amount she borrowed from Shanna to a minimum.

Mr. Mathews laughed. “They are moderate in price. If you’re short on funds, allow me to share my ride since I am returning to the hotel just now.” He met her gaze. “The Menger is a nice hotel. They do not allow rough customers to frequent their establishment. So you will be quite safe.”

Rose hesitated for a minute or two, unsure. Did she dare trust a stranger? Studying him while she checked with her gut, she relaxed, for his blue eyes shone with sincerity.

“What have you got to lose? Alone you will attract unwanted attention, especially on foot. You never know what dangers await.” A carriage stopped beside them as he spoke.

The man had a point.

Allowing him to help her into the hackney and settle her traveling case, she leaned back against the leather seat, and they rode in silence. Staring out the little windows, she searched for her fiancé's face in the sea of people they passed. The breeze blew against her hot face smelling of sea, smoke, and horses. Rose sighed and shifted in her seat. Her backside ached from all the riding, and her legs refused to be folded one more time. Rubbing her knees as she studied her surroundings, she stiffened her resolve, undeterred in her mission. What path she took after this, no one knew because everything depended on what she discovered.

When they arrived at the Menger, Mr. Matthews helped her alight and retrieved her traveling case. She gazed up at the two-story stucco building in surprise. Floor-to-ceiling pane glass windows faced the street on both stories making the building appear very modern and elegant. A peaked roof rose in the front with the words Menger Hotel beneath it, and trees shaded the walkway out front.

"Thank you for the escort, Mr. Matthews." Her gaze rested on the double doors at the front, and she jumped in surprise when her companion took her hand, kissing her fingers.

His blue eyes traveled over her face before meeting her gaze. "If you need something to eat, let me recommend the dining room in the hotel. The food is excellent. I am in room 204 if you need further assistance."

Rose blushed. Handsome and kind, Mr. Matthews would make some lucky woman's heart rate speed up but not hers, not while she had unfinished business with Ranger Chase Calhan. Giving her companion a small smile, she turned toward the entrance to the hotel, and a prickly sensation tickled the back of her neck as if someone stared at her. Glancing around, she detected nothing and no one. Picking up her traveling case, she hurried into the lobby so she could check in and begin her search for her missing fiancé.

Chapter Four

An hour later, Rose stepped out of the hotel and hailed a hackney carriage. She told the driver to take her to a good restaurant and stared out the windows as they bounced along the cobblestone roads. Where could he be? She studied every man they passed, but none of them were familiar. After a nice dinner at a local cantina, Rose returned to the hotel. For four days, she had searched every establishment she could find and came up empty handed. Passing Mr. Matthews several times in the reception area, she accepted an invitation to dinner with him in the hotel dining room. Her funds grew more depleted by the day, and if she didn't find her fiancé soon, she'd have to wire Shanna for more money. She cut her meals back to two a day to preserve what little she had left and ordered hot tea to her room at lunchtime to ease the hunger pains.

On the fifth day, Rose hired a hackney to take her around the entire city. Her fiancé must not be in the area she frequented, or she would've found him by now. Leaning against the side of the hackney, she stared out the window. She could afford one more day in San Antonio, and then she'd have to wire Shanna to buy a ticket home. Disappointment gnawed at her stomach as she surveyed the people on the street with glazed eyes. The driver turned a corner, and Rose spotted a dappled gray stallion tied to a hitching post outside a church.

Aries. Only Chase used a purple woven saddle blanket. Sitting up, she peered out the window with interest as she passed by. A flash of purple caught her eye beneath the well-worn saddle.

"Stop! I want to get out." Hurriedly she paid the driver and stepped out onto the busy street as soon as the driver found a place to stop. Turning back the way they came, she picked up her skirts and ran the block and a half back to the church.

Stepping up to the stairs, she peered up at the cream stucco structure with the stained-glass windows. Chase wouldn't come to a different denomination's place of worship. A cat stared at her with unblinking yellow eyes from the top of the stairs, and she hesitated. Where else would he be? Turning, she stared up and down the street, and a hand-painted sign with the word *Cantina* written in red caught her attention. The sign jutted out from the side of the building above an open door. He would be in there. Putting her inhibitions aside, she walked fast to the open door and stepped through into the darkness beyond.

When she entered, she stopped and waited for her eyes to adjust before continuing. A large open room with a bar met her gaze. Bright woven blankets hung here and there on the cream plaster walls before her, and Spanish music drifted on the smoke-infused air. Rose sniffed the hot, spicy mouthwatering aromas floating toward her from off to her left and assumed the kitchen lay beyond. Tables dotted the floor, surrounded by chairs filled with lingering customers. Loud laughter erupted from the back of the cantina, followed by a man's deep voice, *Chase's voice*. Rose froze. Her breath caught, and her stomach fluttered while she had a stern talk with her wobbling legs.

Her gaze narrowed.

At a table, in the far back, sat her missing fiancé surrounded by cigar smoke and poker chips. He tilted back on his wooden chair and smiled at the men facing him.

Taking three steps forward, her stupefaction soon turned to rage as she took in the entire scene. The table held four other men, all studying the cards in their hands while their pistols rested on the table beside their stack of chips. They puffed fat Cuban cigars and shuffled the cards in their hands.

"I'll meet your bet and raise you two thousand *pesos*." Chase slid a stack of coins to the middle of the table and widened his grin.

Her heart sank, and her fury rose. The love of her life missed their wedding for *a poker game!* Her anger burst into flame like a match on dry tinder. Marching into the room, Rose made a straight line for the table in the far back and her no-longer-missing ex-fiancé. Her heels clicked on the wooden floor, and Chase glanced up as she approached.

Shock crossed his face as his chair legs hit the ground, and he choked on his glass of tequila.

"Darlin'! What are you doing here?" Half rising, he choked again. The surprised squeak in his voice made her angrier.

"Damned if I know. I should be on my honeymoon. The funny thing is my groom never came to the wedding like he promised." Slipping the golden ring from her third finger, Rose stopped beside the traitor and slapped it down on the table with a sound clink. So furious she could barely speak, she placed both fists on her hips and glared. "I cannot believe you left me for a game of *cards*.

I thought, at very least, you got shot or something and couldn't get to Chicago in time. But *this*?" She waved an arm at the table and the four interested men. "I suppose it's better to find out what kind of man I planned to marry before the ceremony rather than months later when I have five kids, and I'm wondering why you don't come home at night. We had an agreement. Take your ring back. I don't want it anymore." The lie stuck in her throat as she faced the hooded gaze of the man she once loved.

"I sent a telegram explaining the situation. Didn't you get it?" He stared at her and ran a hand through his hair. Something behind her caught his attention, and his gaze darted there and then back to her face. "We can't talk here." He reached for her hand, but she jerked away. Frowning, he took a step toward her. "Darlin'—"

"This is what I received! And don't you darlin' me!" She plucked the worn-out parchment from her reticular and waved it in his face. "*Meet you in church. Can't wait!* Well, *I* did!" Her hand shook, and her knees wobbled. Honest to God, she thought she'd fall and clutched the back of the nearest chair for support.

A dark-haired gentleman with dangerous eyes on Chase's left raised his gaze. "Who is this *loco mujer*?"

He ignored the question. "Play the next round without me." He narrowed his gaze on the men in front of him as he tossed his cards onto the table.

Her gaze swiveled to a dark-haired beauty in a white peasant blouse and colorful skirt who sauntered across the room toward them.

She remembered the second telegram. *"Is this Grace?"* Her gaze swept the other woman's dark hair, dark laughing eyes, and pouting lips.

The woman gave a short laugh at Rose's expression.

"You are surprised *Rosa* is here. I am as well, *Mijo.*" The woman's sultry voice dropped a decimal as she leaned closer to Rose's ranger. "I must leave now before I am discovered. *Adios*." Kissing his cheek, she hurried away through the kitchen doors.

Rose narrowed her gaze on the woman's swaying hips, and her fury rose several hundred degrees. How did this woman know her name, and what gave her the right to kiss Chase?

Lifting her hot face to the object of her rage, she ground her teeth together and told the biggest lie yet. "I don't want to marry you anymore. Or talk. I've seen all I care to. Goodbye Chase Calhan. I hope you choke on a chicken bone, marry the town drunk, and die without your spurs on." Turning, she stomped away two feet, ignoring his attempts to stop her, and remembered her promise to find someone new if he didn't show up for the ceremony. Revenge raced through her veins like boiling lava. In a flash, she understood the driving force behind the wicked queens in Mama's stories. He deserved a dose of uncertainty.

Retracing her steps, she rounded the table and approached the younger man of the four, a dark-haired gentleman with white teeth and muscular arms. His black hair gleamed in the afternoon sunlight, and curious brown eyes gazed up at her as she stopped beside him. Before she could change her mind, she dropped onto the man's lap, wound her arms around his neck, and drew his head down to hers for a thorough kiss. Ignoring everyone but the man in front of her, she threw her anger into the act with passion and moaned for effect.

The man kissed her back with enthusiasm, and she froze the second his tongue touched hers. Panic set in.

Why did men have to complicate things that were quite simple? Her advance had nothing to do with him and everything to do with her poker playing ex-fiancé.

Chase caught her arm and dragged her off the stranger's lap. "Touch my woman again, and you'll be smiling with your throat." His silky soft voice sent tremors through her body, and she shivered.

The man's arms dropped like dead weights, and he went still as death.

Rose peeked through her closed lids.

Her fiancé held a knife against the stranger's jugular, drawing blood. Tucking her against his side, he made eye contact with every man at the table. "Anybody who moves will die." Keeping his gaze on them, he clamped her against him and half-carried her toward the back of the cantina.

She had to run to keep up. Furious with his manhandling, she turned on him the second they rounded the corner. "Don't you dare—"

He caught her to him, pinned her against the wall, and kissed the hell out of her. His hands roamed her body and dropped to her hips, pulling her into his. "Rose." He moaned against her lips and drank deep, turning her head to the side for maximum effect. His hot lips plundered her mouth with hungry, tantalizing nips while his tongue mated with hers. "God, I missed you."

Her blood heated, and her stomach did summersaults. Still angry, she leaned back, but he wouldn't have it and tightened his grip. She couldn't think past the taste of his desire and the urgency in his kiss.

"I've thought of you every moment of every hour we've been apart. I want to take you in my arms and love you every way a man loves his woman." His drawl sent shivers down her spine and weakened her knees like smooth Tennessee whisky. The heat of his body drugged her senses, and she groaned in response.

God, she had to get her wayward body under control before she gave in and didn't get the answers she deserved. "We would be on our honeymoon right now if you'd come to the wedding." The pain of his defection still hurt. "I waited for hours in my lace gown, and you never came."

He shook his head and tilted her chin up. "Didn't you get the second telegram? I sent it from the station before I came here and asked you to postpone the ceremony until I settled this thing." A shadow crossed his face, and sincerity shone from his amber eyes.

"No. Just the one saying you'd see me in church. So, I waited. For hours." Her voice trembled, and she swallowed hard.

One of the men at the table laughed, and Rose stiffened. "What thing?"

Chase glanced back at the poker game and shook his head. "It's too dangerous. I don't have the time to explain right now. But you shouldn't be here. You could get hurt or killed, and I cannot lose you." His whiskey-colored eyes bored into hers. "You mean everything to me, Rose. You have to know that. You are my life, and I would never recover if something happened to you." He gathered her closer. "I hoped to avoid this very situation. God, I'm sorry. I never meant for any of this to happen." Holding her tight against his heart, he sighed. "There are things you don't understand. I killed El Diablo and planned to be in Chicago. I thought my war had ended, but before I could board the train, another situation developed." He kissed her hair. "What I'm engaged in now is why I missed our wedding and came to San Antonio. God, I can see you sitting there in your white gown, waiting for me, and the thought breaks my heart. I would never hurt you like that, Rose. Never. Please believe me. You are everything to me, and I ache to show you how much I love you." His kiss devoured her with deep, sweeping strokes of his tongue as he held her close against him.

She sighed with satisfaction. He said the three words she longed to hear more than anything, and she melted in his arms. Her heart picked up speed, and heat seeped through her as he caressed her back and arms. This is the man she traveled to Texas to find. Desire spread through her with delicious anticipation.

Someone coughed beside them. "There's time for kissing and talking later. Delgato could walk through the door any second, and we'll lose this opportunity." The man's deep voice brought her to her senses.

Chase lifted his head and stared deep into her eyes. "He's right." He glanced around. "I need to hide you somewhere safe until this is over."

"I'll watch out for her. You better get back in there before this whole thing goes bad." The deep voice spoke to their right. "I'd trade you places if I could. But we both know if Delgato sees me, he'll know it's a trap and run."

Chase lifted her chin up, and his whisky-colored eyes burned with seriousness. "When this is over, I'll tell you everything. In the meantime, promise me you'll stay here with Sam and don't come out no matter what you hear. Okay?"

"Okay." Her voice trembled with emotion. For the first time since her wedding day, she wondered if she got it all wrong. "I'll stay."

Whatever he read in her expression satisfied him, for he gave her another peck on the lips and strolled back to the poker table. "I'll take two cards." He resumed his seat at the table as if they were never interrupted and took a sip of his tequila.

"You must be Rose." The tall man with dark hair and green eyes beside her held out a hand. "I'm Sam Walker, Calhan's partner." Drawing her back into the shadows, he shook his head at her. "I never seen my partner so worked up about anyone before as he is you. He hears your name and goes all crazy. Now I've met you, I can see why. Welcome to Texas, Miss Rose." He took position to the left of the door and gazed into the cantina. "I just hope like hell we didn't scare Calhan's target away."

A thought crossed her mind. "Who is the woman who left a few minutes ago? Is she Grace?"

"No. Her name is Rozita Sanchez. She works for a Mexican warlord and is responsible for helping Calhan catch and kill Juan Castillo, a general in Mexico's army known as El Diablo. Now, his first in command, a man named Delgato, is in San Antonio to hire guerilla soldiers and get revenge. El Diablo's woman, Maria Garcia, died when we made our move on the general, and we have information Delgato plans to kill Chase and anyone connected to him. Maria is also Delgato's sister, and he's the reason Ranger Calhan missed his wedding." He frowned. "This whole situation in the cantina is a set up to capture the man. If they figure out who you are, they'll kill you."

"I think they know. The woman Rozita called me *Rosa*." She swallowed when he narrowed his gaze on her face.

"Is that a fact? Chase hoped to keep you out of all this. He trusts the woman, but I don't. She may have spilled the beans to Delgato, and your being here complicates things." Moving her farther away from the door, he peered into her eyes. "How did you know we were in San Antonio?"

Her chin lifted a notch. "I know how to find people too. Just because I'm a woman doesn't mean I'm helpless."

He nodded and said nothing while he studied her face.

Her conscience pricked her, and she figured he knew by the way he waited for her to continue. Gazing at him, she confessed her sins. "I read a telegram meant for Chase's brother and rode the train to Houston. Chief Tafford told me he came here."

"And the cantina? San Antonio's a big place." The ranger's green eyes bored into hers.

She told him about Aries.

He ran a hand through his hair and gazed around as if looking for a one-way train to Chicago to stuff her into. "We need to get you the hell out of here." Sam shook his head when he gazed into the cantina and checked his pistol. "Rozita set this whole thing up and gave Chase the information so he could arrest Delgato. My partner won't like hearing she knows about you. This could be a set up for us, as well." He glanced at her face. "Do you have somewhere to go until this is over?"

Rose frowned. She gave Chase her word, she'd stay put. "I have a room at the Menger up the road." She glanced at Sam. "How long has Rozita known Chase?"

"Several years, if I understand it correctly." Rolling

a cigarette, he tucked the end in his mouth. “She gives him information, and he pays her. If I believed anything different, I’d be the first one to break his neck for missing his own wedding.” Lighting a match, he held the end against his cigarette and took a puff.

His words eased some of the sting. “I wish someone would have told me the situation before I left Chicago. I didn’t get his second telegram. I’m not unreasonable, and I would have listened.” Rose put a trembling hand to her forehead. She didn’t feel well, and Sam swirled before her eyes. “I’ve been worried out of my mind about him. And when he didn’t come for the wedding. I wanted to know why.”

Her companion frowned. “He told the truth. He sent you two telegrams. The one you have there, and the one explaining he wouldn’t make the wedding. I stood beside him in Houston when he sent it. Ranger Kaplan gave it to the operator. Calhan is crazy about you.”

Rose frowned as a suspicious thought crossed her mind. “What if Ranger Kaplan didn’t give it to the operator?”

A long silence filled the space between them while Sam puffed on his cigarette. “Now, there’s a thought worth checking up on. The more I think on the situation, the more I don’t like it. You shouldn’t have come, especially not alone. If anything happens to you, my partner will lose his mind. Why don’t you sneak out the back door here, catch a hackney at the corner, and go back to the hotel where it’s safe. I’ll send Calhan as soon as this is over, and you two can work this thing out between you.”

She never got the chance.

Men burst in the front door of the cantina, and a

short, meaty man with a handlebar mustache strolled in, followed by six men with guns on each hip.

"God dammit. There he is." As soon as the men stepped inside, Sam pushed her into a corner and tipped a table in front of her. "Stay put!" He disappeared.

Rose leaned back into the shadows as bullets flew.

More men raced in through the back door and past her hiding place without slowing down. Rapid gunfire filled the air. When a bullet hit the wall behind her, she dropped to her belly and crossed her arms over her head.

Squeezing her eyes shut as lead hit the walls around her, she gritted her teeth when a couple hit the floor out front. Curling up in a ball, traumatized by the sounds of the battle, she held her breath and waited.

Men shouted and bodies fell. She didn't dare breathe or think about who might be getting shot.

"Oh God, Oh God, Oh God." Placing her hands over her ears, she rocked and whispered the words of an old song to keep her mind from conjuring up images of the war going on around her. Had Chase been shot? Or Sam?

She knew the man for five minutes and trusted him with her life. He couldn't die, and neither could Chase. Not until she found out everything and where the hell Grace went. His telegram said he came to rescue her. So, where did she go, and what did these men have to do with her?

The heat, and the worry, combined with her lack of food and sleep caught up to her as a bullet hit the wall with a thud. Something fell from above her, and everything went black.

When she regained consciousness, Chase had her in his arms. His blond head hovered above hers, and concern shone from his warm brown eyes. "Are you okay?"

His sexy drawl rolled over her like a shot of aged scotch, and Rose's stomach tightened. So close, she could see the gold specks in his eyes. She sucked in a shaky breath as his large, warm hands ran over her body, searching for injuries. His scent enveloped her like a fantasy lover, and she trembled with emotion. The familiar smell used to mean excitement, euphoria, and dizzy anticipation. Until her recent experiences.

"Talk to me, darlin'." Chase's warm breath brushed her cheeks while his mouth hovered above her lips. "My heart dang near burst from my chest when I found you unconscious. I thought I lost you, that you'd been shot." His hand shook as he brushed a strand of hair from her face and caressed her cheek. "Don't ever scare me like that again. My life flashed before me, and all I could think about was how empty I would be without you. I couldn't bear to live if you left me."

Rose blinked. "I'm okay." This Chase she loved and traveled for days to find, not the other one who played poker and left her alone on their wedding day. "We're supposed to be on our honeymoon." She swallowed. "Not in the bowels of Texas. And I want to know why."

Chapter Five

Turning her head, Rose stared at the cream stucco wall above Chase's shoulder. "Who is Grace?" She had to know before she gave in to any more of his kisses.

Catching her chin, he turned her face back to his. Surprise flashed across his face as he smiled down at her. "She died a long time ago and means nothing." His dark gaze roamed her body, and desire glittered in their depths. "I missed you, girl, more than I can say." His gaze centered on her face and dropped to her lips. Tugging her up against him, he bent his head to kiss her.

He didn't give her much of an answer about Grace, she noted. Hot and demanding, his lips coaxed a response from her as desire quivered in her stomach. She couldn't repress the shiver of pleasure dancing through her as his hands rubbed her back and massaged her neck. Forgetting all about the last few days, she gave into temptation and kissed him back. God, he felt good, and his kisses drugged her with sweet sensual promise. The heat of his body drew her to him like a campfire on a freezing winter's night.

Sam cleared his throat. "I think we should leave before we attract any more attention. Your girl says they know who she is."

Chase lifted his head. "How?"

His partner shrugged. "Rozita called her *Rosa*."

A frown marred her ranger's brow. "No. I think you

misheard. Rozita doesn't know, or she would have said something to me."

Rose frowned over the amount of trust he had in the woman. She found the fact Sam didn't interesting and changed the subject. "Did you kill what's his name? The big man with the dark mustache?"

Chase smoothed her hair from her face. "No, he's over there with a local ranger waiting for the prison wagon to take him to Houston."

Shaking her head, she frowned. "So, he's the one you came to find?"

Chase smiled into her eyes. "Yes, and thank God we got him. For a minute there, I thought he figured us out."

Clearing her throat, she changed the subject. "You could have been killed."

Her fiancé chuckled. "Not a chance. Delgato and his men did not know what hit them. I had them whipped before they cleared their holsters. Rage is a good thing when it comes to fighting, and I wanted to rip Diaz's throat out for kissing you. Still do. You're mine now and forever. Remember that, darlin'. I will always come for you."

Gazing into his amazing, amber-colored eyes, she trembled. "You frightened me when you didn't come to Chicago like you promised, and I thought something happened to you. When I read the telegram about Grace and then spotted you with Rozita—"

He frowned. "I know, and I'm sorry. With Delgato spreading the word he planned to get revenge on everyone I loved. I had to take care of the situation. I can't make you my wife and put you in danger at the same time. So, I sent a telegram explaining I would be another week or two." Helping her to her feet, he wrapped his arms around her. "I am so sorry I missed the wedding, and I want to make it up to you."

"I'm listening." She tripped when several thoughts danced across her mind.

Outside, Delgato sat against the dirty wall with his hands and feet bound. He wore dark clothes, leather boots, and a frown. Gazing up as Rose followed Chase into the alley, she sucked in a breath at the hatred in the prisoner's eyes when he leaned around the corner to stare at her.

Stepping closer to her six-foot protector for safety, she whispered in his ear. "I hope you plan to come to Chicago with me. I don't believe I'm out of danger at all. Your prisoner isn't dead or in jail. And he's glaring at me like he wants to choke the life out of me."

Her fiancé tossed a glance over his shoulder. "Sam is right. We need to get you out of here." He nodded his head in the prisoner's direction. Four men stood next to the prisoner speaking to his partner. "Sam offered to escort Delgato to Houston for me. So it's you and me, darlin', from here on in. I'm stuck to you like glue on paper."

Sam cleared his throat as he strolled toward them. "Looks like you've got everything under control, so I will be on my way. Be safe, Calhan." Clapping his partner on the back, he grinned at Rose. "I leave him in your capable hands. Keep him out of trouble, will you?"

She smiled back. "I'll do what I can, but you know how he is."

Chase laughed. "Later, Sam." He held her tight against him and steered her out of the alley toward the main road and his horse. "I will get us a couple of rooms at a hotel, and then we can talk about what my hands are capable of."

Rose's knees buckled. If he followed through on half the naughty things he whispered in her ear, she'd die of pure pleasure. And he had a lot of making up to do after the last week and a half. "I have a room at the Menger, so you'll just need one for you. I'd like a bit of dinner, though. I didn't get the chance to eat earlier. I found Aries tied beside the church and went looking for you. I didn't think about food once I found you." The cantina reminded her of Grace. "What happened to Rozita?"

He sighed. "She didn't want to be there when Delgato arrived. He'd figure out who gave me information. I wouldn't have caught El Diablo without her."

Tightening her grip on Chase's arm, she leaned against him. "Rozita's beautiful."

He stopped and turned to face her. "She's like a sister to me. You know you're the only woman I want. You've never questioned me before. What's this all about?"

Rose gazed down at her dusty shoes and then into his eyes. "I didn't get the telegram you said you sent. Do you know how I felt when you failed to appear at our wedding? I'm not like Shanna or Rozita. There's nothing exotic or exciting about me. I'm normal. And Rozita doesn't like me. She thinks you belong to her."

Catching her chin, he gazed deep into her eyes. "What she thinks isn't important." He kissed her hard. "And who says you aren't exciting? I've thought of nothing but making a life with you since the day we met. Let's get some dinner and then have our talk. I'm thinking you need a reminder of where you stand in my life."

Rose sighed with happiness. "Okay, but I warn you, I require a good deal of convincing."

Riding through the streets of San Antonio in Chase's arms soothed the ache she had carried for days. Arriving at the hotel, they put Aries away in a comfortable stable for the night, and Chase gave the bellhop his satchel to put in Rose's room. They ate dinner at a local place he knew a block away from the Menger.

When they finished, they walked toward the hotel, and she soaked in the wonderful feeling of having her one true love beside her. Studying his face while he told her about his life since he left her in Rock Creek, he spoke about his partner Sam Walker and the friendship they shared. She could tell they were close by the way he talked. Chase didn't give respect away, and he had a barrel load for Sam Walker.

A deep, satisfied sigh escaped her lips as the evening breeze touched her hot face. She loved the way his eyes twinkled when he laughed and the wrinkles gathered around the corners. She loved the sound of his voice and the way he smelled of leather, sage, and the outdoors. But most of all, she loved how he belonged to her. Hugging his arm to her side, she inhaled the scent of his skin along with the scent of the river. In a few days, they'd be back in Chicago, and she would be Mrs. Chase Calhan. Gazing up at his wicked laughing eyes, she smiled.

Tightening his arm around her, he bent down. "Keep looking at me like you're doing, and I won't wait until the wedding. I'll take you in my arms and make love to you right now." He paused. "As soon as I knew I wouldn't make it, I sent another telegram, and I can't express how sorry I am you didn't get it. Once I discovered the seriousness of the situation with the cartel, I sent word to Reese and rode for San Antonio. I don't know what I would do without you, sweetheart. My chest hurt worse than anything I've ever known when I thought I lost you."

"Imagine how I felt when I waited for you all day in my wedding gown. And then to read a telegram you sent to your brother…" She shook her head as they walked. "I haven't been able to eat or sleep much for days. You promised me a wedding, a honeymoon, and happy ever after."

He stopped beneath a large tree outside the hotel and turned her to face him. "I don't want to waste another minute. One thing I learned over the past few days is the error of putting something off until tomorrow because tomorrow might not come. The way I see it, marrying and loving you is the single most important thing I will do with my life. With Delgato headed for the noose, I don't want to put it off any longer. I can't risk it. I knew it today when I found you unconscious back at the cantina. I want you in my bed tonight."

Rose bit her lip. "What about our wedding and the family waiting for us in Chicago? Giles has been making plans for months now." Her magical wedding hovered on the horizon.

"I'll marry you anywhere and everywhere in every language and religion there is to make sure you're mine, darlin'. We have a few things to work out between us before we go to Chicago and let Giles have free reign. Tonight is for us. I know how I feel about you, and you know how you feel about me. All I've thought about is you for the last few days. I burn for you in ways I didn't think possible."

Her stomach hitched as she gazed into his whiskey-colored eyes and nodded her head. "I don't think I can wait much longer, either. You're all I've dreamed of for months."

He stared into her soul. "Then let's continue this conversation in your room."

Rose nodded her head, overcome with shyness. The reality of the situation weighed down on her, and she couldn't breathe as excitement raced up and down her body. Oh God! He planned to make love to her tonight, maybe within the hour.

"Take my ring back, darlin', and never take it off again." Slipping the band of gold back on her third finger, he kissed her hand. "You're the other half of me, and I couldn't breathe when you tossed it at me and said you didn't want to be mine."

Rose swallowed hard. She'd never been good at talking, especially when under pressure. "I lied, and I couldn't breathe, either."

Chase strode toward the hotel, taking the stairs in the lobby two at a time, oblivious to the stares of the patrons lounging in the reception area. He grinned down at her. "What is your room number?"

She whispered it in his ear.

When he arrived at the room, he held his hand out. "May I have the key?"

Rose giggled as nervousness fluttered in her belly, along with hot anticipation. Soon she would know all of him and he her. Her knees wobbled, and her breath hitched with excitement.

Everything about this moment felt right.

Holding the key, she noted how his hand shook

when he put it into the lock.

And then the door swung open. He swung her up into his arms and carried her across the threshold.

Kicking the door shut with his heel, he carried her over to the bed. Setting her on her feet, he busied himself with her buttons while his mouth assaulted hers.

"Want to bathe with me? I'm hot, sticky, and thinking of you all lathered up in my arms." His husky suggestion made her mouth go dry.

"Y…e…s." she sucked in several deep breaths to calm her fluttering heart.

"Come with me." Taking her hand, he drew her into the adjoining room.

Rose stared at the gleaming copper bathtub as Chase turned on the water and adjusted the temperature. Thoughts of the two of them naked beneath the steaming water made her breath hitch. "I don't think we'll fit." Her cheeks heated when he turned to survey her from head to toe.

"We will. Let me show you." He stopped in front of her and released the last few buttons.

Shivering when the back of his hands brushed against her back, she trembled against him. Her buttons came loose, and her bodice fell to her hips. Chase drew her dress down until it fell in a pile of blue gingham at her feet, and she stepped out. He caressed her bare arms and then her back until he found the button holding her petticoats in place and loosened them. Her skirts followed her dress, and butterflies filled her stomach. His sensual assault teased her senses while his scent made her quiver with anticipation and her knees knock together.

The running water behind them soothed her nerves

and filled her with tantalizing thoughts. Her breath came fast as she took hold of the buttons on the front of his shirt, and with shaking fingers, she slid them through the holes. She had dreamed of touching his bronzed chest and arms for months now, fantasizing about the event since the first time she set eyes on him. Removing his cotton shirt from his shoulders, her mouth dropped open as she stared at his bronzed beauty embodying everything she dreamed about. Swallowing tightly, she ignored her quivering belly as she ran her hands over his rippling chest and bulging arms, marveling at his strength. Loving the smooth, hard texture of his skin, she bent to taste him.

Chase moaned and thrust a thick thigh between her legs, holding her tight against him. The hard length of his shaft strained against her trembling body, and she cried out, arching closer, unable to believe all this was happening. Soon she would know what it felt like to be joined to him, to feel his hardness deep inside her. Her breath came in short gasps through parted lips as she rubbed against his throbbing shaft, shivering with desire.

His hot mouth teased her ear lobe and the side of her neck. "God, you feel good. Your hands are so soft. I want to feel them on every part of my body. Touch me, darlin'. I like what you're doing."

Encouraged, Rose leaned forward, kissing and licking her way across his chest and down his stomach, marveling at his reaction to the touch of her lips. He must want her as much as she wanted him for him to moan so. Liquid heat settled between her legs. Rising, she squirmed against him. "I like how you—"

He understood despite her inability to speak. "I know." With a growl, he caught the waistband of her pantalets and tugged them down.

Rose's knees buckled.

He caught her before she hit the ground and held her against the hard planes of his chest. "I want you, Rose. I want to feel every inch of your beautiful body and bury my shaft in your sweetness."

She moaned. "I—" Hoping to tell him she wanted him, too, but speech evaded her.

"I want to take this slow, darlin', to make it last. But I've waited for this moment for so long, dreamed of seeing you like this with your lips swollen from my kisses and your body aching for mine. I don't know if I can. I've wondered since the day we met what you would look like naked with your eyes filled with desire and your legs open for me." His wicked eyes roamed her body, touching on her lips, before dropping to her breasts, where her erect nipples strained against the cotton fabric of her chemise, begging for his attention. Rubbing the pad of his thumb over them, he caught her lips in a hot, drugging kiss.

Crying out, she arched toward him.

His hands dropped to her thighs. Catching the hem of her chemise, he drew it from her and added it to the pile of clothing on the floor. With half-closed eyes, he tugged her into his arms. He gripped her buttocks to his bulging manhood and stared at her heaving breasts.

"I want—" Her breath caught. God, soon he would be inside her, and she would know everything. Shaking with the fever of desire, she could say no more.

He turned the water off and unbuttoned his breeches.

Chapter Six

"I know, darlin'. I do, too." He rubbed his raging erection against her trembling belly, and she moaned in response.

Dropping his hands, he made quick work of his breeches. They fell to the floor at his feet, along with his small clothes. The hard pulse of his arousal strained out from his hipbones, mesmerizing her with his size.

She swallowed and shivered with self-awareness as he stepped into the bathtub.

Holding out a hand, he gave her a wicked grin. "Come and join me."

Rose quaked in reaction as moisture gathered between her legs. She climbed in before the logical part of her mind talked her out of it. Settling into the warm water, she gave a gasp of surprise when he lifted her calves and set them on either side of his narrow hips.

He pulled her forward until they were inches apart, and his shaft throbbed against her belly.

She swallowed as he leaned forward to kiss her neck and cup her breasts. Placing her hands on his chest, she stroked him while her gaze roamed his chest and upper arms. She thought him muscular, but without any clothes, he outshone anything she pictured in her head. Her mouth grew dry as she stared at him.

"Touch me." His hoarse voice filled her with wonder.

Glancing up, she met the fiery hunger in his gaze as he placed her hand on his swollen member.

Large, hard, and pulsing with energy, she ran her fingers down the length of his shaft.

He sucked in a breath with a hiss.

Tracing a finger over the velvet head of his manhood in wonder, she glanced up when Chase moaned and shook against her trembling hand.

The raw sound tightened her belly as she stared at his face. With his eyes closed and his head thrown back, she grew curious about her effect on him. Closing her hand around his shaft, she pumped up and down as tremors shook his powerful body. He growled, and after a minute, caught her hand in his. When he opened his eyes, she gazed into a burning inferno of longing and nodded. She understood because she felt the same.

"My turn." His gaze dropped. "God, you're beautiful." Catching a breast in each hand, he molded and shaped them in his palm, murmuring with satisfaction. Rubbing a thumb over each erect nipple, Rose whimpered with pleasure. Pinpricks of ecstasy raced from her breasts to the heat between her legs, and his gaze darkened as if he knew.

When he took her dark pink areola into his mouth and sucked vigorously, she thought she died and went to heaven. Taking more of her into his mouth at her cry of wonder, he tugged harder, and Rose caught the tub's edge for support. Fever burned in her veins like never before as she squirmed against him, wanting him to ease the ache inside her. Lifting his head, he gazed at her with hungry eyes. Fire raced through her, and the ache between her legs grew. Shifting so his swollen shaft pressed lower on her stomach, she squirmed.

"Easy, Rose. You know I want you as much as you want me, but I must make this good for you."

Catching her other nipple in his mouth, he suckled while he caressed its twin. Rose cried out, arching against him. She wanted more. She wanted him to fill her ache and quench the fire inside her.

"Chase!" She managed to get the word out despite the dryness of her mouth and her inability to think straight.

He dipped a hand into the water and slid his fingers between the slick folds shielding her core. With butterfly light touches, he stroked her quivering flesh until she moaned and thrashed her head side to side. She cried out and opened her legs wider.

His chest rubbed against her swollen nipple while his hot lips surrounded the other tugging at her. She whimpered in response, hanging one for dear life. Fire burned between her legs as his long fingers stroked the sensitive nub and filled her with delight. Quivering with a nameless desire, she moaned crying out his name. Her fever burned higher and hotter as she lifted her hips again and rubbed against his hard shaft.

His thick finger penetrated her and withdrew.

Rose sat up straight and gasped aloud, trembling in reaction.

"Lean back, darlin'. You'll like this." The sensual hunger in his gaze slammed into her like a runaway carriage.

She wanted him to take her to his bed and teach her about men for ages and couldn't believe she was here. Doing it. Swallowing her inhibitions, she opened her legs a little wider while she stared into his eyes.

Her heart fluttered like a hummingbird, and languid

heat dragged at her loins. Quaking with expectation, she reclined against the back of the tub.

In slow motion, he leaned forward and tugged a straining nipple back into his mouth. Rose moaned when his hot lips closed around her and shivered with desire.

He maintained eye contact while his finger penetrated her delicate softness, moving in and out with slow, mind-numbing strokes. Her woman's core pulsed with pleasure. The thought of his girth probing her willing flesh made her faint with anticipation.

He knew what she wanted and added a second finger.

She bucked forward with a cry of ecstasy.

"Oh God!" Rose gasped and writhed against him, moving her hips against his hand. The ache increased with each stroke of his hand until she wanted his possession with a fervency she couldn't deny. The urgency to become one with him drove her crazy, and she leaned toward him, panting for relief.

Wrapping her fingers around his pulsing shaft, she stroked him with slow steady motions, sliding up and down his engorged flesh.

He quit breathing.

"Chase. I want—" She lost the ability to speak when he caught her mouth with his.

"I do, too." Lifting her up in his arms, he lowered her passion-moistened core little by little onto his rigid shaft, filling her with his heat.

Every muscle in her body tensed with expectation as she adjusted to his invasion.

"You…I…" She couldn't finish the thought.

He gazed into her eyes while his body shook with desire. "I've wanted this for so long. I don't think I will be able to stop."

Rose closed her eyes. She didn't want him to stop.

"Open your eyes, darlin'. I want to watch you while I make you mine."

She opened her eyes and gazed into his hot golden ones. The intensity of his lust burned into her soul as he pushed his hips higher into hers.

"You're so hot for me. God, you feel good." Pulling back, he surged forward with one big thrust, filling her completely.

Rose gasped as his hard length stretched the inner wall of her hot wet sheath. Nothing about his possession resembled anything she had ever imagined, and she shuddered against him. Heated water lapped against her body as she slid against his slick wet chest. The musky scent of his soap and the salty taste of his skin tantalized her. She wanted more of this connection, more of him.

Many girls spoke of pain their first time. But not her. She'd wanted to be here like this with him for too long for the experience to be anything but pleasurable. The silky folds of her femininity welcomed him with a surge of liquid heat.

"Ride me, darlin'. Take it slow or hard and fast. The choice is yours." Lifting her inch by inch, he settled her on him again. "The more we move together like this, the better it feels."

Rose needed no further invitation and ground down to meet him, marveling at the way her body tightened and thrummed with him inside her. This is what she'd craved, and what she'd yearned to experience for months. Catching his hips, she rode him hard and fast until she gasped for breath, quivering on the precipice of some nameless rapture just out of reach.

"Chase." Her breath came fast between parted lips. Not used to this kind of exertion, she trembled with frustration.

"I'm right there with you, darlin'." He stood in one quick motion, wrapping her legs high around his waist as he strode for the other room with her clutched to his chest.

He caught a thick towel and wrapped it around her naked back before sinking onto the bed with their bodies still joined. Catching her buttocks, he lifted her hips to meet his.

"Is this what you're asking for?" Drawing back, he surged forward, rocking into her and retreating.

"Yes! Oh God, Oh God, Oh God." She found her voice as tremors rocked her body. Moaning aloud, she lifted her hips for more. "Oh God, Oh God, Oh God." She chanted the words as desire held her tight in its grip.

Chase grinned down at her. "God Almighty, you pleasure me like no one ever has. Damned if you aren't the most perfect woman on the face of the earth. You're so tight and slick. I don't think I could take it slow if it cost my life."

"I don't…" Moaning, she threw her head back, unable to complete the sentence.

He must have understood because he rocked harder and faster as her excitement grew. She met his invasion with enthusiasm.

Panting against him, Rose clawed at his back, urging him to thrust harder. Glorious delight shot through her body as he penetrated her deeper and deeper. Dancing along the edge of intoxicating rapture and exhilarating satisfaction, she grew mindless of everything but her quest for release. As ecstasy quivered around his thrusting shaft, she burst up, and over the brink of such exquisite gratification, she exploded into a million brilliant pieces of fiery rapture and died of pleasure in his arms.

Chase caught her to him as convulsions shook her body. Pumping harder until his own release rocked him to the heart of his soul, he moaned as a crescendo of satisfaction roared through his body.

They lay joined together for long minutes, gasping for breath and floating on a sea of mutual exultation.

Completely sated, Chase held Rose against him until the last tremor of their lovemaking ebbed away. Dropping his head to hers, he wiped the perspiration from his brow and tilted her chin up. "Are you okay?"

"More than okay." Smiling up at him, she caressed the side of his face with trembling fingers. "I suspected bedding you would be something spectacular. I never dreamed you could mate in a bathtub. Had I known, I would have lured you to my bathing room months ago."

He laughed. "There are so many ways to give each other pleasure and so many positions to try. We'll be busy for a long time. Do you want to pick the next spot?"

Rose grinned. "Possibly. I'm too tired to think right now, but I will let you know when I've had some sleep and regained my strength."

He kissed her forehead. "So, I can expect to be compromised in the near future?"

"Absolutely. Now I know what you're capable of, I shall expect a repeat performance quite often in as many different places and positions as possible." A lusty yawn followed her statement. "I must plait my hair before I fall asleep, or it will be a mess tomorrow." Rolling to her feet, she fought with her modesty as she strolled nude to the bathing room door.

She caught Chase staring at her naked backside as she stopped in the door.

A giggle escaped when she glanced at the soaking floor and the sodden clothing beside the tub.

"What's so funny?"

"I believe we created a tidal wave or several in our, er, enthusiasm." She held her dripping bodice up for him to see.

He chuckled. "We'll ring for extra towels and clean the place up before anyone is the wiser."

They wrung the excess water from the pile of clothing and wiped the floor down.

Chase took advantage of the bed after laying out their clothing to dry. He patted the spot beside him. "Come sleep with me, Rose."

She grinned and slid into bed beside him. She dreamed of him saying those very words to her several thousand times over the past year. And now she understood how Shanna felt when she lost her virginity to Reese before they were married. She didn't blame her best friend for giving in. Who could say *no* to a Calhan with a sexy gleam in his eye?

****

She woke to Chase's fingers dancing over her flat stomach and dipping down to stroke her quivering thighs.

Lust glowed from his half-closed amber eyes as he stared at her. "Mornin'."

She licked her lips as heat filled her belly and pooled between her thighs. "Good morning."

Light streaming in between the cracks of the curtain danced over his naked chest and arms, highlighting rippled muscle. God, he made her wanton. The morning air smelled of wood smoke from the hearth and aroused male.

Bending forward, he took her in his arms and kissed her, his tongue dipping in. She gave stroke for stroke, returning his kiss with fervor. Curling her lips around his tongue, she sucked.

A moan escaped him. Trailing one hand up to her chest, he cupped a swollen breast, teasing the tight bud of her nipple with his fingers. "I dreamed about you." His husky voice sent shivers of desire racing through her bloodstream.

Wrapping her arms around his neck, she sighed. "Show me." Parting her thighs, she trailed her fingers down his back, loving the feel of his hard hot body.

And he did.

Mid-thrust Rose stilled when someone pounded the wall behind the headboard.

"Can't a body get any sleep?" The angry male voice didn't sound amused by their activity.

She couldn't contain her giggle as memories of Houston flooded her mind. "Let's move to the floor."

"You have a problem making love in a bed?" One eyebrow quirked up and a smile twitched the corner of his beautiful mouth.

She explained about her experience, wiping the mirth from her eyes as she relived the moment through new eyes. "Thank God I didn't knock on the door and offer my assistance."

Chase agreed and scooped the bedding up in one big armful. Catching her in his arms, he lowered her to the floor and resumed where they left off. His hips thrust forward in a steady rhythm, edging her closer to the breaking point. He catapulted her over the edge of sweet oblivion a few minutes later into a sea of exquisite pleasure. Satisfaction rippled through her in pulsating waves of mindless euphoria. For long minutes she lay beneath him, too sated to move.

He took her from behind to find his own release, and she joined him as he exploded in primal rapture.

If only they could remain in this blissful bubble of contentment and joy forever, her life would be complete, and Chase said the same.

The memory would be taken out and relived often in the weeks to come.

Rose chuckled as she wondered what the guests next to them thought about the frequency of the headboard thumping the wall over the next week and made a mental note to ensure they mounted their headboard well at home to avoid embarrassment when they entertained guests.

She didn't realize she could love Chase more than she already did, but each passing day proved her wrong. Waking to his wicked laughing gaze and the sinful things they did together, he taught her things about her body she never knew and tutored her in the art of making love.

"There will never be another woman for me. I have all I ever wanted or dreamed of when I hold you in my arms, darlin'." His deep voice heated the side of her neck, and happiness warmed her insides. He loved her. This, she knew, and every vestige of doubt left her as their time together flew past.

They came together often and only ventured out when they needed food or a breath of air. And Rose loved every minute of it.

On one such occasion, she felt the back of her neck

prick as if someone stared at her from beneath the trees, like the first day she arrived in San Antonio. The sensation often appeared the four days before she found Chase but hadn't since then, and she'd forgotten about it until now. Standing still beside him, she glanced around to see who studied them with such intensity.

He bent to kiss her cheek. "Walk with me to the hotel as if nothing is amiss, and I will come back and see who it is." He whispered the words into her ear and grinned as if suggesting something lascivious.

Rose smiled back, and they continued to the hotel and into the reception area.

Once there, Chase led her to the stairs. "Go up to our room. Lock the door behind you, and I will be back as soon as I can."

Nodding, she walked up the first few stairs as her lover disappeared.

"Miss Tanner?"

Rose paused with her foot on the next stair and turned toward the voice.

Mr. Matthews stood at the bottom of the staircase, smiling at her.

Returning to the bottom, she stopped beside the man. "Mr. Matthews. I haven't seen you around for a few days."

Removing his hat, he made a half-bow from the waist. "I am gratified you noticed my absence. I suspected you were so enamored of your new beau, you'd forgotten about me."

Shaking her head, she smiled. "What can I do for you? I am returning to my room."

Mr. Matthews' smile dropped. "I do not wish to disturb you, but I'm afraid I have a small problem. Since you are the only gentle lady I am acquainted with in the area, I seek your indulgence."

She frowned. "Is something wrong?"

Casting his gaze side to side as if concerned they would be overheard, he leaned close. "I am afraid I ran across a lost child on my walk earlier. She hides in the alley behind the hotel, crying. She is frightened and wants her mother. I do not know what to do."

Rose gazed from him to the back of the hotel and then up the stairs. "I must return to my room. Why don't you take the girl to the reception desk? I am sure the manager will know the correct thing to do to find her mother."

Her companion shrugged. "The problem is the little girl will not speak with me or allow me to touch her. I hoped you would come with me and persuade her to come inside."

Rose sighed. What could it hurt? Shrugging, she followed Mr. Matthews through the hotel and out the back door. Once they were in the alley, she gazed around. But no child appeared, only three short rough-dressed men with dark hair carrying pistols and a wagon waiting behind them.

An uneasy feeling grew in her chest. Twirling toward the door to the hotel, she drew to a stop. Mr. Matthews stood in her way.

"What is this? And where is the girl?" She knew she'd gotten into trouble by the change in Mr. Matthews' expression. His smile dropped like rain on a stormy day, and a scowl appeared.

"Get into the wagon." His harsh command made her shiver.

Her chin rose in defiance as she kicked him in the

groin and turned to grasp the latch to the back door. She never made it, for something hit her on the back of the head, and she fell like a sack of stones.

****

Chase searched the area beneath the trees and returned empty-handed. He remembered Rose telling him someone spied on her the first four days after she arrived in San Antonio and frowned. He didn't like the nagging feeling in his chest.

Taking the stairs two at a time to their room, he tapped on the door. "Rose? Let me in."

Silence followed. A sixth sense tightened a band around his chest as he assessed the unnatural silence. Kicking the door in with a sharp jab of his foot, Chase sniffed. No one had entered since they left to go on their walk. But why hadn't she come to their room like he asked?

Bounding down the stairs, he searched the bottom floor of the hotel but didn't find her anywhere. If she were hungry, she would have waited for him. Panic drummed through him as he took deep breaths to calm his mind. Rose must be here somewhere. There must be a simple explanation for her absence. Anxiety twisted his gut in a knot. He couldn't lose her. Not now. Walking toward the reception area, he rang the bell for assistance, assessing the guests as they walked in and out, busy with their own affairs. Where would she be? Who did she know in San Antonio?

He analyzed everything she said until a name popped into his head. Jonathon Matthews met her right off the stagecoach and escorted her to the hotel the day she arrived. Perhaps his escort wasn't as gentlemanly as she believed. They had not been introduced, but Rose pointed him out on their way to breakfast one morning. Chase frowned. Did her Mr. Matthews have something to do with her absence?

The knot in his gut tightened. He'd seen situations like this before and didn't want to believe his gentle Rose had been abducted. God! The thought made him sick to his stomach. If even one of the filthy bastards touched her, he would tear their heads off. Sucking in another breath, he slowed the rage and focused on priority one—find out everything he could on one Jonathon Matthews.

The manager stepped up to the counter. "Can I help you?"

Smiling at the hotel manager, he leaned against the counter. "I am looking for a friend of mine who is staying here. He goes by the name of Jonathon Matthews."

The manager narrowed his gaze. "I'm afraid you're out of luck. Mr. Matthews checked out about an hour ago in something of a hurry."

Chase described Rose and asked him if he had seen her. Relating the circumstances of their walk and suspicions before they strolled inside the reception area. "I left her by the staircase. She took the stairs up to our room, but now she is missing." After assuring the manager he'd searched the area carefully for her, he leaned forward. "I am a Texas Ranger, sir. If she were here, I'd know it."

Chapter Seven

The manager slid a paper out and wrote a note, slipping it to Chase before announcing in a loud voice he could do nothing to help and walking away.

The ranger flipped it over.

I saw the girl. Meet me behind the hotel in five minutes, and I will tell you what I know. Do not let anyone see you leave. It is dangerous for us both.

Strolling out the front door of the hotel and around to the garden, he searched the trees and bushes for several minutes before slipping behind the hotel.

The manager waited beside the back door, pale with anxiety. "Several young ladies have gone missing from the Menger in the past few months, and every time there is a man with dark hair and a mustache who invites them in and requests a room for them. He is the man you called Mr. Matthews but goes by a different name every time." He wiped his forehead with a shaking hand. "I believe he is abducting the women and taking them to Rio Grande City to be sold."

Chase's stomach tightened and his chest grew heavy. Dammit to hell! He had dealt with this sort of thing before and didn't want to think of his Rose being taken. "Why haven't you reported your suspicions?"

The manager glanced around them. "I reported to the sheriff, and he told me he'd investigate the situation. But a week after I made my complaint, they abducted me on my way home and beat me. Mr. Matthews brought three men with him, and they told me if I talked to the law again, they'd kill me and my wife."

The ranger nodded. "What makes you think they are taking the women to Rio Grande City? Why not Mexico?"

The manager leaned close. "I heard them talking about a partner in Rio Grande City." His voice dropped to a whisper. "Your Mr. Matthews spoke to the woman you described, and she followed him out the back door here." He pointed to the area around him. "If anyone asks, I know nothing and said nothing." After making his statement, the man disappeared into the hotel without looking back.

Chase saw red. Several long minutes passed before he could think straight enough to study the area. There were two horses and a wagon coming and going in the last hour. Following the wagon tracks into the street, he noted they turned west for Rio Grande City.

With trembling hands, he wiped the perspiration from his face. Rose must be terrified. He should have warned her about strangers. Especially men who met single women at the stagecoach office or train depot. Too trusting and sweet to understand the evil he met every day, she would make excuses for the man, for Rose possessed a heart as big as the great outdoors.

Shoving his panic to the bottom of his boot, he sank to his heels and studied the tracks. He might miss something important if he let his hot head rule his thinking. Emotion clouded the judgment and provided a luxury he could not afford. Jamming his hands into his pockets to keep them under control, he fantasized about strangling Mr. Matthews.

Classic human traffickers contacted their victims, usually at the train depot or stagecoach office, and appeared as kind, helpful folk offering assistance in a strange city. Luring their victims to hotels of their choice, they kept track of their mark's behavior while they plotted the best time and place to make their abduction. The man who watched them must work for Mr. Matthews and made his move once Chase walked away.

He hurried around front and up to their room. Rose must be so frightened and alone. Rage grew minute by minute as he packed her clothes in her valise and gathered his personal items from their room. Turning in the door on his way out, he spoke into the silence. "I'm coming for you, darlin'. You know I will, and God help the men who did this to you."

Taking his horse from the hotel stables, he rode to the telegram office and sent Reese a message informing him of Rose's disappearance, mentioning Mr. Matthews and his suspicions.

They will take her to Rio Grande City-Stop

The center of human trafficking-Stop

Saving Grace-Stop

Do not tell Mama I love her-Stop

I will do it myself- Stop

Copying the telegram, he paid the operator to send the important information to Chief Tafford as well. He would need all the help he could get.

Turning to leave, the telegraph operator stopped him. "You're getting a reply."

Chase waited while the clerk deciphered the message. Chief Tafford kept a wire and operator inside the ranger office, and his quick response came as no surprise although his message set him back on his heels.

Sam Walker dead-Stop
Everyone dead-Stop
Attacked five days out of San Antonio-Stop
Unknown armed men-Stop
Delgato free-Stop.
Investigating information leak-Stop
Chief Tafford Houston Division
Texas Rangers

Shock and disbelief rocked Chase's world. What the hell happened? Holding the telegram from Chief Tafford, he reread it shaking his head in denial. None of this made any sense. Sam brought four deputies with him, could shoot better than most gunfighters, and proved time and again to be one of the best rangers he ever had the privilege to work with. Sam made sure he doubled back and kept watch on his back trail. The perpetrators would have to know his partner's method, what trail he took, and have a Goddamned army because Sam was one of the toughest sons-of-bitches who ever lived and wouldn't have died easy.

With Delgato on the loose, Rose would be his number one target. He must find her and get her the hell out of Texas and back to Chicago, where Reese could protect her. Then, he'd recapture Delgato, and this time, he wouldn't just arrest him. He'd kill the bastard for what he did to Sam and the others. Chase shook his head. Sam Walker dead. The notion took some getting used to.

Exiting the telegraph office, he stepped out onto the street and rolled his shoulders. It took twelve days of hard riding to reach Rio Grande City. Good thing he'd done this before because he knew how the traffickers operated and where they'd take her.

****

Rose curled up in a ball in the back of the rumbling wagon and sucked in air through the thick cloth over her head. Her hands and feet were bound, and her head hurt where Mr. Matthews' men struck her back at the hotel. Biting her lip, she felt like a fool for believing the man and his lies. Never again would she trust someone she didn't know.

Thank God she tucked her reticule into her pocket before leaving the room with Chase. The weight of her pistol comforted her and gave her hope, although panic never strayed far from her mind. Dropping her head, she forced her body to relax and thought hard about her situation. Her friend Shanna had been abducted, and her life threatened. Talking about her experience afterward, she advised Rose to never show fear. Shanna made it out alive, and so would she. Forcing a serene expression when all her kicking and biting made no difference, she shrugged and grew still, waiting for her opportunity. Mr. Matthews and his friends planned to sell her to the highest bidder in Rio Grande City, and her reluctance to conform to their demands made them angrier. Her fiancé's image gave her the courage to inform her captors they were dead men walking.

They dropped a hood over her head in response.

Chase would find her and kill the bastards who hurt her. Twisting her wrists against the rope, she sighed. Too thick and too tight, her binding would soon make her wrists raw.

Listening to the rumble of the road, a cow mooed nearby. Wondering how long she had been unconscious, she calculated they were several miles from San Antonio and security. The wagon slowed and men spoke in rapid

Spanish. She frowned and sucked in a breath of air. A herd of goats must be close because she heard their bleating and got a whiff of their pungent odor. Fighting nausea, she held her stomach until the urge to puke passed. The smell of the animals, coupled with the heat in the back of the wagon, made her sick to her stomach. Someone whistled, and the bleating grew distant as the wagon rumbled on.

Licking her dry lips, she squirmed onto her other side and wished for a drink of water. The sun beat down on her and made her dizzy.

"Hey!" She yelled, hoping the men would hear her above the noise of the wagon, and called again.

Movement came from the front of the wagon, and someone leaned over her. They poked her shoulder.

Jerking away, she yelled at the top of her voice.

"Jesus Christ, what do you want?" Mr. Matthew's voice came closer and into the back beside her. He jerked the hood from her head. "What's the problem, now? I told you to be quiet."

Rose ducked to shield her eyes from the sudden brightness of the sun. "It's too hot. I need water."

One of the men up front said something in Spanish, and the one still leaning over her laughed.

Mr. Matthews sighed. "I am not getting paid enough for this. They told me you would not be a problem, and if I'd known what a pain in the ass you were, I would have asked for more."

Glaring, she folded her arms. "Who told you I wouldn't be a problem? The man you had watching me? A lot he knows. How well can one know anyone from a few peeks through the bushes? I need water, or I'll die before I get wherever you're taking me. If I do, all this will be for nothing because you won't get paid."

Her threats worked.

With an oath, Mr. Matthews grabbed the canteen from its hook by the front seat and twisted off the cap. "Here."

Tilting her head to the side, she smiled sweetly. "I can't open it or drink from it on my own because—" Holding her bound hands up, she waved them in his face.

Mr. Matthews said words Rose had never heard before, and she used to tend the counter at the mercantile for saddle-weary drifters and cowboys. She knew more swear words than most.

Holding the canteen up to her face, he allowed her to drink greedily.

Her captor took it away before she finished and twisted the cap on. "I'm not giving you any more. If you were a good girl and did what you were told, I would be nicer."

Keeping her expression serene, she answered. "If you don't give me enough, your employer will be displeased. What use will I be to him if I'm unconscious?"

Mr. Matthews growled and gave her another drink. When she finished, he gave her a good glare. "This trip won't be over fast enough for me."

Rose smiled. "For me, either, because when my fiancé finds you, you will wish you never laid eyes on me."

Her captor frowned. "The ranger is your fiancé?" Turning to one of the men, he said something in Spanish, and the three men held a heated conversation.

She studied their faces with interest. They must know Chase's reputation and didn't like the risk he presented. Her hopes sank when after a few minutes, Mr. Matthews shrugged. "You will be delivered before the ranger has a chance to rescue you. Our reward for abducting you is worth too much to give in now. But we do thank you, Miss Tanner, for alerting us to the danger."

Panic rose high in her chest, and she struggled to keep her expression bland in the wake. Forcing her mind to think of other things than who paid them to kidnap her and why, she turned her face away. Having no enemies of her own, she concluded this must be connected to Chase in some way.

The man beside her dropped the cloth back over her head, and Rose lay down wondering if her fiancé knew of her abduction yet. Having no idea how long he had been gone searching before he arrived back at their room, she figured he must know her predicament by now.

A sudden thought crossed her mind. But how would he know about Mr. Matthews and what direction he took her? Panic rose to her chest and tightened before sound reason intervened. Her ranger tracked criminals for a living and would find her. She repeated the words over and over in her mind for comfort. How could she know the charming man who escorted her to Menger Hotel could be capable of such a horrible thing? Her captor's charm dropped the second he got her alone. After her initial protests involving a lot of kicking and biting, she quieted down. A bullet in the head did not appear on her list of things to do today. Knowing the criminal mind as he did, Chase would see through Mr. Matthews' façade and come for her. He had to.

She must have dozed off because the next thing she knew, cool air blew across her, and the wagon slowed to a stop. The men murmured, and everyone but Mr.

Matthews and Rose climbed out.

"We are making camp here." Her captor's clipped voice startled her.

Sitting up, she stretched as much as she could until Mr. Matthews removed the hood from her head.

Surprised to see darkness and stars, she glanced up. "Where are we?"

He stared at her for several minutes, ignoring her question. "I'm going to take a chance and cut the rope around your feet. But I warn you, don't try anything, or I will put a bullet in your head and tell my employer you were shot trying to escape."

Rose nodded. The right opportunity would come. It might not be tonight, but soon.

Removing a knife from his boot, Mr. Matthews cut the ropes around her feet.

A whimper escaped despite her determination to remain aloof as blood returned to her limbs along with pin and needle pain. Holding her hands out, she hoped he would relieve her of those bands as well.

Laughing, he shook his head. "After all the scratching and biting you did? I don't think you'll have the use of your hands for some time because I'm not cutting you loose."

Rose shrugged and crawled to the back of the wagon. Scooting her legs off the edge, she slipped to her feet and held the side for support as pain shot up her legs, and her knees wobbled. All the kicking made her sore. So, she gave her limbs a minute to adjust to her weight.

Mr. Matthews jumped from the wagon beside her and walked toward the fire his partners lit.

After a minute, she made her way into the clump of trees and searched for a private area to take care of her needs. Afterward, she wandered around for a few minutes to get her bearing, wishing she had paid more attention when Shanna explained how to tell which direction to take by the pattern of the stars.

Staring up, she jumped when the metallic click of a gun hammer being drawn back sounded next to her ear. Turning, she faced a furious Mr. Matthews.

"Camp is over there." He indicated his left. "What were you doing out here all this time?"

She shrugged. "Watering my garden and plotting my escape by the stars. What else would I be doing? I've had a hood over my head all day." She nodded at his gun. "You can put your gun away. I know if I made a dash for freedom, you'd catch me before I got very far. My skirts and petticoats would slow me down, and you have horses."

Coyotes howled in the distance, and Rose shivered, reminding her frantic heart she'd made it a whole day without Chase and still lived.

Her captor noted her discomfort and laughed, letting the hammer down on his pistol before sliding the weapon back into the holster he wore on his side. "If you try to escape, I'll tie you to the nearest tree and cover you in blood so the coyotes tear you apart."

Gripping her arm, he forced her back to the fire where the men sat, turning a jackrabbit on a spit.

Rose's stomach revolted at the sight. She tried the tough meat once and entertained no plans to repeat the exercise. "Is there somewhere I can lie down? I'm not feeling well."

Mr. Matthews glanced at her. "I'll get a blanket." Nudging his chin toward a spot on the far side of the fire, he turned toward the wagon.

She gaped. Did he expect her to sleep in the dirt with the snakes, spiders, and occasional scorpion? She turned and followed. "I think I'll sleep in the back of the wagon."

The man shrugged. "Suit yourself. If you plan to escape in the night, I might point out I'm the best tracker in Texas." His gaze narrowed on her face. "I will find you and make you regret your decision."

She didn't bother to answer because he lied. Her fiancé was the best tracker in Texas and followed their trail, even now. She knew the truth of the statement in her heart.

Climbing into the back of the wagon where Mr. Matthews threw a blanket, she curled up in a ball and drew the woolen fabric over her as best she could. Staring up at the night sky, she spoke to the moon and stars about Chase.

Chapter Eight

How could she be so foolish as to trust Mr. Matthews? She allowed him to recommend a hotel and escort her there. Her naivete put her in harm's way, and he took advantage of the situation. Did he follow her and Chase when they went out, or did someone else? Perhaps one of the men sitting beside the fire kept them in sight. She remembered the prickly feeling when she first arrived. Puzzling over the whole affair, she rolled to her side and stacked her hands under her head. Mr. Mathews made a point of kissing her hand, betraying her as Judas did his master. The act must signal a new target to the man watching from the bushes. If so, who paid them to single out women, and why abduct her? If this involved Chase, as she suspected, one of them would have to know her name and face.

A man beside the fire said something, and Mr. Matthews' voice drifted toward her through the darkness. "No. We must deliver her untouched. We won't get paid otherwise."

The voices died away.

Rose swallowed the lump in her throat as icy fear wound its tentacles around her chest. Jumping at every little sound, she lay for hours staring into the darkness, alert for the bulky shape of a man intent on compromising her.

"Stop it." Her voice sounded odd to her ears, and she

wished for the hundredth time she carried a blade on her thigh like Shanna. If she did, she could cut her ropes and disappear into the night. Until the sun rose high in the Texas sky. Rose bit her lip. She wouldn't last one day alone in the heat, and she knew it.

One problem at a time. Studying the blinking stars overhead and reciting rhymes made her heart rate return to normal. If they attempted to force their attention on her, she'd drop them in their tracks, one way or another. All she had to do was pretend to be Shanna.

****

Chase sent Rose's valise to headquarters in Houston before checking his knives and added a few more to the belt he wore across his chest. Some men called them bandoliers and filled them with extra ammunition. But he filled his with throwing knives. Following a bad experience with guns as a youth, he preferred to do his fighting with blades and wielded them with fatal precision. He'd need plenty for the action he knew he'd see before he rescued his fiancée. Once he got her somewhere safe, he'd finish Delgato. After packing food and water, he swung into the saddle and patted his dappled stallion, Aries. "Let's go, boy. Rose needs us."

Turning his mount's head west, he nudged the beast into a gallop, calculating they would catch up in a day or so. Narrowing his gaze on the horizon, he frowned. Women were captured and sold in Rio Grande City as well as Mexico on a regular basis. Many organizations paid men to hang around the train depot and stagecoach offices in search of single women. Did the villains have their eye on Rose the second she stepped foot into town? Rose mentioned Mr. Matthews met her by the stagecoach office and offered to find her a place to stay.

He frowned. Or did her disappearance have something to do with him? Many of his enemies would like nothing more than to find something or someone he cared about. For this reason, he hadn't said anything about Rose to anyone but the captain and Sam. Thank God he killed the worst of them, El Diablo. For if he were alive and the man responsible for her capture, she would already be dead. Killed this same time last year, El Diablo topped his list as the meanest son-of-a-bitch he had ever met. A man who reigned as king, raping, murdering, and plundering an entire region and several villages he considered his. Abducting local girls and visitors alike, he either sold them or added them to his harem. When Chase first investigated his case, he spent months searching for the bastard. But the devil struck like the rainstorms in southern Texas in the summer, violent, sudden, and gone without a trace.

He got his first big break when he met Rozita, and she informed him she would do whatever she must to see El Diablo receive the justice he deserved. Having no love for the man, she wanted him dead for what he did to her and her sister. Her tip on the location of the bastard's Texas headquarters got him close enough to plan an attack, and she proved to be an invaluable asset since.

El Diablo's headquarters turned out to be a beautiful white stucco villa with a ten-foot wall in Eagle Pass, Texas. Keeping the area under constant surveillance until he knew for sure the general and his men were all inside, he kept three rangers busy full time. Few could recognize the man, but Rozita did. She mentioned he stood medium height with black hair and a mustache. The man wore a signet ring depicting a devil's trident on his right little finger.

When Chase caught sight of the man entering the villa, he gave the order to attack. A few sticks of dynamite, some nitroglycerin, and a bunch of knives later, El Diablo's reign of terror died with him. Frustrating in the extreme, Delgato's body had not been among the dead within the compound, although the general's was.

Sighing, Chase shook his head, regretting not tracking the man down and shooting him then and there. In his defense, he figured with El Diablo out of the equation, peace along the border would be restored. But Delgato hosted other ideas. And for the past year, he occupied the number one target on Chase's hit list.

Did the bastard have something to do with Rose's disappearance? Frowning, he trotted Aries over a hill and down the other side. The man would know her name and face from the cantina in San Antonio, which is why he must die.

The bastard had plenty of time to orchestrate the whole event after being free for five days. A lot could happen in a week. According to Rozita, Delgato vowed revenge for El Diablo and his fallen soldiers after he discovered his boss's body alongside his favorite woman, Maria Garcia.

The woman also happened to be Delgato's sister.

The upper part of their bodies lay beneath a heavy cement column, crushed beyond recognition. Chase identified El Diablo by the heavy gold ring on his littlest finger, where his hands clasped tight around Maria Garcia. As if in his final moments, he sought to protect her from disaster.

Chase didn't like the casualties they found inside the villa when they sifted through the rubble. The servants and whores didn't deserve to die along with the man who made their lives a living hell. He commanded his men to save as many as they could because he didn't believe in the ravages of war. If a person were innocent, they should live and do so on their own terms.

The first night out of San Antonio, a full moon lit his path, so he kept going figuring he could catch the wagon if he kept up the pace. Once the sun rose, he studied both sides of the road for tracks, calculating he'd be on the bandits come nightfall the fourth day. Thoughts of Rose kept him going, despite his weariness, knowing she must be terrified. He avoided any thought of what they might be doing to her because he couldn't afford to lose his focus. Rage burned bright in his veins, and he swore whoever the bastards were, they would die.

"I'm coming for you, darlin'."

He stopped at midnight the second day for a little rest. Clouds covered the sky, and he couldn't see as well as he'd like. Concerned he might miss something important if he kept going, he made camp and took care of Aries. The next morning, he made coffee and chewed on jerky. Rinsing out his cup and canteen, he packed his meager belongings and hit the trail. Rose and getting her to safety occupied his thoughts as storm clouds darkened the sky. Swearing at the unexpected turn of bad luck, he nudged Aries into a trot, determined to make some distance before the wetness washed their trail away. Nothing would keep him from finding her. Nothing.

****

Rozita Sanchez dressed with care for her meeting, hoping her somber brown skirt and cream blouse conveyed trust and honesty. Nervousness tightened her stomach because the boss entertained suspicions about her part in the attack at Eagle Pass. El Diablo showed up at the wrong time with his men. But she could not be blamed. How could she know Maria entertained the son of her lover's enemy even as the devil snuck into the compound to catch them together? Her simple plan to get rid of the competition and become the master's favorite blew up in her face, literally. And Delgato never liked her, seizing the opportunity to whisper doubts in the master's ears about her involvement. She must convince them all of her innocence or die by Delgato's decree.

Smoothing her skirt and pinching her cheeks for color, she adopted a nonchalant expression to hide her anxiety. No one must suspect her part in any of this.

Memories of the past filled her breast with rage as she relived being captured with her younger sister, Consuela, four years ago, along with the other girls in her village. Taken to El Diablo's stronghold twenty miles inside the Mexican border, he kept women under locked guard before they were sold to the highest bidder. Men traveled for miles to view the goods the devil put on display until, one by one, the other girls were sold, and Consuela and Rozita alone remained. When the last of the girls were carted away, Rozita and her sister were relocated to El Diablo's women's quarters, where they joined his harem and learned the ways of men.

Muscular and dark, the devil ruled the compound, and his word was law. Feeling her way through the horrors of the situation, she soon discovered a hierarchy existed within the harem. The most favored received privileges, expensive gifts, and freedom. At the top, Maria Garcia ruled them all. Tall, buxom, and beautiful, she reigned as El Diablo's favorite with her long, flowing, ebony hair, dark almond-shaped eyes, and perfect curves. Her suites took up the entire third floor of his lavish home.

Determined to enjoy the luxurious life and freedom of Maria Garcia, Rozita rose in the hierarchy and soon occupied the second most favored position. The master slept in her bed when he and Maria were out of sorts. And for a short time, she reveled in her power. On one such occasion, El Diablo took Rozita to San Antonio on a business trip, promising to buy her a diamond ring she fancied. While he conducted his meetings, she wandered the shops alone, spending all the money she brought with her.

When she returned to their hotel to cajole more from her master, she found him pacing the floor for her return. Announcing he planned to leave for Mexico within the hour, he hurried away to prepare. Maria had forgiven him, and he burned to return to his favorite's bed.

Ordering Rozita to pack her things, he never once glanced back to see how *she* felt.

Furious at the turn of events, Rozita kept her anger hidden while the need for revenge fired her blood. She wanted the ring. She wanted power, and she wanted El Diablo's money. Gathering every expensive thing she could, she rode in silence toward the compound, knowing the ring would have to wait for another time. If Maria and the master made up, it could be weeks, perhaps months, before he offered to buy Rozita more jewelry. In order to live the life she deserved, something must be done about Maria.

Pausing on her way through the corridor one day in their Mexican stronghold, she stopped outside the door as El Diablo and Delgato talked. A Texas Ranger out of Houston asked questions about him and killed several of his men in his search. Something must be done for the ranger probed too close for comfort.

The master planned to keep Maria at Eagle's Pass for several weeks for safety, and he ordered Delgato to keep an eye on her.

Deep in thought, Rozita left the compound with a plan. Why settle for baubles when she could have it all? Traveling to Houston to find Ranger Chase Calhan, she gave him the location of El Diablo's Eagle Pass residence and swore her master would be there at a certain date. Smiling over her cunning plan, she rode away happy. With Maria out of the way, she would soon have the devil eating out of the palm of her hand. All the lovely wealth, power, and freedom his top woman enjoyed would be hers to wield according to her own pleasure. Her simple plan should have worked, except El Diablo ordered his men to Eagle Pass the day before the rangers attacked.

He came to kill her lover.

Because the master occupied the villa when Chase blew it up, Delgato suspected she had a hand in the attack.

And somehow, she must atone for her mistake.

Anxious about the man's attitude toward her following his escape from the rangers, she worried he would discover her part in his capture. If he did, she would need powerful allies…and another plan to rid her life of his presence.

"The boss will see you now." The deep voice broke into her reflections, making her jump in alarm.

Rising to her feet, she smiled wide and sailed past the armed man at the door. Once inside, she fell to her knees before the gleaming oak desk. Reigning supreme as the most powerful man in Mexico, she must have the boss's favor if she were to survive. Delgato had not forgiven her for her part in El Diablo's death.

"Why have you come?" His black glittering eyes narrowed.

"I come to seek your favor, *El Jefe*. I have been accused of many lies and wish to speak the truth. What can I do to assure you of my loyalty?" Trembling, she lowered her gaze, hoping her voice did not reveal the frantic beat of her heart. This man could snuff her life out with a flick of his fingers.

He snipped a fat cigar and lit the end while he kept his gaze on her face. "What do you know of Ranger Calhan's woman?"

"You were wise to enlist Ranger Kaplan. His presence in the ranger station is invaluable, but he is stupid. His plan to capture *Rosa* in Houston failed, and she escaped. The woman followed Ranger Calhan to San Antonio. My sources say she has been abducted by some locals and taken to Rio Grande City. She will be no problem to whoever you send to kill her, for she is colorless and weak. I hope this information pleases you and alleviates any doubts you have about me."

The dark gaze of the man behind the desk studied her for several long minutes. "I will give you one more chance. Send the men to find this woman and bring her to me. Alive. Kill everyone else. Your debt will be paid when I have Ranger Calhan and his woman in my villa. See to it there are no more mistakes."

****

Rose huddled beneath the blanket as sheets of rain poured down on them. Closing her eyes, she envisioned Chase riding up and shooting her captors before taking her in his arms and kissing her senseless. She sighed. Mr. Matthews had no idea what kind of trouble he bought when he tossed her in the back of the wagon and hauled ass for Rio Grande City. But Rose did. Chase Calhan would tear him apart once he caught up to them, and nothing would stop him.

A series of thunder clouds gathered overhead, and her smile dimmed along with the darkening sun. The rain would wash their tracks away, and her fiancé would not be able to find her. Chanting nursery rhymes to keep her mind from dwelling on her present situation, she didn't allow fear to enter her thoughts until the rain poured down in torrents. Too sudden and too violent to sink into the earth and make tracking the heavy wagon easier, the water raced downhill, creating a flash flood.

Rose sat up and gazed over the side. How would Chase know which way they took when the wheel tracks disappeared before they traveled twenty feet? Gritting her teeth, she whispered soothing words to calm her heart. "Chase tracks criminals for a living. A little gully washer won't slow him down. He will find me."

Closing her eyes, she replaced her nursery chants with prayers while the weight of her pistol reminded her she had a chance if she used it wisely.

"No one can track us in this rain." Mr. Matthews chortled with glee. "Even the great Chase Calhan." Gazing into Rose's downcast face, he chuckled. "You worried me for a bit there with all your talk about his prowess as a lawman, but he isn't coming. We've backtracked our trail, and Calhan isn't following us. Best get used to the idea you won't see him again, and about this time next month, you'll be serving a new master on your back."

Rose glared. "The only thing happening in the next month is your rotting bones bleaching in the sun. Chase is the best ranger in the district for a reason. Do you suppose a little rain will keep him from finding me?"

Her captor's eyes narrowed. "I told you; he isn't coming. He would be closing in by now."

Her heart sank. Mr. Matthews made a good point. Staring up at the bleak sky until they threw the hood over her head, she curled into a ball beneath her blanket. Chase had to find her, had to be looking. Envisioning him tracking their wagon kept her hope alive and gave her the courage to keep her wits about her. He wouldn't let her be sold or ravished. He couldn't. Memories of their talk the day she arrived in San Antonio played in her mind. "*Remember one thing, darlin'. I will always come for you.*" And she would be ready. Swallowing her fear, she put her mind to laying out her garden at Chase's Texas ranch. He would come.

The rain poured down for an hour, and when it stopped, she shivered beneath her sodden blanket. "Are we stopping soon? I'm cold, I'm wet, and I'm hungry. If you leave me like this, I'll catch my death, and your hope of getting paid will die with me."

The hood lifted off her head, and Mr. Matthews skinny face appeared nose to nose with hers. "We've had this talk before, and I'm getting tired of you using the same excuse on me. Keep it up, and I'll shoot you dead and tell the boss you were wasted effort."

She smiled. "Then he'd shoot you." Saying the first thing which popped into her head, she didn't realize her statement contained truth until her tormentor paled. Tucking the information away for future use, she tilted her head. "So are we stopping or what?"

"Drive into the next village. The princess wants to rest." Growling, he took his seat.

Chapter Nine

Rose draped the sopping blanket over the side of the wagon box and wrapped her arms around her middle to hide her trembling. Thank God Shanna gave her pointers on being abducted, or she'd be terror-stricken.

They rumbled along for another four miles before a farmhouse appeared on the horizon, and Mr. Matthews sent one of the men to speak to the farmer.

He offered them the barn and a bed of straw for the night. When her captor pointed at a stall, she protested and walked toward the stairs leading to the loft. She stopped when he stepped into her path.

"You stay down here with us."

Tilting her chin in defiance, she opened her mouth to tell him what he could do with his suggestion when a slow smile spread across his face.

"I could always make you sleep with me."

Rose snapped her mouth shut, marched over to the blanket in the straw he indicated, and rolled her body up in it. Scooting as far from the men as she could with her limited ability to use her hands, she turned her back and feigned sleep.

Mr. Matthew's laughter followed her. "Any more back talk, and I will take you to my bed."

Rose grimaced, wishing she remembered to not show fear. Her abductor recognized her terror when he mentioned sleeping with him and pounced on it like chicken on a grasshopper. Somehow, she must get him off balance again, or her life would be unbearable. Thoughts of another man touching her rolled her stomach, and she scooted farther away until she came up against the back wall of the stable. Turning so she faced the room with her back protected, she surveyed the area and men's positions. Having no idea how she would defend her virtue with her hands bound together and her pistol inside her reticule, inside her pocket, she'd be damned before she let them take advantage of her.

The night grew long and cold, and she slept very little. When at last the sun peeked over the horizon, Rose sat up, leaned against the wall behind her, and ate the porridge Mr. Matthews handed her without comment.

He wouldn't allow her to see the farmer or his wife to thank them for the hot food. "We don't want them to see your face. The less they know about us, the better."

When Rose insisted, the man turned, his glimmering blue eyes in her direction. "Go ahead. Show your face to them. But if you do, I'll kill them, so they can't tell anyone you were here."

Her heart sank. Mr. Matthews squashed her plans in one fell swoop. She had hoped to pass a message to Chase if he came asking about her.

Clamoring into the back of the wagon, she sat with her back against the seat. Running a hand over the blanket still looped over the side of the wagon bed, she discovered the hot Texas sun sucked the moisture out of it in the few hours since it rose. Rose closed her eyes. "Please, God, help Chase find me."

Two hours later, they rumbled over a high spot and surprised a wild bull drinking from a creek at the bottom. He stood directly in their path with his massive head turned in their direction. Snorting fire and pawing the ground, he shook his head in anger.

Gripping the blanket in her lap, she bit her lip. Chase told her about the wild bulls he came across in his work and advised her to give them a wide berth.

"Heeyah!" Mr. Matthews rose to his feet and shot his pistol into the air. "Get out of here! Go on! Heeyah!"

The noise enraged the bull further. His snorting grew louder, and he lowered his head, pawing the ground with his mammoth hooves, making the earth rumble.

The hair on the back of Rose's neck prickled with tension as she held the side of the wagon in a death grip. Mr. Matthews re-bound her hands the night before, and now she wished for the use of them. When the bull lowered his head, she didn't wait around to see the outcome. Bailing over the opposite side of the wagon, she ran for her life.

Glancing back, she witnessed Mr. Matthews shoot the bull in the head, but the bullet didn't slow him down, and he kept coming. He hit the side of the wagon with a crash, and the wood splintered, knocking the equipage sideways.

Mr. Matthew sailed over the side and landed several feet from the wagon while the other men flew in the opposite direction. The bull circled and lowered his head for another pass, bellowing with rage as he tipped the wagon over on its side.

Three more shots rang out behind her as she ran for the nearest oak tree. Unsure how to climb with her hands bound together, sheer terror got her several feet above the ground.

Bracing her body with her feet, she leaned against a large branch while she searched the area behind her for the angry beast. Another shot rang out, and Mr. Matthews yelled. Not sure how this answered her prayers, but she accepted the gift with gratitude. Anything to keep her abductors from dragging her farther away from Chase created a welcome diversion.

Once Rose grew certain the bull had left the area, she shinnied her way back to the ground and ran. She made it twenty feet before a bullet hit the ground in front of her. Stopping cold, she turned around to face one of Mr. Matthews men behind her with his gun leveled at her chest.

"This way, *Senorita*."

Nodding, she plodded back the way she came with drooping shoulders. Her escape almost happened. If her hands were free, she could use her pistol and even out the odds. With the weapon, she had a decent chance of escape.

They found Mr. Matthews kicking the wagon and cussing. "Dammit to hell and gone!" Jumping up and down, he kicked the wagon again. "The damn horses ran off when the bull rammed the wagon and broke their hitch. We must find us new horses and fast, or that goddam ranger will be all over us like flies on day-old milk. We must get out of here."

"I thought you said he wasn't tracking us." Rose smiled, enjoying the man's frustration. Her prayers worked, after all.

Mr. Matthews glared and stomped away to talk to the men out of earshot. Two of them walked away while the other one forced her to sit by a tree with his pistol pointed at her head, waiting for their return.

A farmer, several miles outside the small town, sold them five horses.

Her captor cut the ropes, binding her hands before they mounted up.

His small blue eyes stared into hers. "If you try to escape, you will wish you hadn't been born."

Her chin lifted. Every captive focused on escape. Her as well. Nodding, she disguised her grimace when the rope fell to the ground, and blood flowed into her cold hands. "Thank you."

Working her hand back and forth, she circled her wrists, conscious of the weight of her pistol in her pocket. Climbing into the saddle, she followed Mr. Matthews while the other men rode behind her to keep her in line.

For the first three days, she slept under the armed stares of the men. To be truthful, slept is an exaggeration of what occurred. She tossed and turned all three nights for fear of what might happen if she dozed off. Mr. Matthews taunts of sleeping with her played and replayed inside her head.

On the fourth night, after their brush with the wild bull, her captor declared he planned to get some rest and lay down by the fire with his head in his saddle. His deep snores filled the night moments later while his men held a heated discussion in Spanish and glanced in her direction. Fear curled in her stomach, and anxiety tightened her mouth as she inched her reticule from her pocket and removed the pistol.

"If you touch her, I'll kill you." Mr. Matthews voice drifted across the camp from the fire.

His men stopped talking, turned away, unrolled their blankets, and lay down on different sides of the fire.

Sighing with relief, she turned to face the men and slipped her pistol down by her side out of sight. Tonight, she would make her move.

Midnight stole upon the silent camp beneath the silver light of the moon. Crickets chirped, and a slight breeze rustled across the dry earth. The scent of sagebrush and mesquite filled her senses.

Rose waited until she figured all the men were asleep and slipped from her blanket. Pocketing her pistol, she stole on silent feet toward her horse. Keeping her gaze on her captors, she led her mare from camp and walked back the way they came. Once she figured they were far enough away to not be heard, she climbed into the saddle and nudged her mount north toward San Antonio. Kicking the mare into a gallop, she bent close, holding tight to the reins.

She had no idea how far she had traveled before a bullet whizzed past her head. Thundering hooves pounded the dirt road behind her, and Rose flattened her body against the mare's neck, kicking her in the side. More shots sounded behind her. She turned her horse to the left to avoid the line of fire as the pounding hooves got closer. Suddenly fire burned her shoulder and knocked her from the saddle. She landed hard, tumbling across the ground, heels over head, until she stopped with a bone-jarring splat. Her frightened horse reared and galloped away leaving her wounded and alone.

Lying face-down, sucking breath into her flattened lungs, dizziness washed over her. Not sure if she lived or not, every part of her ached as she took stock of her injuries. Both arms worked as well as both legs. Nausea rose in her throat, and her head hurt like hellfire. Rolling to her left side, she wrapped her arms around her middle and focused on breathing.

Her pursuer caught up to her a few minutes later and

damn near trampled her. Rose tucked and rolled to get away from the thundering hooves, landing in a clump of bushes with a groan.

"Where the hell did she go? I could of swore she fell to the ground after you shot her." Mr. Matthews' voice bellowed from off to her left.

She didn't dare breathe. Her shoulder burned, and her head swam from her sudden movement, so she focused on a leaf near her face, drawing in short breaths. Removing her pistol from her pocket, she waited.

Then more gunfire shot through the night as horses galloped past and men shouted. Furious activity exploded around her for several minutes while Rose curled up into a tight ball to avoid detection. She had no idea who the interlopers were until a minute later when a large hand grabbed her by the hair and yanked her from the bushes. A man in uniform held her up for inspection. Swinging the pistol in her captor's direction, she fired off a shot fighting with her might to get free.

The man gave a howl of pain, dropped her to her feet, and clutched his shoulder.

She took the opportunity to turn and ran as fast as her aching body would let her.

Out of nowhere, a horse knocked her to the ground, and a hand jerked her pistol from her fist.

"She is here, *senor*. I have her *pistola*." The deep voice sounded smug with delight, and she wanted to punch him in the throat.

The hand turned her to the man in uniform with a bloody shoulder. His fuzzy image swam before her eyes as he lifted his hand to strike her.

Rose knew no more for some time.

When she awoke, she lay on her side facing a large

fire. Her hands were bound, as well as her feet. But this time no pistol rested in her pocket offering a chance to escape.

Great. Here we go again. Blinking, she moved her arm to cover her face and discovered someone had bandaged her wound. Her shoulder burned, and her body ached as the events of her near escape flooded her mind. They took her pistol, whoever they were. Her split lip and swollen eye where the soldier hit her tingled with pain. Where did they take her? Gaping up at the night sky, too sore to turn her head, she sought out different patterns of stars, hoping they told her the answer. Men's voices drifted toward her from the fire, and a horse snorted nearby, frightening the life out of her.

Easing onto her other side, she gazed around her. She lay on a blanket in the dirt, and her mare stood tied to a small tree several feet away. Rose frowned. How long had she been asleep?

The man in uniform walked toward her with a scowl on his face and his shoulder bandaged. She should practice more. If her bullet were two inches to the left, he wouldn't be here. Reese would tell her to slow down and breathe before squeezing the trigger.

Rozita Sanchez accompanied the soldier, sauntering behind him with a sneer of contempt. Her brightly colored skirt and ruffled blouse were at odds with the sour expression she wore.

Stopping in front of Rose, she crouched down. "The men want to kill you for the trouble you make, but I have other plans. *Mi jefe* wishes you to visit him at his villa, and so you live." Picking up a strand of Rose's hair, she stared at it. "I do not understand what *Senor* Chase sees in your pale face and skinny body when he can have a real woman anytime and does not." Grimacing, she dropped the hair and rose to her feet. "It does not matter, I suppose, for soon you will belong to other men, and *Senor* Chase will die."

Her fiancé trusted this woman, and she wasn't nice nor a friend but evil. "What do you mean he will die? Calhans don't die easy." She repeated Shanna's words the day of her almost wedding and lifted her chin in defiance.

The woman ignored her question. "Tighten her binding so she cannot escape again. You are lucky I happened to be in the area and arrived to check on you. If this stupid woman escaped, your life would be over like so." She snapped her fingers in the soldier's face.

Rose swallowed the lump of fear in her throat. "When Chase discovers what you've done, he'll kill you." Glaring at Rozita with all the hate she could muster, and she could muster quite a bit, she spit on the ground at her feet.

The crazy woman laughed. "He will be dead before he gets the chance. *Mi jefe* will make certain this time."

Rose stared after her as she walked away. This time?

The soldier grumbled as he sank to his heels. Grabbing her hands, he tightened the twine until she cried out. "Rozita is right about one thing. You're damn lucky she showed up this morning because I planned to put a bullet in you for the mess you made."

She glanced at him. "What mess? I'm a captive. It's my job to get away."

The soldier glared. "We were supposed to find the men who abducted you and kill them. The general wants you brought to the villa, but when we attacked the camp, you were gone. The men who abducted you got away, and now, I must hunt them. The general wants no witnesses."

Talk about out of the frying pan and into the fire.

"The horses are ready, *senor*." A man approached wearing a wide brimmed hat and cotton clothes. He wore a multi-colored sash tied around his waist and woven sandals.

Rose stared. She had no idea such clothing existed. The shirt had no collar and the pants flared out at the bottom. Both articles were simple and devoid of decoration.

"We're coming." The soldier grabbed Rose by the arm and jerked her to her feet.

Swaying as pain and dizziness took control, her vision darkened, and she grabbed the air around her for something to hold on to. She came into contact with the soldier. Snatching her hand back, she took a step to the side. She'd take the darkness and whatever came with it rather than rely on him for help.

Rozita appeared at her side. "No, no *senorita*, you must live until we arrive at the villa. We have a surprise for you."

Rose doubled over and dry heaved onto the ground at the woman's feet. *Senorita* Sanchez could go to the devil.

The soldier handed her up to a swarthy man who smelled like cigars. Settling her on his lap, he wrapped his arms around her and kicked his horse into a gallop.

She held on in fear of her life.

Chapter Ten

Her hope of rescue diminished with every mile they traveled south, and she wondered if Chase knew about the village where they got their horses or the fact she'd been shot when she tried to escape. Keeping her eye on their back trail, she hoped to see a rider, but none appeared.

When they stopped to water the horses, Rozita laughed at her. "*Senor* Chase will not find you. He is miles from here and does not care you are our prisoner."

Rose folded her arms over her chest and glared. "You lie. He won't be fooled by you because he chases *banditos* for fun. When he finds me, your life will be over like so." Snapping her fingers as the woman did earlier, she imitated her haughty stance. *Banditos* constituted the only Spanish word she knew other than *si,* and she threw it into the conversation to sound smart. The other woman intimidated her, and she didn't know why.

Rozita threw her dark head back and laughed. "*Senor* Chase believes I am his friend and a victim of El Diablo's cruelty. I helped him kill his enemy, and he trusts me." She glanced sideways at Rose and smirked. "No one knew of his woman, but me. He tells me everything."

The other woman lied, and Rose knew it. Wondering where Rozita's hostility derived from, she said the first thing that popped into her head. "You think of Chase as more than a friend."

As soon as she said the words, she knew they were true and noted the flush on the other woman's cheeks. "To him, you are nothing but an informant, a source who helped him catch El Diablo. He speaks of you as a sister." Depriving the woman of her fantasies involving her fiancé tasted good.

Rozita glared. "*Senor* Calhan stares at me with longing in his eyes." Strolling closer, she tossed her head. "Are you certain the lawman wants your white child's body when he could have me?" Running her hands through her long black tresses, she indicated her full bosom and rounded hips. "I am everything a man desires."

Rose pinched her lips together. With her woman's body and full pouting lips, she didn't doubt men wanted her. But Chase belonged to her, and she wouldn't give him up. Twisting his ring on her finger, she didn't back down. "Chase isn't all men. He's had plenty of opportunity to accept your…invitation, but he hasn't because I'm the woman he cares for."

The truth of her words hung in the silence between them, and the dark-haired beauty's eyes flashed. She said nothing more as she strode to her horse and motioned for the men to mount up.

Twisting her hands in her lap to ease the rope cutting deep into her wrists, Rose heaved a sigh of relief and stared at the brush. Dust from the horses' hooves made her eyes water. Chase thought of the other woman as a sister and said as much when they discussed her in San Antonio. He couldn't hold Rose in his arms and make love to her like he did if his heart belonged to someone else. She kept her thoughts quiet. She riled Rozita more than she planned to and made the decision to say nothing more.

The soldier dropped her to the ground in the evenings, where another man gave her water and a dried biscuit. They allowed her a moment of privacy out of view of the guard but within earshot twice a day. The experience proved both humiliating and embarrassing. Rozita threw a scratchy woven blanket at her the first night, which Rose folded so she slept between the rough layers of the blanket. In the mornings, she received the same fare, a drink of water and a dry biscuit. They rode like the fiends of hell were on their trail, and she sympathized with the horses. Sweat dripped from their bodies, froth foamed from their mouths, and their sides heaved whenever they stopped.

Four days and nights of relentless travel and dry biscuits later, they arrived in Laredo.

Riding to the back of a local church, they stopped. Rozita's dark eyes flashed over Rose's pale face as she stepped down from her horse and indicated to the armed men beside the church door she wanted Rose removed from her captor's horse.

They caught her numb arms and dragged her off, forcing her to stand.

A whimper escaped her dry throat as blood pricked her stiff legs and feet.

The other woman smiled with satisfaction. "Now I have delivered you, I go to find *Senor* Chase. He will come to Laredo to search for you, and I must be ready." Her eyes filled with tears and dripped down her rosy cheeks in a flash. She changed from laughing to crying in a matter of seconds. "How do I look?" Her voice broke as if she had cried for hours, and a hiccup escaped. "Will *Senor* Chase believe I am heartbroken over his loss of you?"

Rose gaped at the transformation, unable to think of a single thing to say.

Rozita laughed as she sauntered away. "*Senor* Chase is not the only one who hunts for fun."

****

He studied the ground from every angle, looking for sign. The hard-packed dirt road did little for tracking, and after searching both sides of the road, he found their tracks. Experience told him he didn't have a lot of time, and the sons of bitches had a half-day's ride on him. Rio Grande City harbored the bastards who sold women and the buildings they kept them in before being sold. He'd rescued a senator's daughter two years ago and knew a local ranger in Rio Grande City who kept his eyes peeled for trafficking.

Chase stopped as soon as he spotted a telegraph office to send the man a description of Rose. He told the ranger in Rio Grande City to communicate through Chief Tafford because he couldn't afford to wait for an answer, and he couldn't afford to not know what the ranger found. Human traffickers tended to be consistent if anything, and everything about Rose's abduction pointed to the ring in Rio Grande City. From Mr. Matthews meeting her at the stagecoach office to the man following them through town and the fact their room showed no signs of forced entry.

He also sent a message to Chief Tafford to see if he learned anything new about her abductors.

Remounting, he rode hard to make up for lost time. Every minute that passed meant his woman could be in more trouble, and he couldn't bear to think of his sweet, gentle girl hurt or afraid. Hour after hour, he rode as if the jackals of hell nipped at his heels. Even the rain didn't slow him down, and he kept the pace as long as he could. When it stopped, he made camp and hung his clothes on sagebrush to dry in the hot sun while he rubbed Aries down with a dry cloth. He stopped four days into his journey when he discovered he hadn't eaten for two of them. With a groan of impatience for the curse of being human, he built a fire and cooked some salt pork and beans. Leading Aries to a stream, he let him drink while he rubbed his shiny coat. Then he turned him out with a hat full of grain and settled beside the fire with his bedroll and saddle.

He awoke to the sun coming over the horizon and Aries nickering by his head. Rolling to his feet, he gazed around and discovered he'd slept all night and well into the next morning.

Cursing, Chase splashed water on his head and made a cup of coffee before resaddling his horse. He kept his thoughts busy with details about his surroundings to keep his mind off Rose and what she might be going through. The stone in his stomach grew with each passing day, and he felt as though he were anchored with a heavy weight.

He would find her in time. He had to. Life without his Rose wouldn't be any life at all. Weary to the bone, he glanced at the sky. He's lost a half day sleeping while she traveled farther away from him. Ignoring the tightness in his chest, he urged Aries to go faster.

Topping a small incline, he discovered the destroyed wagon and stopped to investigate. They must have surprised a wild bull when they topped the ridge above the draw. Dropping to his haunches, he studied the tracks, circling the broken wagon until he found Rose's small prints running away. With trembling fingers, he touched one, and emotion choked his throat. Alive and well, at least at this point, with a strong even gait. Rising, he followed the tracks one of the men made to a farm and analyzed the situation. They bought horses from the farmer and continued their trek to Rio Grande City. For five sets of horse prints traveled together, one of them lighter than the others. Rose.

Hope and anxiety for her current welfare twisted a blade in his gut. She must live. They had so much to see and experience together. He wouldn't let this be the end. Stepping into the saddle, he continued.

Later the same day, he froze when he came across her escape attempt. Ten horsemen rode up from the south and surprised Mr. Matthews' band.

Fury blinded him while he investigated the scene and discovered blood on a patch of bushes. By God, if they hurt her, he'd tear them to pieces. Rage filled him with a new source of energy as he studied the ground. Three of Mr. Matthews' horses continued toward Rio Grande City while the other two grazed nearby on prairie grass. The sign indicated three of the attacking horsemen followed Mr. Matthews, his companion, and Rose, while the other horsemen rode back the way they came. Chase frowned. Who the hell were the new riders, and why did they attack? Why would they follow the survivors unless they planned to kill Matthews, Rose, and the other rider?

He needed help. Finding the nearest telegraph office, he sent a message to Chief Tafford updating him on the situation. Then he sent a telegram to the chief of the Rio Grande City Rangers informing him of

Matthews' arrival.

For the first time in Chase's life, he wasn't sure he'd make it in time, and the weight in his stomach settled lower. Racing after them, he knew Mr. Matthews and the rest would want to deliver her fast, especially once they caught scent of him following them. He found several places where they backtracked, checking their trail, and shook his head. They must know somewhere between them, the other three riders lurked.

Ten days after his fiancée's abduction, he rode into Rio Grande City and stopped in front of Texas Ranger headquarters. Tying Aries reins to the post out front, he made his way inside to give the commanding officer his report.

Requesting permission to search all the local traffickers, he kicked every door down and searched every corner, but no Rose.

Weary and discouraged, Chase dragged his body back to the ranger office and took a seat in front of the chief's desk. They gave him news. A woman fitting Rose's description had been spotted in a different part of town.

Striding from the office, he joined three local rangers and planned an attack. Kicking down a door in a disreputable hotel, he stepped inside to discover a woman tied to the bed with a hood over her head. With a sinking heart, Chase removed the hood. His woman possessed a shapelier body with longer, darker hair. Removing the hood from the woman's head, he shook his head at his companions. "This isn't Rose."

Leaving the other rangers to deal with the situation, he walked outside to vent his anger. Sick to his stomach and mad as hell, he beat everything in arm's reach.

Where the hell did they take Rose?

An hour later, he strode into the chief's office and resumed his previous seat.

"I have a message for you from Chief Tafford." The commanding officer handed Chase a telegram and leaned a hip against his desk.

Ranger Calhan Texas Rangers Rio Grande City, Texas-Stop

Rozita has information about Rose- Stop.

Meet her in Laredo. One week -Stop.

Kaplan a spy-Stop

More information later-Stop

Chief Tafford, Texas Rangers, Houston, Texas-Stop

Thanking the officer for his help, he strode from the office using every swear word in his considerable vocabulary to express his frustration.

Kaplan

So much made sense. The way Rozita knew about Rose, the way Delgato's men knew what trail Sam took with him in chains, all of it. The traitor made sure he read every transmission going through the Houston office and sold the information to whoever offered to pay.

Chase worked his hands, envisioning them around the man's neck and wanted to gut the other ranger for getting Sam killed.

Rozita. Laredo.

He came the wrong damn way and swore in Apache, Navajo, and French with a little Spanish for good measure. The men who attacked Matthews must have taken Rose south with them. Delgato must be involved if Rozita wanted to meet. Did Kaplan sell information to him about Rose, too? Chase punched the outside wall and stared at the busy street in front of him. He didn't want to think about what might be happening to his love at this moment. She would have to be strong a little longer.

****

They locked Rose in the back room of the church with twenty other women, all of them young and terrified. Some of the women sported bruises and black eyes, to her shocked dismay. Somewhere a man deserved to be whipped. Gazing at the variety of females filling the room, she wondered where they all hailed from.

Leaning close to the small, blonde-haired girl she judged to be eighteen or nineteen, she struck up a conversation. “Hi, I’m Rose. What’s your name?”

“Silence.” A tall man appeared in front of them with a whip in one hand. Crouching down to eye level, he smacked the handle of the whip on his open palm. “You’re new here, so I will not punish you this one time.” His gaze swept her face and dropped to her breasts.

Catching a whiff of cigar smoke and cheap whiskey, she damn near threw up on his brown cotton shirt.

“The rules are simple. No talking allowed. Keep to yourself, or you’ll wish you had.” Rising to his feet, he snapped his whip in warning and asked if she understood.

Rose averted her gaze and said nothing keeping her chin down. Assuming her silence meant her acquiescence, the man smiled and snapped his whip as he walked away.

Once he left the immediate vicinity, she inspected the girls around her. Two of them bore marks from his whip, and she wondered what infraction they committed to warrant such a thing. Talking?

Afternoon and evening passed. As the night grew cold and lingered on, Rose huddled into a corner with her arms around her middle and dreamed of Chase with his warm amber eyes and gorgeous bronzed body. What she would give to be with him at this moment. If the devil rose from the floor bartering for her soul, she'd give in without hesitation to spend one more night in her fiancé's arms.

Replaying every moment they spent together to keep her terror at bay, she grimaced when she remembered the scene at the cantina in San Antonio. Rozita must pay for betraying Chase. Her emotions threatened to choke her as she dwelt on what could be happening at this moment. What if the evil woman succeeded and killed Chase or subdued him? Icy fear trickled down her spine. Who would rescue her, and of more importance, who would rescue *him*?

"You're the one who puts the spark in my step and the fire in my eye. My heart beats for you, darlin', and no one else. I will come for you." Her fiancé's words replayed in her mind and settled around her heart. She must believe he would know the scent of danger, even on Rozita. The thought created peace in her soul, and she drifted off to sleep as the first fingers of dawn lit the morning sky.

Startled awake when the guards entered with a bucket of cool water and a plate of biscuits, she brushed her hair from her eyes and gaped in amazement. The girls fell on the food like wolves on their prey, and she didn't stand a chance of getting close. Her stomach twisted with hunger as the last biscuit left the plate clutched tight in a very dirty fist.

The blonde-haired girl sat beside her and handed

Rose a biscuit. "You must be fast if you want to eat. I'm Hannah."

Smiling, she accepted the food. "Thank you." Whispering the words, she glanced around for the guard who had threatened to whip her.

"It's safe to talk for a few minutes after they feed us. The guards go somewhere to eat, and nobody is outside the door to hear. They return in fifteen minutes." The girl bit into her biscuit with relish.

Taking a bite of her own, she glanced at the pale face beside her. "How long have you been here?"

"Two weeks. They took me from my daddy's farm outside Laredo while he plowed the field."

Rose digested the information. "Did they hurt you?"

"Quiet. They're coming back." Rising to her feet, the other girl walked to the other side of the room and took a seat in the opposite corner.

Leaning back against the wall and nibbling on the dry biscuit, she surveyed the group of girls. Somehow, she would help them all escape. Whoever captured them deserved to be hung, and once the women were safe, she'd make sure the villains received a just reward.

Chapter Eleven

The bright Texas sun filled the tiny room with stifling heat, and the humidity clung to them like a steam bath. Wiping the perspiration from her face, Rose licked her lips and wished for a cool drink of water.

When the evening meal of biscuit and watery soup arrived, she clasped the clay dish of liquid and drank, ignoring the sparse vegetables floating within. While ingesting her biscuit, she learned Hannah had been engaged to a young man on a neighboring farm named Theodore. Planning their wedding for the fall, Hannah worried he would be too late to save her.

"Too late for what?" Certain she knew their fate, she wanted to see what the girl suspected.

"I'm not sure, but I think whoever is in charge sells us as servants or something. I've heard the guards talking about how much some of the girls were worth."

Rose eyed her newfound friend, unsure of how to explain the harsh reality of what they faced. She didn't get a chance to speak again before the guards resumed their posts and night settled upon them.

The next day, several armed men arrived and carried five of the girls out screaming. The crack of a whip snapped through the air, followed by a cry and then silence.

Rose swallowed hard.

Boots shuffled outside the locked door,

accompanied by the sound of something dragging across the floor. Men's voices argued outside the structure, and another girl cried out.

Gaping in surprise, she wrapped her arms around her middle. Did they kill one of the girls? "Every week, they come and take more of us. I fear when my turn comes." Hannah's face paled as she turned toward the wall. Great tears rolled down her cheeks while she whispered fervent words to an unknown source above her head.

Her as well. Squeezing her eyes shut, she prayed alongside her friend, each silent in their supplications.

Afterward, the days fell into a pattern. Twice a day, they received biscuits and water, and once every two days, the guards arrived to take away more prisoners. Spending her time thinking of Chase and the glorious day he would arrive on Aries to rescue her kept her sane.

Until it didn't.

On the fifth day, Rose had enough. Studying the movements of the guards over the next two days, she formed an escape plan in her head.

Distracted from her thoughts by the arrival of a new batch of terrified women ranging in age from eighteen to twenty-five, she considered rushing the door and bolting for freedom. Before the thought finished being formed, heavy boots clumped across the wooden floor of the church toward their door and stopped. Saluting guards stepped aside for the newcomer to enter, and all grew silent.

Glancing up, Rose froze as every ounce of blood she possessed turned to ice in her veins. Choking, she scooted back against the wall as *Delgato* sauntered into view, followed by ten armed men.

Inspecting the women as he strolled past, he asked

questions in Spanish. When he stood in front of her, he stopped, saying nothing for long terrifying minutes while she quaked against the wall, unable to meet his gaze.

For the first time since they took her captive, she wondered if she would live to tell the tale.

The man's cold, soulless eyes stared at her, chilling her to the bone, and a smile curved the thin lines of his cruel mouth. "This one is special. Check her binding and triple the guards. I have a new location for her. No one is allowed to touch her unless I say so."

Speaking slow, deliberate English so she would understand, he lifted her chin with one finger to meet his hate-filled gaze. "Welcome to Laredo, Miss Tanner."

Rose kept her expression neutral until Delgato strolled on to the next girl, giving his instruction in Spanish. Chase better hurry the hell up because the message she read in the evil man's eyes told her she wouldn't like what he planned.

The wagons arrived next, and one by one, they selected five girls and hauled them away. Their cries of fear and pain reverberated in the silent room as the armed men demanded obedience.

And then another wagon appeared.

Hannah cried out, squeezing her hand when the guards nudged her to her feet with their guns and ordered her to follow them out.

Sick with fear and anxiety for her friend, Rose searched the area for a way to help. What would become of them, and why the hell hadn't her ranger come by now?

Furious with the situation and her inability to control her terror, she rushed at the man holding Hannah's arm, knocking him to the ground.

"Come on!" Tugging the frightened girl away from the guards and the back of the church, she turned around. "We must go through the front of the church. It's the only way out!" Dashing through the priest's office and into the main area, she picked up speed, dodging parishioners. People knelt in front of a large crucifix and sat on long wooden benches praying. While others lit candles for remembrance, gazing up in amazement when the girls burst through the door.

Rose paid them no mind as she dragged Hannah toward the entrance of the church. They made it out the front door and onto the cobblestone drive before she paused to allow her eyes to adjust to the sunlight.

Bullets pelted the ground around their feet, and both women froze.

"Take one more step, and you're dead." Delgato and two of his men rounded the corner of the church with their pistols cocked and ready.

Swallowing, she squeezed her friend's fingers. "I'm sorry, Hannah. Whatever happens, I will find you and get you back to your farmer. You will marry the man you love, and I will help you. I give you my word."

Hannah nodded as they jerked her away from Rose and marched her around to the back of the church.

Her chin rose when she turned to face Delgato.

"I should shoot you for the trouble you've caused. Because of your defiance, the local sheriff will know of this place, and we must relocate our operation." Spitting on the ground at her feet, he fondled the butt of his pistol and spun the chamber. "You are worth more than all the girls together. For this reason, you live."

"Ranger Calhan will find you—"

"Spare me the speech, *senorita*. Your ranger will not

find you because he is too busy chasing your abductors all over Texas." Laughing at some private joke, he nudged his chin in her direction. "Bring her."

Biting back her retort, she glanced around, thinking hard. If they gave her fiancé false information to keep him from finding her, she must let him know she had been here if he did make it to Laredo. Wrenching her hair bow from her long braid, she stepped back against the church and stuffed it in a crack between two stones. Chase would see it and know he followed the right path.

The guard jerked her down the alley to the back of the church. Weak from lack of proper food and water and her recent run, she stumbled. A gun nudged her in the back when she slowed to catch her breath. Straightening her spine to hide her fear, she rounded the church and stopped dead at the sight of a carriage. Everyone else had gone, and the church yard stood empty. Her rebellious mind ran through several possible scenarios for escape before a hood dropped over her head.

Bucking and squirming, she hoped to knock the guards off balance so she could get away, but something hit her over the head, and everything went black.

****

Chase discovered Mr. Matthews and his men on his way out of town. Recognizing the horses and the two men tying them to the post in front of the Broken Spur Saloon, he turned around and drew to a stop beside the hitching post. Finding the bastards produced a hint of encouragement in his rage-fueled world. Eyeing the dandy climbing the stairs to the boardwalk, he slid to the ground and tied Aries up. With one hand on a blade in his bandolier, he rolled his shoulders in anticipation. The bastard must pay for taking his woman and, with a little persuasion, would tell him what they did with her.

"Hold it right there, Matthews. Put your hands above your head and turn around real slow." Chase held his knife easy.

Mr. Matthews paused with one foot on the wooden stair leading to the boardwalk. "Is there a problem?" Turning, he faced Chase with a smile.

The ranger narrowed his gaze as one of Matthews' men inched his way to the left. Chase withdrew another knife without breaking eye contact. "Where is Miss Tanner? Did you deliver her to your foul friends? Or did the men who attacked you take her?"

"Who?" The bastard's eyebrow climbed upward in surprise. "I'm afraid I don't know what you're talking about."

Fury flowed through the ranger's veins like molten lava. "I know you took her from the Menger Hotel in San Antonio because I followed your tracks. You have one chance to tell me where she is. Don't waste it." He motioned to the man on his left. "Move back beside Matthews, or you die.'

The other man made the mistake of reaching for his pistol. Chase's knife hit his throat before he cleared the leather, toppling him to the ground.

Mr. Matthews turned to run, but the ranger knocked him unconscious with a fist to the face.

The last man froze in place, and a dark stain appeared on the front of his trousers as Chase tossed another knife into the air and caught it.

"*Donde esta la chica?*"

The man shrugged, saying nothing.

"You know something, and I intend to find out what it is." Bending to cuff Matthews, he took his gaze from the man for a split second.

The man took his opportunity and palmed his gun.

A knife flew through the air and lodged in his throat. Taking two steps, he fell dead with a surprised look on his face.

Shaking his head, Chase tugged Matthews into a sitting position and leaned him against the wooden stairs to wait for help to arrive. He figured with the size of the crowd gathered around him, the other rangers would soon show.

In the meantime, he wanted answers. Nudging the unconscious dandy with his boot, he got no response and asked one of the onlookers to fetch him some water.

Ranger Toleman elbowed his way through the crowd several minutes later. In his late twenties, he'd been a ranger for five years and had seen more than a man his age should. Tall, with brown hair and hazel eyes, he drew a quick, accurate pistol and possessed the heart of a lion.

Chase explained the situation, and the other ranger nodded.

"He's waking up. Let's get him to the office for questioning." Ranger Toleman nodded to the crowd. "Y'all go about your business."

They threw the dandy over the back of his horse and tied him to the saddle. His muffled shouts grew louder.

Mounting Aries, the ranger led Matthews' horse across the street.

Half-away back to headquarters, a shot rang out, and their captive quit squirming. Still, as a corpse, blood dripped onto the cobblestone road beneath him as his horse whinnied and reared with fright.

Chase tightened his hold on the reins. "Easy, boy."

Someone killed the bastard before he got the answers he needed. Using every swear word he knew, he handed Matthews' mount's reins to Toleman and galloped off in the direction of the gunfire.

For two hours, he searched for the killer until the waning sunlight made him call it off. He figured whoever shot Matthews didn't want him to talk and knew something about Rose. Discouraged and mad as a wet cat, he rode back to the ranger's office and drew a chair up in the chief's office.

The chief looked up. "What did you find?"

"Not a goddamn thing." Setting his hat on the desk in front of him, Chase walked to the stove to get a cup of coffee. Sipping the black brew without another word, he let the silence settle over him and drew a deep breath. He'd make a mistake if he didn't calm down.

Setting the cup beside the stove, he adjusted his bandolier and ran a hand through his hair. "I'm hightailing it for Laredo. Rozita is my only lead now." Shaking his head with frustration, he tapped the heel of his boot on the wooden floor. "I want answers."

"We'll get whoever shot him." Ranger Toleman walked into the office and handed Chase a bundle of food. "You'll need this. God speed. If you need anything. Send a wire. We're happy to help."

"Thanks."

Four long, hot days later, Chase arrived in Laredo and rode for the sheriff's office. Tying his horse out front, he bent his head and walked inside.

In his mid-forties, Sheriff Hernandez stood five feet two with thinning black hair, bright brown eyes, a small mustache, and a beer belly. "Ranger Calhan, it's nice to see you again."

"Likewise." He updated the sheriff on the situation. "Do you know a man named Delgato?"

"El Diablo's right-hand man? *Si.* But I have not heard of him in this area for some time. Do you think he is the one who abducted your fiancé?"

The ranger nodded. "He's a suspect." Removing his hat, he ran a hand through his blond hair. "I received a message from a trusted source telling me to be in Laredo in a week for information about Rose. If she is in Laredo, Delgato is involved, and I hoped you had news."

Sheriff Hernandez nodded. "Tell me the story from the beginning."

Chase poured a cup of coffee and sat back down. Relating the events from the morning he arrived in San Antonio until he rode into Laredo, silence filled the office when he finished.

The sheriff tilted his head, studying his companion. "And you trust this woman, Rozita Sanchez?"

Chase shrugged. "She's been a great source of information in the past. Her information led me to El Diablo's compound and later to Delgato."

"Who you captured and lost when he killed your partner. Does this woman have reason to betray you?"

A frown furrowed the ranger's brow. "Rozita lived in the general's harem for several years. With him dead, she has no one to fear, and her only ambition is to get her sister away from the compound in Mexico. Together they plan to make a new life. He holds her sister captive in El Diablo's old villa."

Sheriff Hernandez folded his hands over his beer belly. "Does Delgato know she betrayed his master? If he does, he will take revenge on everyone connected to her."

Chase agreed. "She's desperate to get her sister out and needs me to help her."

The sheriff dropped his boots to the floor and leaned forward, resting his arms on his desk. "What are you going to do?"

The ranger swallowed the rest of his coffee and rose to his feet. "I'm going to get something to eat and do some looking around while I wait for Rozita." He paused. "I'll be at the La Posada if you find anything."

" 'Night."

Riding toward his favorite cantina, he thought of Rose and prayed for her wellbeing. A sweet, tender girl like her should be snuggled beneath a satin comforter, full and warm, not shivering and hungry in some godforsaken hole. Weary, discouraged, and mad as hell, he stepped from the saddle and strode inside to get some food. Halfway through his plate of spicy enchiladas and refried beans, Rozita slid into the chair opposite him.

"You got here fast." Chase studied her while he sipped his beer.

She gazed side to side as if to make sure they were not being watched. "As did you. I have a message for you. Your woman is here."

The knot in his stomach tightened as his informant confirmed his worst fear. Losing his appetite for everything but strangling the men responsible, he shoved his food aside. "Tell me where."

Chapter Twelve

"Something isn't right. Are you sure your cousin said farmhouse? We've searched every damn farm for miles, and there's no sign of Rose." Losing all patience, Chase whirled around to face his companion. "We've been at this for three goddamn days now. Every time we get close, they move her. I'm the best damned ranger alive, and I can't get a jump on whoever has my girl. I want to know how they stay one step ahead of me." Eyeing Rozita with suspicion as the sheriff's conversation played in his head, he narrowed his gaze on her face. "How sure are you about your informant? I don't like wasting time. Rose could be in terrible danger, and I'm running around like a rooster without a head on slaughter day. I swear to God, if something happens to her, I will kill everyone involved." He narrowed his gaze on her face. "Including you."

Rozita glanced at him. "My cousin knows how important the woman is to you. We will find your *Rosa*."

Pausing when she said the name *Rosa*, he fingered the handle of a throwing knife. Sam and Rose both told him Rozita knew in San Antonio. Chase mounted his horse. "You keep searching. I'm going back to Laredo. If Delgato has her, there's a trail. I'm certain he plans to take her to Mexico if he hasn't already."

"Wait, *Senor* Chase. She is here. My informant would not lie to me." Rozita paled in the afternoon sun.

At her denial, the ranger growled. “Maybe not, but you do. I trust my intuition more than your information.”

Turning, he galloped back to town, arriving late in the afternoon, hot, tired, and cranky as a man in red woolen underwear in the middle of a heatwave. Stalking into the sheriff’s office, he plopped down in a chair, too furious to speak. *“Where are you, girl?”* Staring at the ceiling, he analyzed everything he knew to date.

“I have news for you. Someone has been using the old church on Juarez Lane for a holding area. Several townspeople say two women ran through the church a week ago. From the description the witnesses gave, one of them is your Rose.” The sheriff breezed into the office and leaned against his desk, studying Chase.

“Why am I hearing this now instead of when I got here?” Jumping to his feet, his weariness vanished like a tamale on Thanksgiving Day. Placing his hat on his head, he strode for the door.

“I didn’t get the report until yesterday and sent my finest officer to investigate. I had no idea there were women being held there or the possibility your fiancé could be one of them until an hour ago. I’ll follow and show you what we found.” Running to keep up, he huffed his way to his mount.

Chase rode hard for the church, not caring whether the sheriff kept up or not. Rose had been in Laredo all this time and must be frantic with fear. Cursing and galloping down Juarez Lane, he stopped outside the church. Sliding to the ground, he tied his horse to the post while searching the area for sign. Something pink caught his eye as he walked across the sparse hard ground toward the front door of the church. Crouching down as he neared it, he tugged on the end, and a pink bow slid out from between the stones. His stomach twisted. Mud splattered and limp, her scent still clung to the abused satin ribbon.

His chest tightened.

And he knew in his gut she left it there for him to find.

Lifting the bow to his nose, he sucked in the faint scent of lilac and closed his eyes at the memory of her beautiful face. His hand shook when he shoved the bow into his pocket and rose to his feet.

"Good thing your girl has some spice in her. If she hadn't run away, we wouldn't have discovered this place. Who would have thought to search a church for stolen women?" Sheriff Hernandez strode toward him after tying his horse to the hitching post. "Come with me."

As they searched the back of the old church, Chase's anger grew with each passing moment. The stench coming from the buckets used for human waste in the corners overpowered them. The filthy floor and aroma of unwashed flesh added to the mixture, turning his stomach. God, the heat in here would be unbearable in the middle of the day. Scratches in the stucco walls a foot from the floor caught his attention. Kneeling beside a tight corner, he ran his trembling hand over the letters C *H A S* and swallowed the lump in his throat. His Rose slept in this corner.

Rising to his feet, he stared at the wall to get control of his emotions. Terrified and alone, his love left signs for him to follow. She had the fortitude of a soldier and the soul of an angel. Unable to stay in this dismal place a second longer, he strode toward the back door. "They took the women in and out the back door to avoid detection."

The sheriff hurried to keep up. "We figure they corralled between fifteen to twenty women in here at a time."

"Where's the priest? He's the one I want to talk to. He'll know all the details." Chase pushed his emotions aside and focused on the details around him. Any mistake he made now would be fatal.

Sheriff Hernandez shook his head. "Father Juan is missing. No one has seen him since yesterday."

"Then they either killed him so he wouldn't talk, or he holed up somewhere." Sitting back on his heels, Chase studied the tracks in the dirt behind the church, where they loaded a couple of wagons and a carriage. The wagons turned south out of the churchyard, and the carriage traveled west. The transportation vehicles would be impossible to track across the cobblestone roads of Laredo. Turning around, he studied the exterior of the church. If he were a rat of a priest with abducted women in his church, he'd have an escape planned in case someone discovered his secret. Strolling around the outside of the church, he knocked on the walls in several locations, bending close when the noise changed pitch. Stepping back, he studied the outer wall and strode for the back door.

"What are you doing?" Sheriff Hernandez kept one step behind him.

"Catching a rat." Entering the priest's office, he studied the east wall. The main room of worship contained a small notched-in area next to the priest's office, while the outside wall remained straight. Gazing around, he grabbed the fire poker and struck the wall of the notched-in space in several places.

The wall crumbled in, revealing a small square room.

"Holy tamales." Sheriff Hernandez stepped forward with his hand above the butt of his gun.

Chase struck the wall again, and a large piece of plaster fell in, followed by a cry of pain.

"Stop!" A terrified voice called out.

Not slowing down, the ranger struck the wall until he could reach in, grab the priest by his frock, and remove him from his hidey-hole.

Five foot three with black hair and brown eyes, Father Juan wore a brown frock and a frightened expression.

The ranger dropped the small man on the floor and withdrew a knife. "Who paid you to hide women in your back room, and where did they take them?"

Trembling with fear, the small priest gazed up. "I know nothing."

Chase held him by the hair with a knife to his throat a second later. "Who paid you?" The silky soft question hovered like the angel of death above the man's head.

The priest glanced at the sheriff, leaning against the opposite wall with his boots crossed, picking dirt from his fingernails with the blade of his knife.

"Sheriff Hernandez will not interfere. So talk." He repeated his command in Spanish so there could be no misunderstanding.

Swallowing, the priest dropped his head. "*Senor* Delgato pays me coins for the church if I allow him to use my storage room."

His instinct never let him down. Somewhere in his gut, he knew the evil little man had taken his woman. "How does a man of the cloth allow women to be mistreated in church?" Tightening his hold, he glared down at the priest. "Where does he take them?"

The priest trembled. "I do not ask questions. I did not know what *Senor* Delgato kept back there or where they go after the leave."

Chase snorted. "You're telling me you didn't ask questions when the women cried out for help, as I'm sure they did? Or what happened after?"

Staring down at the floor, the priest shook his head. "I do not question *Senor* Delgato. I have a family to think of."

Sick to his stomach, Chase resisted the urge to slit the priest's throat on principle. "And what of the families of the women locked in your storeroom? Those women are sisters, daughters, perhaps wives of someone. You don't think they deserve a chance to live?"

The priest shook his head. "*Senor* Delgato only takes virgins. They bring him more gold."

Gripped the handle of his knife so hard his knuckles showed white, he forced the man's head back to meet the fury in his. "So you do know something despite your claim of innocence."

The sheriff placed a hand on Chase's arm. "Let me take it from here. I will lock Father Juan up and notify his superiors. I'm sure they won't like what he did any more than we do."

With reluctance, the ranger let the priest go and slid his knife back into his bandolier. He straightened. "If Delgato has these women, he's headed for Mexico, picking up where El Diablo left off. He'll auction them off as soon as he has enough to make it worth his while."

Cuffing the priest, the sheriff led him to the door. "And your woman? What will he do to her?"

He already knew. "The bastard will use her to lure me into a trap and then kill us both."

"Ride fast, my friend, and keep me updated. Once you have this monster, we'll need to locate the families of the women he has captive."

His words fell on an empty room. Chase was already leaning forward in his saddle as he raced toward Mexico.

****

Rozita leaned against the wall of the church where she could hear everything the sheriff and Chase said. She'd followed the ranger back to Laredo and stood outside the sheriff's office to hear their conversation. They told her to keep the ranger busy for a few days and then bring him to Delgato. He suspected her, and she would have to find a way to regain his trust. Tagging along behind the sheriff to Juarez Lane, she kept out of sight while they did their investigation. Smug with delight over the entire affair, she nearly passed out when they found Father Juan. Delgato would be furious when he discovered what happened. He'd made sure he hid the priest well before he left. Damn the ranger to the depths of hell. He would ruin everything if she did not do something quick. Slipping forward along the outside wall of the church, she withdrew her pistol from her waistband. Inching her way toward the open door, she hoped for a clear line of fire, but the ranger walked back and forth while he spoke, making it difficult to get her shot.

Her agitation grew by the second. Delgato would be furious when he discovered the priest talked and would administer punishment for his failure, torturing him and his family. Shifting her angle, she closed one eye and took aim. If she shot the priest now, hers would be a mercy killing.

She must have made a noise, for Chase stilled and glanced toward the door.

Freezing in place with her heart in her mouth, she didn't dare breathe. If he discovered her presence, her ruse would be over, and her life with it. She recognized the threat of death in his eyes earlier, and no amount of lying would get her out of this one. Her breathing resumed when the ranger turned back to the priest and continued his questions.

Holding her body still, she listened to everything Father Juan said. Delgato would require a report, and she must give every detail, or he would kill her. When the priest blurted out that Delgato only took virgins for gold, Rozita closed her eyes and shook her head. Stupid man. He sealed his death with those damning words, and her boss would expect her to deal with the situation. Flattening her body against the wall, she waited for an opportunity.

The ranger strode through the church, and a few seconds later, his horse's hooves pounded away into the distance. Peeking through the half-open door, she kept her eye on her target as the sheriff helped him to his feet and led him to the front of the church. A wicked smile curved her full lips as luck shifted in her favor. Sliding along the outer wall of the church, she waited until the sheriff turned his back. With one quick shot between the eyes, she killed the priest and ran down the alley as fast as she could. Sheriff Hernandez would never catch her. His large belly prevented him from moving with any speed, and she could run like the wind when necessary. Dodging through several yards and businesses, she kept her eye on her back trail to make sure no one followed her. Once she reached safety, she slowed her pace and sauntered toward the tavern where the men waited.

Ordering a beer, she sat at the table with the rest of the men but didn't divulge information about the priest or the ranger. Delgato would learn of today's occurrence from her and no one else. The men made a habit of taking credit for her kills, and Rozita learned the hard way to keep her bragging to a minimum. What the men didn't know about, they couldn't take the glory for.

After drinking and playing cards for a reasonable amount of time, she left the tavern and circled through town to lose any nosy followers. Entering her cousin's house under cover of darkness, she saddled her mare and checked her guns. Her plan was to catch Chase at the border and convince him Delgato took Rose to Nuevo Laredo. Despite her failure to keep the ranger busy and out of Mexico, she had a job to do. With a kick to her mare, she galloped after the desperate ranger, determined to keep her word and prove her loyalty. With so much at stake, her life, her position, and her livelihood, she knew every second counted. Pinching her lips together, Rozita vowed she would never bow to anyone, man or woman, again.

****

Chase crossed into Mexico a half-hour later, riding for Nuevo Laredo and a tavern he knew Delgato's men favored. Riding up in a cloud of dust, he slipped to the ground, tied his horse out front, and tipped his hat forward before strolling inside.

Dim and filled with cigar smoke, the tavern contained several customers sitting at the bar and a half dozen playing poker. None of the men were the ones he sought.

The barkeeper glanced up as Chase walked in. "No shooting or fighting allowed." He spoke Spanish as he poured tequila for one of his customers.

The ranger took a seat at the bar. "Have Delgato's men come in today?"

Frowning, the barkeeper switched to English. "Why do you want them? They are bad *hombres*. I do not want trouble here. It is too expensive to keep my place open." Waving his arms around at his various customers, he leaned forward to make his point. "Please leave, *senor*."

Chase ordered a shot of whiskey and placed extra coins on the counter. "I want information."

Biting one of the coins, the barkeeper tucked it in his vest, splashed the liquid into a glass, and set it in front of him. "The men you seek have not come to my bar today." Wiping the long wooden counter down, he refilled the ranger's glass. "Why do you look for these men? Mexico is beautiful with many distractions." He indicated a dark-haired woman wearing nothing but her underwear leaning on the end of the counter. "You should take advantage of the scenery. Your night will be so much more pleasurable if you do, and you might live to see another dawn."

The ranger set his glass down. "I'll live to see it either way, and I have no interest in your hospitality."

Shrugging, the barkeeper walked away. "Have it your way but don't act surprised when you wake up dead. Any fighting and you pay the damage."

Taking his whisky to a corner table to wait, Chase put his back to the wall and tipped his hat low over his face. His mind turned to Rose. Instinct led him here, and deep down, he knew they kept her somewhere close. What happened to Rozita after he rode off? She had a habit of disappearing, and he hadn't given her absence much thought because she usually brought back more information. Their fruitless search among the farmhouses outside Laredo angered him and his gut told him the woman kept him busy while they moved Rose from under his nose.

"*Rozita doesn't like me. She thinks you belong to her.*" Considering his fiancée's words, he frowned. Did she? Or did she work for Delgato? If she did, why turn on him and get him arrested? Unless she secretly worked for an unknown source with a hand in the game. Tossing the rest of his whiskey down his throat, he signaled for another drink. If Rozita led him on a wild hog hunt out of jealousy or spite, he'd cut her heart out.

Replaying everything from the moment Rozita informed him Delgato would be in San Antonio until now, he stopped short. Rozita may or may not be acting out of jealousy, but one thing for damn sure stood out in his mind. She lied about too many things for this to be an accident. Who knew where her true loyalties lay? Not him. And somewhere, out there, Delgato groomed his Rose for the auction like a prime heifer headed to the breeding pen.

With shaking hands, he picked up his glass. If his sweet Rose hadn't created a scene at the church, he'd still be kicking open farm doors and searching barns.

Hour after hour passed, and not one of Delgato's men entered the bar. Discouraged and mad as hell, Chase slammed a coin on the counter to pay for his drink and turned toward the door.

Slipping the coin into his pocket, the barkeeper leaned forward and whispered. "I have a room upstairs. I'll give it to you cheap."

The ranger froze. “Why?”

Glancing around to see if they were overheard, the man continued. “I, too, am interested in the women Delgato has. My daughter is missing.” Wiping the counter next to Chase’s elbow, he made an offer. “If I help you catch the bastard, will you rescue my daughter?’

Giving a quick nod, he placed a couple of coins on the counter.

“Lupita will show you the way.” The barkeeper tucked the coins into his vest pocket. “Be friendly so the men think you are taking advantage of the services we offer, and I will speak to you when it is safe.”

Throwing an arm around Lupita’s shoulders, he let her lead him up the stairs. When they stopped at the end of the hall. Lupita unlocked the door and handed Chase the key. “Let me know if you need anything else, *senor*.” Her smile told him she would be willing for anything he had in mind.

Shaking his head, he wished her a good night. One woman caught his blood on fire, and she wasn’t here. No other female interested him in any way.

With a twist of her lips, Lupita walked away.

Closing the wooden door and turning the key in the lock, he walked toward the window and drew the curtains closed.

The barkeeper gave a short knock two hours later, and when Chase let him in, he gave detailed instructions on how to find El Diablo’s compound and two other strongholds.

“This is where the auctions take place. If Delgato has your woman and my daughter, they will be here.”

After studying the hand-drawn map, he thanked the

barkeeper and tucked the map into his shirt pocket.

At midnight he walked downstairs to stable his horse. Throwing the saddlebags over one shoulder, he returned to his room and locked the door. The streets were quiet. Above the town, stars twinkled, and the moon lit a silver path across the stark ground. He stared at the moon, and his heart ached as he considered his tender-hearted woman. "I'm here, baby. I *will* find you, darlin', and bring you home. Hold on a little longer. I'm coming for you."

Chapter Thirteen

Rose swallowed the lump in her throat when the carriage rolled to a stop.

Men's voices shouted, and boots ran back and forth while Delgato's voice called out in rapid Spanish. More running feet raced by, followed by the scent of lavender and honeysuckle. A woman stood beside them, speaking in Spanish, and she shrugged. Familiarity with the language would come in handy about now. A hand took her arm in an iron grip and tugged her from the carriage. Tripping, she stepped over uneven ground and into a cool area.

Someone ripped the hood from her head, and Rose blinked. She stood in a small tavern with five other girls, one of them Hanna. Her friend kept her head down and trembled like a lamb before the slaughter.

She didn't know the other girls' names, but she recognized them from the church. Gazing at them, an interesting observation popped into her head. She noted they were all blonde-haired and blue-eyed. Fear wound around her belly as her gaze dropped to their hands. Every one of them was tied, gagged, and terrified.

A small, slender woman stood beside her using the same voice she heard while hooded in the carriage. "I am Consuela. Do as I say and no harm will come to you." Speaking in English so everyone would understand, her gaze swept over the cluster of captives.

None of the girls answered or made eye contact.

Consuela smiled. "Good, we understand each other. Follow me." Leading them outside to an outhouse behind the tavern, two armed guards stood nearby while they all took a turn. Marching them back inside to the main room, they were served hot, watered-down soup and a dried biscuit.

Rose sniffed the food, and Consuela laughed.

"It is not poison. Eat. You will feel better. Once the food is gone, I will show you where you may rest."

Not trusting the small thin woman, she sniffed again. Fooled once before by a kind man offering to share his carriage got her into this mess, and she had no intention of being fooled again. Taking a cautious sip from the end of her wooden spoon, she found the soup tasty and filling, to her surprise. Gazing up, she met Hannah's frightened eyes. "It's going to be all right. The soup is good."

Eating every bite, they smiled at each other when they finished. If they died, it would be together and with a full stomach.

Guards herded the women up the steep stairs to an attic room where five narrow cots covered with a single blanket filled the empty space. Rose had the impression every captive girl stayed in this room before they continued their journey south.

"You shall sleep here. Two guards are positioned outside the door and beneath the window. Do not try to escape. You will be shot if you do. Someone will wake you in the morning at the appropriate time." Closing the door behind her, a key turned in the lock.

Staring at the door and then the other women, she crossed to the window and drew the cotton curtain aside.

"There must be a way out of here." Gazing down with dismay, she discovered their chamber at least fifteen feet from the ground, a straight drop from the attic window to the hard-packed earth beneath.

"You heard the woman. We will be shot if we try." One of the girls whispered.

Pressing her face against the pane, she noted two armed men beneath the window talking. Glancing up, they lifted their guns and waited.

Stepping out of sight, Rose wished for her pistol. With the full moon high in the night sky, the countryside would be visible for miles, making tonight an excellent opportunity to escape. Staring out at the scrub brush and cacti, she wondered why Chase hadn't caught up to them yet.

Unless…A mental picture of Rozita with big tears rolling down her high cheekbones flashed across her mind. What if he believed the woman's lies? Gazing up at the stars as panic tightened her chest, she bit her lip. Chase promised he would always come for her, but what if he didn't?

Shanna wouldn't wait around to be rescued, and neither would she. Her freedom depended on her wit and ability. And no one else.

"Do you see anything?" Hannah stood at her side, gazing up at the stars.

"Armed guards." Turning, she gazed at her friend. "We will figure out how to escape by keeping our eyes open and our fears quiet. We won't give them the satisfaction of seeing us upset."

Smiling, her friend leaned against the side of the window. "You sound like my Theodore. He always has something good to say despite the situation."

Rose's gaze returned to the sky. "Did you ever wish you could see what the moon and the stars do? Maybe our men are gazing at the same stars and the same moon right this minute. The notion makes me feel closer to mine and not so afraid."

Hannah sighed. "How do you think of these things? I do feel closer to Theodore and not as frightened as before."

"Someone's coming." One of the girls stood with her ear pressed to the closed door. "They're walking up the stairs."

Hurrying to their cots, the women climbed beneath their blankets as the key turned in the lock and the door swung open.

Closing her eyes, Rose feigned asleep.

"They are all here." Consuela's voice spoke from the door.

Boots approached her bed, stopping beside her, and Rose resisted the urge to squirm.

"See this one is kept separate once we arrive at the compound. She will not be sold with the rest. I have a special surprise for her." Delgato's deep voice sent shivers down her spine.

"*Si.*" Consuela answered. "What has this one done?"

The deep voice chuckled. "All you need to know is I have a special interest."

"Does my sister know?" Consuela's voice sounded hesitant.

Another male chuckle. "I know of her because of Rozita. I also have a man who reports on the rangers. So, I know everything."

Ranger Kaplan's face popped into her mind for some reason, and she feigned a snore.

"Oh." Not sure if the woman sounded relieved or curious, Rose struggled with the idea of her being the traitor's sister.

The feet walked away, and the door closed, followed by the click of the lock and silence.

"Who is he?" Hannah's voice drifted toward her from the right.

"Delgato." Keeping her voice even, she closed her eyes and hoped to come up with a plan. Shanna would no doubt scale the outside wall, drop to the ground, slit the guards' throats, and disappear into the night. She couldn't do any of those things and must think of something more practical.

"Why are we being sold? What do they want with us?" Another voice floated on the silence of the room.

Sitting up, she imparted what wisdom she possessed. "The worst thing you can do is show them we're scared. We will escape and return home one way or another. For now, we'd best get some sleep and look for a way out tomorrow."

"What if there is no tomorrow?" Another voice joined the conversation.

Clenching her hands into fists, she answered. "There will be because I won't accept anything different."

Silence followed her statement.

"My fiancé is Ranger Chase Calhan. He's been tracking me since San Antonio. I know he will find me and rescue us. We must believe there is another answer than the one these people plan for us. I refuse to be bought or sold."

"What if we don't have a choice?" A different girl chimed in.

"We always have a choice. Make up your mind and

keep your eyes open."

She didn't sleep at all and jumped every time the boards in the hall floor creaked. Crickets chirped outside their window, and coyotes howled in the distance. Tucking her thin blanket beneath her chin, she pictured her fiancé the way he appeared when they first met, wicked smile and all.

Rozita said he must die. Wrapping her arms around her middle, she concluded she wouldn't let him leave her again. If he didn't come rescue her, she'd do it and then go rescue him.

Consuela woke them before the sun rose above the horizon and led them downstairs for a bowl of watery boiled wheat.

Rose scooped hers into her mouth and swallowed, not wanting to eat but knowing she must keep her strength up. All desire for food fled after the first few days of captivity, and in her emotional state, everything tasted like sawdust anyway.

After breakfast, they were allowed to use the outhouse before being rebound, gagged, and loaded in the back of a wagon. Dropping hoods over their heads, the guards commanded them to lie down while someone threw straw over them to hide their presence.

Closing her eyes, Rose focused her attention on the sounds around her. Some of the girls cried; their sobs and hiccups audible above the rumble of the wagon wheels. She understood their frustration because she had a hard time keeping her own panic under control.

The hood and the straw soon became claustrophobic. Sweat broke out on her brow, and fear coiled tight inside her belly as they rumbled farther away from everything she knew.

Terrified, she did what she always did and thought about Chase. Visions of his wicked grin and knowing eyes calmed her nerves. She relived the glorious moments she spent in his arms until her lids drooped and her sleepless night caught up to her.

The next thing she knew, the wagon bumped over a cobblestone road. The air cooled, and the smell of hot musty straw dissipated in the slight breeze. Voices shouted, and horses whinnied. Activity swarmed around them as women's voices mingled with the deep rumble of men's answering ones. Wherever they were, they were no longer alone.

When the wagon slowed and drew to a stop, Rose held her breath and waited.

The equipage jolted as someone climbed into the back and shouted in Spanish. Several of the girls cried out as the wagon rocked side to side telling her they were unloading their captives. A hand grabbed her by the arm, and another removed the hood from her head.

Blinking, she stared around her with curiosity. Evening filled the area around her with shadows as the sun sank in the distance.

Standing inside a courtyard surrounded by a high stucco wall, a large two-story cream stucco building loomed over them on her right. Large paned windows glinted in the sun, and men with rifles were everywhere.

A few women dressed in expensive clothes stood in a group laughing and pointing in their direction. Turning her head, her gaze caught on four of her companions, still bound and huddled together off to her left. The man who held her by the arm jerked her forward, away from the others.

A beefy black-haired man with pistols riding low on

his hips and a bandolier filled with bullets stood between her and the girls. He ordered the guards to escort Hannah and the rest toward a door on the bottom floor of the huge building.

When she took a step to follow Hannah, the guard jerked her backward.

"You stay." Withdrawing a knife from his belt, he took a step toward her.

So, the man understood English. Stiffening, she held her breath and lifted her chin as he approached.

But he did nothing more than cut the gag from her mouth and re-sheath his blade.

Relief washed over her in a giddy wave, and she wobbled in place. "I'll find you, Hannah. Remember the moon and stars." Standing helpless as the others were led away, her resolve to help them all grew.

Her friend threw her a grateful look and stared hard as if drawing strength from her for whatever lay ahead.

Rose pasted a smile on her face in response.

"You make empty promises. You will never see them again."

She knew the deep, bitter voice, and her breath caught.

Freezing as Delgato strolled toward her from the shadows, she lifted her chin a notch. "I keep my word." Were she to believe she'd never see her friends again, she'd curl up and die on the spot. There must be a way out of this hell hole.

The evil little man sneered. "Your companions will be sold and on their way to their new masters before the end of the week. There is nothing you can do to stop it."

He didn't deserve an answer, so she kept her gaze on the other women until they disappeared.

"What do you want them for? Who are they being sold to?" Not expecting an answer, she asked her questions to keep the devil talking. Not sure she cared to know what fate they planned for her, she stalled for time, hoping to figure out a way to escape.

"There isn't one."

Rose glanced at Delgato's evil smiling face. "Isn't one what?"

"A way out. The gates are closed and locked at night. Guards patrol the grounds watching every door and window. Even your Texas Ranger will be unable to rescue you from here. This villa is a fortress. We made corrections to our defenses after *Senor* Calhan took us by surprise in Eagle Pass."

Understanding dawned. "This is El Diablo's villa?" Gazing around, her heart leaped into her throat and threatened to choke her. "Why am I here?"

Smug satisfaction shone from his eyes as he ran a finger over her cheek. "Your ranger will follow your trail, and soon he will arrive at the villa. I have planned for this day for weeks. Your death shall be long and painful while your ranger watches. There shall be a great celebration after you die. Then Ranger Calhan will be hung upside down in shame while his blood seeps from his body and soaks the earth in penance."

Rose clapped her hand over her mouth. She envisioned it all in her head as he spoke, and unable to contain her revulsion, puked all over the ground. Dropping to her knees, she dry-heaved for several minutes, shaking with the intensity of her emotions. When the convulsions stopped, she wiped her mouth with a piece of her petticoat. Dear God. Staring at the ground, she fought to regain control. Swiping a hand across her eyes, she discovered they were wet with tears.

"Take her to the women's quarters and send for Consuela." Delgato spat with contempt at the ground beside her and stalked away.

A guard hauled Rose to her feet and dragged her through the same door as the other women. She had a quick impression of stucco walls and colorful tile floors before being forced up a steep flight of stairs and marched down an empty, desolate corridor. Her escort stopped beside a wooden door halfway down and withdrew a key from his pocket. Unlocking the door, he threw it open and tossed Rose inside before she had a chance to think.

Rising to her feet, she took one step before the door swung shut, and the key turned in the lock.

Tugging on the door even though she knew it wouldn't open, she stared with unseeing eyes at the shiny grain and resisted the urge to weep. A large window on the opposite side of the room beckoned, and with a cry, she dashed across the floor to throw the plain cream curtain aside. Long wooden boards nailed across the front made it inaccessible, and Rose swore, striking the wooden planks with her fist.

Turning on her heel, she took inventory. A narrow cot with one colorful woolen blanket stood in the center of the room. Against the far wall, a small table held a wash basin and no mirror. Turning to her right, she noted a ceramic chamber pot standing in the corner. Her gaze returned to the bed where a bible lay beside the scratchy woolen blanket. The small chamber contained nothing else.

Stifling a sob, she glanced toward the window. She couldn't even see the stars here. Anguish filled her soul and spilled out over her cheeks. Throwing her body onto the cot, she cried until she had no more tears left. When the last hiccup died away, Rose lifted her swollen face. The darkness of night weighed heavy on her, and she discovered they hadn't even given her a candle to light her dreary world. Wrapping the blanket around her body, she rolled onto her side. Now she knew what Delgato planned, she thanked God Chase had not found her and prayed he would stay away.

Chapter Fourteen

Rose stiffened when the key turned in the lock a few hours later. The hinges squeaked as the door swung open, and a candle appeared, revealing Consuela's unsmiling face.

"Put the food on the table and leave us." Stepping aside to let the beefy man enter with a plate of food, she said nothing more.

Roast chicken assailed her senses, and despite her best intentions, her mouth watered. Sitting up, she hugged her blanket to her chest.

The man put the plate of food on the small table along the far wall beside the wash basin and walked away, stopping in the doorway.

"Leave us. I have a message from *El Jefe* which must be delivered in private." Snapping her fingers at the man, Consuela frowned.

The door closed with a thud.

The woman waited for a few minutes before turning to Rose. "Hurry and eat. I took the food from the kitchens after they served the main party in the dining room."

She blinked. "You brought me food? Why?"

The woman shrugged. "Why not? I remember when they brought me here and how frightening this place is. Let me help you where I can."

Stepping onto the colorful Saltillo floor, she hurried to the table. Weeks passed since she smelled or ate anything as wonderful as the plate of roast chicken paired with beans and rice.

Consuela indicated the wooden utensils beside the plate. “Eat. I don’t have long before I am missed.”

“What about the other girls? Did they eat? Where are they?” Rose asked questions in between mouthfuls of food.

“Your friends? They enjoyed a nice dinner and a bath. They sleep in the lower room. Do not worry. They are safe for tonight.” Consuela gave her a small smile.

“Thank you.” She ate all the food and placed the plate back on the table. “What will happen to them?”

A deep sigh escaped the other woman. “They will be fed well for a few days, bathed, and dressed. The general will host a party at the end of the week, which will include several rich men who will bid on your friends. They will be sold to the highest bidder.” She shrugged. “There is nothing you can do for them but pray.”

Not accepting the situation in the least, she shook her head at Consuela. “There is always a way. I must find it.” Walking back to her cot, she sat down. “Hannah is engaged to a farmer out of Laredo. They planned to marry in the fall. Alice has a beau she’s sweet on, and Amy just started courting a young man from a nearby town. They have their lives planned out and their future ahead of them.”

“And what about you? Delgato tells me you plan to marry the ranger who attacked El Diablo’s villa in Eagle Pass.” The woman gazed upon her with sympathy. “I, too, once had a fiancé.”

“I do plan to marry him, and I figured he’d rescue me before this, but after my last run-in with Rozita, I’m not sure anymore." Wondering if she would regret this conversation, Rose tugged the blanket over her.

Consuela shot her a quick glance. "You know Rozita?"

"I do." Unsure of where the conversation would lead, she didn't elaborate.

The other woman frowned. "Rozita is my sister. She will lead your ranger here to die."

Swallowing, she wondered if she just made an enemy out of the one almost-kind person she'd met. "I didn't know you were related."

Sadness shone from Consuela's eyes. "We have grown apart. We want different things."

Turning away, she spoke fast. "I have been gone too long. I cannot leave the candle. When I come during the day, I will be cold and distant. Do not give the impression anything is different. I will do what I can to help you and your friends. Sleep well." She tapped on the door for the guard to open it. "Bring the empty dishes." Tossing her command at the beefy man, she walked away.

The door closed, and the key turned in the lock with a loud click.

Rose sank back on her cot, bemused and thanking Providence for sending her a little comfort. Tucking her blanket around her, she reveled in the first ray of hope since her abduction and drifted off to dream of Chase.

****

The clang of keys and the squeak of the hinges as the door opened woke her the next morning. Sitting up, she clutched the blanket to her chest like a shield and waited.

Two men entered her chamber with a metal tub and

set it on the floor, followed by women and young girls carrying vessels of hot water.

Consuela entered with her nose high in the air. "You are to be bathed and escorted to the dining hall." Placing simple cotton clothing and undergarments on the cot, she waved another woman into the room bearing a thick towel and soap. "You must be quick. Delgato wishes to eat with you."

Gaping at her in surprise, she wondered what Delgato wanted with her. He already divulged his evil diabolical plan in torrid detail.

Snapping her fingers in Rose's direction, Consuela frowned. "Do not keep him waiting, or you will be whipped instead of fed." Sweeping from the room with a regal air, she resembled nothing of the kind woman from the night before.

Waiting until the key clicked in the lock before she moved, Rose stripped and collected the soap from the cot. Sinking into the heated water with a groan of satisfaction, she bathed and washed her hair. Then she stepped from the water, towel dried, and dressed as fast as she could in the plain clean undergarments, colorful skirt, and ruffled cream blouse. Tying a wide woven belt around her waist, Rose brushed her hair out with the bristled item she found rolled up in the clothes. After days of riding in a wagon with a hood covering her head, her hair resembled a rat's nest. The key turned in the lock, and the door swung open as she finished plaiting the back of her hair.

Consuela entered and glanced around the room. "Take her to the dining hall."

Rose followed the beefy guard down the steep stairs and around to the front of the massive villa. They walked down several corridors and through a large room filled with beautiful velvet furniture and gilded portraits before entering a large dining room. A massive wooden table ran the length of the room, with chairs pushed up on either side. A gold piece of fabric ran down the center with gold candelabras and platters of food. The walls were cream plaster with gold detail. Paintings and mirrors hung here and there, creating an elegant atmosphere.

Her gaze stopped short on Delgato sitting on one end of the table. In full military dress, he glanced up when the guard announced her presence.

Freezing in the doorway, Rose put a hand to her throat, unsure if she wanted to sit with this man despite the savory aromas making her mouth water.

Black, glimmering eyes skimmed over her, simmering with hatred and rage. His small black mustache twitched as he stared into her soul, and a fake smile twisted his cruel thin lips. “Welcome, *Senorita*.” Waving a thin hand at the chairs on either side of his, he beckoned her closer. “Come join me.”

The guard indicated a velvet chair to the man’s left, and she lowered her body to the seat, gripping the arms in case she needed leverage to expedite her departure.

He waved a hand at the platters of roast pigeon, duck, and partridge and the bowls of fruit. “Eat. Then we talk.”

Placing a sliver of duck and some fruit on her plate, she stared at them and wondered if this were her last meal. She should eat, she supposed. If he didn’t kill her immediately, she’d need the strength to escape. Picking at her food and too upset to do it justice, she ignored how the duck melted in her mouth, the juicy sweetness of the grapes popped, and the refreshing deliciousness of the guava sated her appetite.

Gazing at the man seated opposite her, she waited for him to speak.

He ate a disgusting amount of food, belching and licking his fingers with relish. Waving his cup in the air every few minutes, a frightened girl in a dark skirt and blouse hurried to pour him more wine.

Rose kept her gaze on him while she wiped her fingers on the fine linen napkin beside her plate.

Used to eating in the Delaney living room while Shanna's servants waited on her, this experience couldn't be more different. Her friend's dining room burst with laughter and smiles while this dining room reeked of darkness and fear. A shiver ran down her back as she gazed around at the guarded doors knowing she couldn't leave unless the Delgato commanded. Shanna would pretend she didn't notice and search for a weapon. Her glance dropped to the knife next to her fork.

Picking up a knife, she selected another slice of duck, cut it into bite-sized pieces, and set her knife on the edge of the table. As she ate, she used her elbow to scoot it closer to the edge while her companion enjoyed his food.

When he turned his head to signal he wanted more wine, Rose slid the knife into her lap, then into the pocket of her skirt. Rising to her feet, she wandered the room to draw his attention away from the table, giving every painting and portrait her undivided attention.

Wiping his mouth with his napkin, the evil little man dropped it onto the table and rose to his feet. He joined her in front of a portrait depicting a beautiful dark-haired woman wearing a red scarf and little else.

"Who is she?" Proud of the way her voice stayed steady, Rose lifted her chin and sucked in a deep breath to calm her nerves.

Standing shoulder to shoulder, she discovered they were the same height and frowned. She never experienced such a thing in a man before.

"Maria Garcia. El Diablo's one true love and my sister." His voice grew bitter and filled with rage.

Nodding, she walked away.

"Don't you want to know what happened to her?" Swiveling to face her, he caught her arm and turned her toward the portrait.

Pretty sure she knew all she cared to, Rose backed up a step, shaking her head.

He took a step forward. "She had a lover El Diablo knew nothing about, the son of his enemy, a powerful warlord who robbed the villages and tradesman belonging to my master. When he learned of this affair, El Diablo gathered his army and rode to Eagle's Pass, where Maria entertained her lover. He caught them by surprise, and as he carried out justice, the Texas Ranger and his men attacked. They shot El Diablo and threw nitroglycerin in the windows, dropping the building on them all."

Wrenching her arm from his grasp, she folded them over her chest. "What does this have to do with me?"

A cruel smile twisted his lips. "It is fitting for the ranger to experience the same pain he caused El Diablo. For this reason, you are here. My foreman wanted to sell you with the others, but I convinced him my plan was best. The ranger shall watch as another takes his love's maidenhead." His gaze wandered over her from head to toe. "I am the man who shall perform the act in remembrance of Maria." His smile sent chills down her spine. "After which, you shall be given to my men to kill as they see fit."

Rose's knees knocked together, her mouth went dry, and her heart rate climbed. Delgato should be shot between the eyes for the things he planned. And if she still had her pistol, she'd pull the trigger with no regrets. Her chin rose, and she tucked her shaking hands behind her back. "What of the other girls? They have nothing to do with this. Let them go."

Throwing his head back with mirth, her captor laughed. "They will be sold. There is money to be made and women to pleasure." He stared at her breasts and then at her lips. "I would sample you now, but it is important the ranger is present when I take your virginity."

Slipping her hand into the pocket of her skirt, she grasped the handle of the knife, wanting to bury it in the evil man's black heart. "What if I don't cry? What if I'm not a virgin? What if the ranger kills you before you have a chance to carry out your horrible plan? A great many things could go wrong."

His eyes darkened to pitch black as his rage grew to the point he frothed at the mouth. "I will see justice is done! Ranger Calhan will pay the price, and you will die!"

A calculating glint entered his eye as he gazed up and down her body with contempt. "If you are not a virgin as you suggest, I will take you now and slit your throat when I am done." Taking a step toward her, he grinned with malice. "I could toss your severed head to *Senor* Calhan as a welcome gift."

Taking a hurried step backward, she gripped the

knife handle in readiness. “I said *what if*? I only pointed out there could be other outcomes besides the one you have in mind.”

He caught her braid in one quick motion and twisted her head backward.

She froze in place. Inching the knife to the pocket opening, her breathing grew shallow, and she tensed in preparation for her attack.

His eyes glittered as his head descended toward hers. “Do not play word games. There can be no other outcome. Are you a virgin?”

Swallowing hard, she added unrepentant lying to her list of sins. “Yes. Now let me go.”

Staring into her eyes for several long minutes as if he searched for the truth in their depths, he released her and flung her away from him. “If I find you lied, I will have your skin cut from your body inch by inch.” Stalking from the room, he ordered the guards to take her away.

Rose fell back against the wall and sucked in a shuddering breath, trembling in the aftermath. Her captor had anger issues up to his eyes. Thank goodness she hadn’t been forced to use the knife. She needed weapons to help the girls escape. Dropping the knife back into her pocket as the beefy guard took her by the arm, she grimaced as he marched her back to her room.

Rose didn’t breathe normally until the key clicked in the lock, and the guard’s footsteps retreated down the steep stairs.

Catching a glimpse through the door on the lower level as the guard hurried her past, she caught sight of Hannah and the others.

Pacing her little chamber back and forth, she wiped

the perspiration from her brow and made plans.

An hour later, Consuela appeared. “How did breakfast go?” Her whisper told Rose the guard stood in the corridor.

She grimaced. “Not well. I must get away before Chase comes. What Delgato has planned is evil, and I cannot allow him to do the things he says.”

Compassion shone from the other woman’s eyes. “I understand more than you think. I do not want any other women to go through what I did, and I will help where I can.”

“Thank you.” Smiling, she leaned closer. “Can you help me get the other girls away?”

Glancing at the door and back at Rose, Consuela bit her lip. “I will return tonight.” Turning around, she sailed from the room with her nose high.

Rose walked to the window and spent the afternoon digging nails out of the wooden planks across her window with her knife. When a board came loose, she scooted her cot across the room to the back wall beside the little table and hid the boards beneath it.

By nightfall, she removed all the boards and could gaze out to her heart’s content. When the guard clattered up the stairs with her evening meal, she drew the curtains across the window to hide her remodeling and sank onto her cot.

Strolling inside, he glanced around the room before setting the tray on the little table. “Eat.” After barking his command, he left, locking the door behind him.

Tonight, she could see the moon and the stars. Grinning, she picked up the bowl of soup and drank it without tasting it. After the guard returned for her dishes and the door shut behind him with a click of the lock, she hurried to the window to talk to the moon and stars about Chase.

Chapter Fifteen

Rose studied the movements of the guards over the next three days, making notes on when they took their breaks and when they changed shifts. Her window faced the back of the villa, so only parts of the grounds were visible. The two guards who came on duty at dinner liked to play poker and smoke cigars, disappearing for hours. They emerged and took up position when they knew their superior had arrived to check on them.

Her four friends were fattened like cattle before the slaughter, fed the best food, bathed every day, and had special oils rubbed into their skin and hair. Delgato ordered new clothes made for them and different hairstyles created to see which one brought out their best features.

Consuela kept Rose informed and passed messages back and forth between them. Although risky, the woman enjoyed the intrigue, using every opportunity she had.

On the day of the big party, Rose cornered her when she carried in the noon meal. "What if we make our move after dinner when the girls take their walk? We can sneak them through the south gate, and no one will know until they come to prepare them for the auction. They will have two hours to run before someone sounds the alarm." The women ate in the dining room, where Rose met the general for breakfast. From there, they would take them through the kitchen and out the back door to the grounds.

"It is dangerous. We will need a distraction to keep the men busy." Consuela sat beside her on her little cot. "If we are caught, they will shoot everyone involved."

"I know." Rose got up and paced. "But we don't have much time. Delgato said they would be sold tonight at the party. We must do this now, or it will be too late."

Consuela rose to her feet. "I do not want Delgato to realize I am involved yet." Biting her lip, she glanced toward the closed chamber door as if she heard a sound and frowned. "I hoped Rozita would be here."

Glancing back, Rose raised an eyebrow in surprise. "Why?"

"I have my own revenge planned out." The other woman's chin rose, and anger flashed in her brown eyes. "My sister betrayed me, and I have not forgotten."

"They must not discover your part in this. If I could do this without you, I would." Twisting her hands together, she sank back onto the cot. "I wish we had more time, but I can't let the girls be sold. They don't know what's in store for them."

"But you do?" Consuela's gaze swung around to Rose's face.

"Yes. Chase and I were together in San Antonio. I know what it is to have a man." Lifting her gaze to meet the other woman's surprised expression. She shrugged. "He missed our wedding in Chicago to arrest Delgato. I traveled to Texas for answers, and well, once we sorted everything out…"

Understanding shone from the other woman's eyes. "You are in love, and you could not withhold the natural desire to be together. I sympathize with your plight, but if Delgato finds out, he will not wait for *Senor* Chase to come. He will kill you, and Rozita will kill your man. He trusts her and will not believe she is capable of such a thing until it is too late. My sister is an excellent liar."

"I know." Jumping to her feet, Rose resumed her pacing. "Chase told me he thinks of her as a sister, and she didn't like it when I told her what he said. She wants him."

Consuela laughed and shook her head. "Rozita wants to be the center of every man's attention. Her pride cannot allow another woman to receive what she believes she deserves. Her elevated opinion of her own attractiveness knows no limit. She does not believe in love or honor, not even for family, and will stab the ranger in the back with the same lack of conscience she stabbed me."

Stopping, she turned to Consuela in surprise. "Your sister stabbed you?"

The woman nodded. "When we first arrived, we were as your friends, innocent of men, and hopeful of rescue. A wonderful man from my village courted me, a blacksmith who owned his own shop. In my village, owning a business at such a young age is a big thing, and my man enjoyed an elevated position among the people. His name was Mario. I loved him with every beat of my heart, and he me." Gazing across the room with a dreamy expression on her face, she sighed.

"He was taller than I with thick arms from his work at the forge. He had black hair, brown eyes, and a mustache that tickled my mouth when we kissed." Her expression changed and her voice fell flat. "Then the *banditos* raided my village, capturing Rozita and I. We were brought to this place, as you were, to be sold as slaves. My sister did not believe such a thing could happen to her, but I knew by the look in the general's eyes it would. We were served good food, such as your friends eat now, and given beautiful clothes.

"On the night we were to be sold, we were dressed in our new clothes with our hair up in elegant styles. I stood beside Rozita as man after man approached and looked us over. You do not know of the humiliation. They looked at our teeth and smelled our necks. The men ran their hands over my body. They touched my breasts and hips." Her eyes flashed with anger as she related the experience. "I did not know what to do. I had never been close to anyone but Mario, and even he did not touch me as these strange men did. Frightened, I moved closer to Rozita for courage. She laughed at me and told the men of my fear." Consuela's voice dropped.

"I realized then; the men excited my sister. She enjoyed their touch and asked them for more, basking in the attention they gave her. Until El Diablo walked into the room." Her face flashed with fear, anger, and then resignation. "He gazed at Rozita and then at me. Whatever he read in my sister's face excited him, and he ordered the other men from the room. His favorite woman, Maria, arrived moments later to take us to his harem." Swallowing, she lifted her chin as memories of her pain raced across her face. "There, he took our innocence and destroyed whatever hope I had with Mario forever."

Rose ached with empathy. Gazing at the other woman's expression, her heart twisted in two, and she swiped at her cheeks as tears ran down her face. "I am sorry. If I had known. I would have rescued you for Mario. This cannot be the end of your story. Somehow, I will find a way to help you get the happy ending you deserve."

Sadness shone from the other woman's eyes as she smiled. "You have a kind heart, *mi amiga, un gran corazón.* For this reason, I help you now. You are a good woman, one of the best I have known, and many women come through this villa."

"What happened with Rozita? Why doesn't she live here anymore?" Frowning, she studied the older woman's face.

Anger and hatred flashed in her brilliant eyes. "My sister rose in the hierarchy among El Diablo's many women. Soon she became his second favorite and had whatever her heart desired. The master gave Maria a beautiful diamond pendant, and when Rozita discovered this, jealousy and greed blackened my sister's heart.

"One night, I caught her in the corridor with the pendant in her hand on her way down from Maria's apartments. I knew she stole the jewels and urged her to put them back before anyone discovered what she did. She refused, saying she deserved the pendant more and intended to sell it on her next visit to Eagle Pass.

"The next day, Maria discovered the jewel missing, and El Diablo ordered the villa searched. The guards inspected every room and everyone's personal property. They found the precious pedant in my basket of clean clothing, and I knew who put it there. Later the same day, the master invited my sister and me to a special dinner, just the two of us, to discuss the theft. Rozita lied, claiming *she* found *me* on my way down from Maria's apartments. When El Diablo questioned her about her loyalty to him, she turned and stabbed me with her meat knife so he would know to whose side she gave her loyalty."

Consuela drew the front of her blouse down so Rose could see the jagged scar on her shoulder.

"What happened?" Anxiety for her friend made her heart rate accelerate. Thank God El Diablo didn't kill her for this supposed infraction.

The other woman shrugged. "He ordered me to be whipped and demoted. I serve the women he captures until the day I die. The master rewarded my sister with a trip to Eagle Pass, and she is free to travel wherever she desires. No one believes the truth of what happened, and I have paid the price for Rozita's sin. We have not been close ever since. My sister does not care whom she hurts. She is more interested in money and power than love and family."

"So, being demoted is a good thing, right? He didn't consider you part of his harem after, did he?" There must be a rainbow in this storm somewhere.

Shaking her head with resignation, Consuela sighed. "My position is worse. I am the woman he sends his associates to when they come to visit. He barters my body to every man he does business with. This is the reason I wish to get revenge."

"And you should. I will help you in any way I can. With any luck, Mario is still around and in love with you."

A lone tear trickled down the other woman's face. "He married two years ago and is happy in his new life. I would not expect him to wait for me." Shrugging, she gave a bitter laugh. "I have nothing to offer him if he did hold me in his esteem. I have been well used and am unworthy of such a good man."

"No!" Rose didn't agree. "This is not your fault, and a man who truly loves you would understand."

"It does not matter anymore. I will see Rozita receives justice for her lies, and then I shall find a different life." Lifting her chin, she smiled. "We don't have much time. If we plan to help your friends escape, we must work out the details."

Gazing up at Consuela, she nodded. "I wish I could go back and help you before all this happened, but you are correct. We must make plans before my friends suffer the same fate."

"I shall have my turn at revenge." The older woman's face adopted a blank expression as she changed the subject. "For now, we focus on the girls. One of the guards with a key to the gate is sweet on one of the servant girls. I will get the key from her."

"Perfect," Rose announced. "Leave the door ajar, and I will make an escape attempt. The guards will come to catch me, giving you time to get the girls out and the key returned before the men discover what happened."

"They might shoot you." The other woman warned. "Are you sure you wish to risk your life for your friends'?"

She nodded. "And for yours. But I do not believe they will shoot me. Delgato is committed to getting his revenge."

"As am I." Consuela's eyes glittered as she strode toward the door. "Wait until the women are in the back of the villa before you make your escape. I will wait for the alarm to sound before I get them out."

"Okay." On impulse, she hugged the other woman. "No one should suffer through what you did, and I'm sorry no one arrived to rescue you."

Grimacing, she stopped with her hand on the latch. "I had Rozita. At least, for a while." The door closed behind her with a soft thud, and the key turned in the lock.

Pacing her chamber like a caged animal until dinner arrived, Rose went over the details of the plan and prayed it worked. Consuela did not come with the guard to deliver her plate of food, and placing the tray on her table, he walked away, leaving the door ajar.

Gazing at this odd phenomenon in amazement, she considered the guard and wondered if he were in on their plans. Did he leave the door open by accident or on purpose?

Popping his head inside, he gazed at her. “I must watch the corridor at the bottom of the stairs as well tonight. So, I warn you. Do not try to escape. I left the door open so I can hear you from my post.”

Rose nodded and walked away to retrieve her tray, wondering for the thousandth time where Chase could be and why he hadn’t come to rescue her yet. She ate her fried fish, beans, and rice without tasting them and wandered to the window when she finished. Drawing the drapes aside, she gazed down and noted Hannah and the girls walking the grounds!

Should she take the knife or not? Patting her pocket for reassurance, she bit her lip. If she were caught and searched, they would take it from her. On the other hand, if she got into trouble, she would wish she had it. With a growl of frustration, Rose slipped the knife into a crack in the plaster behind her bed and slipped from the room.

Stepping off the last stair, she searched the area for the beefy guard, but no one appeared. Shrugging, she glanced down the corridor in both directions and tip-toed to the nearest doorway to hide. Silence filled the lower floor, and she nodded in relief. Peeking around the corner, she continued toward the front of the villa, surprised she hadn't run into at least one guard.

And then she did.

Rounding the next corner, she came face to face with one of the men who transported them.

Glancing up, he let out a bellow of rage, sounding the alarm.

Rose dashed through the elegant sitting room and down the next corridor, retracing her steps the day she arrived until she stood outside the villa in the evening air.

The guard's volume grew louder as he approached, and the men in the yard stopped to stare at her.

Now she had their attention. She made an all-out dash for the front gate.

Men shouted, and feet pounded behind her. Someone shot a gun, and a bullet whizzed past her head.

"Do not injure her! Remember our orders!" An angry booming voice called out.

Ignoring the chaos behind her, Rose zig-zagged until she arrived at the front entrance. As the massive gates swung closed, she gave a giant leap, diving through the narrowing space. Twisting as she propelled through the opening, she hit the hard ground with a thud at full speed.

She knocked the breath from her lungs on impact and lay there gazing at the scrub brush, wondering if she'd died. When she could suck in some air, she rolled onto her back and stared up at the hot, wavy sun while she caught her breath.

Delgato's angry voice shouted from the other side of the gate. "Get her, you damn fools."

Rose rolled to her feet and ran as the gate creaked back open. Bullets hit the ground all around her. Behind her, a horse whinnied, and hooves pounded the earth coming closer and closer.

"Stop, or I swear to the sacred mother I will kill you." Delgato's bellow brooked no argument.

She stopped dead, hoping her distraction worked and her friends made their escape.

"Turn around." The man's deep voice dripped with rage, so she complied.

His glittering black eyes speared her to the spot while he waved his pistol at her with one hand and reigned in his dancing horse with the other. "Give me one reason why I shouldn't kill you now."

Her mouth grew as dry as the Chihuahuan desert, and her heart threatened to pound out of her chest. Wiping perspiration from her brow, she gazed up at him. "If you kill me, the ranger won't walk into your trap."

He stared at her with hard, narrow, calculating eyes.

For a second, she wondered if she said the wrong thing. She knew he wanted Chase and figured he wouldn't shoot her until he did. Although risky, her attempt to run would be worth the effort if the girls got away.

Delgato lifted his pistol and pointed it at her head without saying a word. Pulling the hammer back, he took aim.

Rose didn't flinch and lifted her chin in defiance. "I would rather die with a bullet to the head than the way you have planned. So go ahead. Shoot."

Uncertainty stretched for an eternity until he let the hammer on his pistol back down. Laughter erupted from his mouth as if he couldn't contain his mirth. "By God, I like you. If I didn't have plans for the worthless ranger, I'd take you into my stable."

Rose whispered a silent prayer of gratitude to Chase for unknowingly saving her from a fate worse than the fiery pits of hell.

The guard caught up to them by the time Delgato holstered his gun.

Waving his hand at Rose, he glared at the men. “Get her back to the villa and find out who is responsible for her escape.” Turning his mount around, he galloped for the gate and disappeared inside.

She walked all the way back with a rifle in her back. A hundred feet from the gate, a flash of light in the scrub brush caught her attention. Glancing over, she caught movement, and for a few seconds, she thought Chase found her, but then nothing.

Staring at the bushes and willing them to move again, a tiny light flickered in her eyes.

Tripping, she fell to her knees as tears welled up in her eyes. He *had* come for her!

The guard behind her jerked her to her feet and shoved her forward. “Walk.”

Rose kept her head down to hide her joy as she trudged wearily back to the villa.

When the gates closed behind them, the beefy guard glared at her and backhanded her face. “This is the way you repay my kindness?” Grasping the rope, he bound her hands tighter than ever, and she changed her mind about him as she spit blood onto the cobblestones. He wasn’t nice, and he hadn’t been helping. It didn’t matter, though. Chase had come, and soon she’d be free.

Chapter Sixteen

"Did they get away?' Rose whispered the words when Consuela arrived with her dress for the party. They only had a few minutes alone.

"Yes. My brother is on his way to Laredo and will drop them outside the sheriff's office. They will find their way from there." Consuela whispered as she sat the pink silk gown on the cot beside Rose. When she straightened, her face twisted with dislike, and she spoke in loud, angry tones. "You are to bathe in scented water and wear this gown." Her voice dripped with ice as she snapped her fingers for the servants to carry in the tub and water. "When you are finished, a woman will do your hair. I will collect you afterward." Lifting her nose high, the woman swept from the room with a disapproving sniff.

Rose kept her head down while the servants filled the tub, knowing Consuela had a part to play in keeping anyone from suspecting her hand in the women's escape.

As her punishment, Delgato ordered five lashes, and Rose could barely move for the pain. But a sore back and stiff limbs were a small price to pay for the girls' freedom.

Her beefy guard had been shot for leaving her door ajar. So had the guard who owned the key to the south gate. Quaking for her part in their deaths, she didn't touch the hot soup Consuela supplied. Rose had never met a man like Delgato before and marveled how he could take life with such recklessness.

Her ears rang from verbal abuse heaped upon her when her captor discovered the women's escape. He knew she played a part but could do nothing more than order her whipped for it. Whatever plans he had for her were more important than shooting her along with the two guards.

Stepping into the warm water with a groan, she allowed the young servant girl to help her bathe and wash her hair. Once the beautiful gown clung to her body and the laces were cinched, Rose turned away and pretended to drop her slipper beside her cot. Sliding the knife from under her pillow, she dropped it into the pocket of her gown while the servant girl bent to retrieve her slipper. Thanking the girl, she put her slipper on and sat in front of the small table while another servant dried and combed her hair. Curled high on her head and threaded with pearls, she resembled the old Rose once more. So much had changed since she sat in front of her mirror at Delaney Estates and grumbled about Chase missing their wedding. The face staring back at her no longer blushed like a virgin or shied away from danger. The gaze holding hers in the mirror possessed a new strength she did not have before boarding the train for Houston.

Rubbing the knot in her stomach with the palm of her hand, she knew with certainty tonight would change everything. Delgato planned this occasion with care, and whatever happened, she saved five lives this day. Lives he no longer controlled, and the knowledge made her proud.

Consuela appeared at the door. "Follow me."

Taking a deep breath, she slid her hand into the

pocket of her gown and clasped the handle of the knife. The cold silver handle reassured her, promising a chance at freedom.

Her friend led her to the main floor and around to the long dining hall without saying a word. Laughter and music filled the air, along with the sweet scent of floral garlands twisted around the doorway, and tall vases filled with blooms stood in all the corners. Elegant guests holding champagne flutes lingered in the corridor and filled the dining hall.

When they stopped, her escort squeezed her hand. "It will be over soon."

Unsure of how to feel about her comment, she gave a slight nod to Consuela.

"Ah, there you are." Delgato stood at the other end of the room dressed in a tailored suit and holding a glass of tequila. He beckoned for Rose to come to him. "I would like to introduce you to the general."

A black-haired man stood beside him. Thinner and close in height, his black gaze simmered with interest and hatred.

Glancing around for avenues of escape and finding none, she complied with reluctance.

"General, this is Miss Tanner." As if his words explained everything, Delgato took her by the elbow and steered her forward to face the older man by his side.

By everything she noted so far, Delgato planned to proceed with the auction, despite the fact her friends were gone. This man must possess great wealth and power for her captor to beam with such interest in the exchange.

"Indeed." The thin man nodded in her direction.

Rose swallowed as her stomach clenched with

apprehension. Something didn't feel right. Dipping into a small curtsy, she rose and met the general's glittering eyes with indifference. Whatever else she did, she must not let them see her fear.

Casting her gaze around, she noted very few women attended the event. Those who did spoke in quiet tones in a corner while the male guests roamed the halls like cocky roosters.

She peeked at the men beneath her lashes, hoping to recognize them at some future event. If they ever stepped foot in the United States again, she would testify of this night and see them prosecuted for their crimes. Women were not objects to be bartered and sold.

Delgato took her elbow, making her jump in alarm. "It is time to begin."

Dipping her head to gather strength, she gave her nerves a stern talking to. Somehow, she must make it through this night, no matter what happened. She thought of Shanna, Reese, and the twins, of her parents and friends in Rock Creek, and of the Calhans, but mostly of Chase. It no longer mattered whether she had fighting skills or not. All those people were part of her life, and she was part of theirs. Love was all the superpower she required, and she would live through this because the twins deserved her as their aunt. Shanna deserved her as her best friend, and Chase deserved her as his wife. She loved them with all her heart, and they loved her back. Her heart swelled to overflowing, and in response, her chin lifted along with the darkness hovering over her.

Chase would make his move tonight, and she must be ready. Stiffening her spine, she met the general's gaze, and her chin rose another notch. Hope and courage fluttered in her breast like twin pennants of freedom.

Delgato steered her through the crowd toward two closed doors with guards,

The general kept pace on her other side, and Rose had the impression they herded her like the condemned to the hangman's noose.

Tugging from her captor's grasp, she glared and took a step away.

He chuckled beside her. "It is too bad I shall not get the chance to have you. I would have enjoyed breaking you."

She refused to give way to the anger and panic his words created. She ignored how her stomach swirled with apprehension.

A servant at the door offered her a glass of champagne.

Rose shook her head.

Delgato's gaze narrowed. "Do not presume upon my good nature. You do not want me as an enemy. Take the champagne. You may wish you had it before the evening is through."

He had a point. "I accept your offer of champagne, but you are not my friend." Staring straight into his shiny black eyes, she kept her gaze steady to make her point.

Her captor handed her the glass. "Take it."

She did.

"I have been both kind and generous to you. Had I not taken a liking to you, you would be dead. You should thank me for all I have done." Her captor stopped in front of the two doors. He grasped a small gold bell from his pocket and rang it. "It is time to begin."

Everyone turned toward him, talking excitedly as the double doors to the ballroom were opened and the guests hurried inside.

Reclaiming her elbow, Delgato guided her to the front of the room. Rows of chairs were arranged before a low wooden platform, and her companion took his seat in the front. Once more, she sat on his left, and the general sat on his right. When everyone had a place, her captor clapped his hands.

A large bald man in evening clothes entered through a door to the right of the stage and strode to the center of the wooden platform. "Good evening. I am Eduardo." Waving his hand to introduce a small muscular guard who stood beside him, he grinned. "And this is Emilio.

"Bring the first one in." Eduardo beamed at the audience, and Emilio hurried to the door on the right, returning with a frightened blonde-haired, blue-eyed girl.

The crowd clapped with delight.

Rose froze in place. She only rescued five of the girls. How could she forget there had been twenty women in the church room? Clenching her teeth and gripping the arm of her chair, she intended to rise and give Delgato a piece of her mind when a guard approached and whispered in his ear.

Her captor whispered with the general and frowned. Waving at Eduardo to continue, he ordered the guard to keep their guest busy until the auction ended.

The hair on her neck stood on end. Chase must be inside the compound. Gazing around, she met Delgato's amused expression.

"Do not allow your mind to give false promises of hope. There will be no rescue for you. You belong to me, and my men have things under control."

Rose swallowed. "I will never belong to you."

His eyebrow arched. "No?"

"No." Her emphatic answer hung suspended between them until Delgato leaned toward the general, and the two held a whispered conversation.

Leaning as close as she could stomach, she hoped to overhear their conversation, but they spoke too quietly.

When they finished, Delgato nodded and rose to his feet, glaring at her. "The general will keep you company while I see to our guest." He paused. "A word of warning. My friend does not possess the same kindness or forgiveness I do." Turning around, he disappeared.

Grimacing, she turned her attention to the front of the room. Neither word could be used with any believable amount of sincerity in relation to her captor. Folding her arms over her chest, she took deep breaths. She would not be frightened. Not with Chase so close and not with hope hovering over her.

"Sold for ten thousand pesos to the gentleman with the cane." Eduardo's voice boomed over the murmur of the crowd making her shiver.

Gaping in astonishment, she could not believe her eyes. They auctioned the girl away right in front of her while she did nothing to stop them. The girl cried out and fought Emilio as he hauled her away. Her screams filled the ballroom and out into the corridor. An elderly man with a big nose and a cane walked past her, following Emilio from the room.

What the hell—

Shots ricocheted through the corridor outside and struck the heavy wooden doors with a thud. Rose turned in her seat as the general's hand gripped her arm.

"Stay where you are." Turning, he waved a hand at Eduardo. "Proceed. Until we are forced from our seats, the auction will continue."

"Bring in the next item." Smiling at the crowd, Eduardo waved a hand at the door to the right.

A small, brown-haired woman of eighteen or nineteen entered the room with bound hands and bruises on her cheeks.

Rose gasped in outrage. "Let her go! How can you do this to these women? Let them go!" Rising to her feet, she intended to wrestle the girl from her captors when the edge of a knife pressed into her side.

Men shouted, and more bullets hit the walls and door outside. Half-turning toward the door, she expected to see Chase striding toward them.

"Sit down, Miss Tanner." The general stabbed his blade into her side and wetness spread from the wound.

Gasping in pain, she sank into her chair and gaped at the dark red stain on her gown. Sucking in a breath, she pressed her hand into her side to stop the bleeding. No general would get the best of her. She had too much to live for.

Eduardo hurried on. "This item has plenty of spirit, as you can see by the scratches. Some lucky man will have the enjoyment of breaking her. Who will start the bidding?"

Rose opened her mouth to protest when her companion gripped her hand, threatening to break her fingers. Cold sweat broke out on her brow.

"If you make a disturbance again, I will kill you. Sit still and be silent." His gaze narrowed onto her face, and Rose knew why he and Delgato were such friends.

Wiping terror from her forehead, she marveled at the surreal events as dizziness tilted the room sideways. Pressing tighter against the wound in her side, she dipped her head. Nausea rose in her throat as she glanced up.

The small, brown-haired woman's eyes were glazed over as if she had been drugged, and Rose shivered with revulsion. How could they treat women this way? And where the hell did Chase go? Not daring to turn her head, she dropped her gaze to the floor and considered her options. She would need stitches and a bandage before she could run with any speed. The guards stationed in front of the doors would stop her before she made it two feet. And then there was the matter of the general's wicked blade. She dare not antagonize him further without a sound plan, and help.

They auctioned off five more women while she sat in a state of shocked disbelief, unable to do a thing to help. All the while, the sound of guns and shouting filled the corridors of the villa. Only the ballroom remained untouched.

Staring at each man who purchased a woman, she vowed she'd get the women back while her mind cataloged the battle in the distance.

Her heart ached, and the pain in her side made everything else pale in comparison. Shouldn't Chase be kicking in doors to find her? Rose pressed harder into her side and winced. A loud crash reverberated behind them, and she dropped her chin, focusing on every noise in the corridor beyond.

The general signaled, the guards hurried into the corridor, and Eduardo announced the auction over, thanking everyone for attending. The remaining guests fled, leaving them alone.

Rose leaned over and dry-heaved all over the polished tile floor.

The general chuckled at her discomfort and held out his hand to help her up. "As you have no doubt guessed, your ranger is in the villa. Come, we must see what keeps Delgato. He will be sad he missed the auction. We bet which item would make us the most money. Tonight, I won a thousand pesos on the second bid. We received a lot more for her than Delgato thought we would."

Rose dry-heaved again.

An explosion shook the foundations of the villa, dropping her to her knees with a whimper.

The door behind them crashed open, and a bloody Delgato staggered in with a knife in his chest. "I failed. Forgive me…"

The general's face paled beneath his darkly tanned skin. Gazing from the wounded man to the door behind him and back, terror flashed across his face. "We must leave." Plucking a pistol from his waistband, he shot Delgato between the eyes.

She gaped in stupefaction.

Fear flickered in the general's glittering black eyes as he grabbed Rose by the arm and hurried her through the door behind the platform.

"Chase!" She dug her heels in, screaming with every ounce of strength she had.

The general hit her over the head, and blackness swallowed her whole.

****

When she regained her senses, she lay in the back of a carriage bouncing along at a violent pace. The carriage jolted and bucked as the horses ran over the rough dirt road. Rose shook her head and righted herself. A warm hand settled on her arm. Turning, she met Consuela's concerned expression. Holding a finger to her lips, she shook her head to indicate she shouldn't speak. "When will we stop, general? I am weary, and the prisoner may wake soon."

Rose glanced in front of them.

The general held the reins with both hands, slapping the horses with them to urge them faster. "We cannot stop. The bastard ranger will catch us if we do. I must make it to my family home before sunrise. He does not know of its existence, and we will be safe there while I gather more men."

Rose raised an eyebrow at Consuela.

"Your ranger attacked the villa and killed the guards. Delgato lies dead in the ballroom. The general slipped out the back door with you while the ranger searched the compound." Glancing at the general to make sure they were not being overheard, she continued. "I ran into the courtyard after the last explosion. The general had you over his shoulder, and I begged to come along."

Rose closed her eyes. Her head hurt, and her vision blurred. "Chase will follow.'

Consuela nodded. "He is behind us. This is why the general is so frantic."

"What does the general want with me? All he has to do is stop and let me go to my fiancé. Delgato is the one responsible."

Consuela gave her a quick glance. "We will talk later."

They crashed and bounced for several hours. A full moon lit their way as they wheeled past sagebrush and cactus.

The general kept his eye on their back trail. "He's catching up to us. We'll have to take refuge in the ruins."

The first fingers of dawn lit the sky in brilliant shades of orange and red, and they wheeled into the scarred remains of a once magnificent home and drew to a stop with a flourish. The floors and roof were gone, as were the doors and windows. Only the tall, impressive shell remained, with a few crumbling inner walls creating a labyrinth of stone solitude.

The general jumped from the carriage with a curse. “Get out and make yourself useful.” His gaze speared them both before staring at Consuela. “Do you know how to shoot a gun?”

She nodded her head, and the general handed her one of the pistols by his side.

“We don’t have much time. I will make my stand here.” He pointed to a wall in the middle of the ruins. “You will hide there.” He pointed at a half wall adjacent. “He will walk along this path to meet me. When you have him in your sight. Shoot him.”

Rose lifted her head from the carriage seat. “What you suggest is murder and a hanging offense in the States. Chase has three brothers who will not rest until you are brought to justice or dead.”

Swinging around, the general narrowed his gaze on her face. “So, you live.” He strode toward the carriage. “They will never discover what happened to either one of you. This is Mexico, and my country will believe my testimony.” He grabbed her arm. “I’m grateful you did not die from your wound because I have need of you for my plan to work. You will help me kill the ranger.”

“Never.” Every fiber in her body stiffened at his suggestion.

Tugging on her elbow, he waved his knife in her face. “Do not make me hurt you again. Come along like a good girl.”

Stepping from the carriage, she caught the seat

beside her as dizziness claimed her. Slipping her hand into her pocket, she grasped the handle of her knife. Now was her chance.

When he tugged on her arm the second time, she tripped. Righting her body, she swung her knife around to strike him, but he knocked it from her hands with a laugh.

"I wondered how long it would take you to strike out at me. I'm sure you believe you are clever, but I knew you had the knife all this time. Delgato informed me of your deceit."

At her surprised expression, he sneered. "Did you believe he would not notice it missing?"

Backhanding her across the face, he sent her flying backward into a heap on the ground. "If Maria could not escape me, what makes you think you can?"

Rose winced and felt her teeth with her tongue, sighing when they were all accounted for. Her cheek throbbed from the blow, and the scene swirled around her head. "Maria…?" She said the word and wiped blood from her lip with her hand. Understanding flashed across her mind the next instant. "Maria Garcia. Who are you?"

Chapter Seventeen

Chase approached El Diablo's villa with caution while his heart thumped in his chest. After all this time, he'd found her.

Rozita made some paltry excuse to not get close to the villa during the day, so he left her. He knew she double-crossed him with Delgato, so her excuse not to accompany him to the villa came as no surprise. Either way, he had to get Rose the hell out of Mexico and back to Chicago to safety. He didn't give a damn what Rozita did and would deal with her later. Right now, rescuing the love of his life held top priority,

Sneaking through the brush until he hid next to the front gate, he waited for an opportunity to slip inside unnoticed. He didn't expect Rose to come barreling out and face plant into the ground a hundred feet from his hiding spot.

Chase forgot to breathe. So goddamned beautiful, she took his breath away wearing a dress anything but elegant. His heart stood still in his chest when he gazed at her pale face. Damn, was she a sight for his weary eyes.

Crouching behind the bushes, preparing to scoop her up before the bastards discovered what happened, he narrowed his gaze when Delgato and his men rushed through the gate.

Slipping a knife from his vest, he studied the scene.

When the bastard drew his gun and aimed it at his woman, he flipped the blade over in his hand and took aim.

The next second, Rose stopped running and turned to face the bastard. Fire flashed in her eyes, and her chin lifted in her go-to-hell, damn-you face.

Surprised, he gaped. This gorgeous furious woman glowed with life and bore no resemblance to the frightened women he envisioned while on her trail. Shaking his head in wonder, he turned his gaze to her captor, prepared to drop him on the spot. The man chuckled at something his darlin' said and rode back to the gates.

Chase ducked low into the bushes to escape detection with his ears peeled for sounds from his woman. When he peeked out, anger turned his blood to molten lava. Sporting a bruise on her cheek, with her head held high, she marched back to the confines of the compound with an army of guards behind her.

Lifting his knife, he held the blade flat and angled the blade at the sun. If he could get her attention, he'd let her know his location. The sun glinted on his blade as he aimed the light toward Rose's face and waited.

She glanced at the bushes and tripped.

Chase grinned. She'd seen his signal and knew he'd come for her like he promised. Waiting for her to gaze his way, he held the blade flat to signal her again. Sometime in the next few hours, he'd again hold his love in his arms.

The gates closed behind the men, and he spent the rest of the afternoon inspecting the layout of the villa and planning his attack. Groups of people arrived from all directions, most of them men, Chase noted. Delgato must be having an auction tonight in keeping with El Diablo's reputation. Slipping into the back of a covered wagon, he rode inside the gate undetected.

Finding the supply room where the ammunition, gunpowder, and dynamite were kept, he placed bundles of dynamite in strategic locations one at a time. He spent the rest of the afternoon getting them into position without being spotted. As dusk approached, his task got easier as the shadows covered his activities. One man against an army of guards did not have great odds, but with the element of surprise, he had the advantage.

Once the guests arrived and the compound settled down, Chase slipped into the lookout posts and took the guards out. Then he sidled through the shadows toward the guard barracks, where he hid his first two bundles of dynamite. He lit the fuses, and all hell broke loose.

Everything went according to plan until he stepped inside the villa and came face to face with Delgato and a group of soldiers. Using all his skills to stay alive, he assessed his position. A line of four guards stood in front of a double door leading to an inner room. The other men danced around the corners, hoping to lead him away. The more he studied their movements, he realized they were determined to keep him from the inner room and what must be Delgato's auction. The guests and Rose must be in there.

His enemy took position in the center of the room, holding his sword and beckoning him forward. Chase killed the guard off to his right with a quick throw to the throat and relieved the man of his sword in time to deflect Delgato's blow. He took out the other three men in between strikes with his enemy, cutting a swathe across Delgato's chest, which would have dropped a normal man to his knees. But the man only stumbled, swinging his sword around. The battle grew fierce, and Chase missed his mark twice, paying dearly for it with deep cuts on both arms and one to his ribs. Soldiers ran down the halls firing their pistols, their heavy footsteps thundering in the empty corridors. Chase dropped them with his knives or the sword when they entered the fray.

Guests exited the large double doors, a few at a time, making a wide circle around the two men fighting with blades. Catching a glimpse into the room, he detected the back of Rose's head sitting next to a black-haired man with a handle-bar mustache. *El Diablo?*

Chase stilled. How could this be? His shock gave Delgato the advantage, and he raised his sword, aiming for the heart. Sidestepping at the last second, the blade missed his heart and slashed the upper arm. Whirling to the right, he rushed Delgato and stuck a blade in the bastard's chest before racing around the corner to set off the last bundle of dynamite.

Running in the opposite direction, the explosion knocked him to the ground. When he lifted his head, no sign of Delgato could be seen, but the double doors to the ballroom were thrown open, and guests poured into the corridor. Chase dodged his way through, but as he approached, the double doors swung shut, and a guard appeared with a pistol in his hand. He aimed at Chase's heart and died of a knife wound to the chest a second later.

Catching the doors in both hands, he swung them open.

"Chase!" Rose's scream ripped through the large room toward him, and his heart damn near burst from his chest at the terror in her voice.

Racing into the room, Chase's heart beating at a furious rate, his hand hovered over his throwing knives, but the room remained empty. A door to the right stood ajar. Running through it all the way to the back of the compound, he stopped in time to see a carriage disappear through the back gates with three passengers.

Swearing, he spit on the ground and leaned against the outer wall to catch his breath. The wounds he received from his fight with Delgato bled freely. Ripping the sleeve off his shirt, he tied it around the deeper one on his upper arm. Swaying from loss of blood, he gritted his teeth and stepped away from the wall. He had to get to Rose before the devil killed her. Stumbling through the gates and around to the clump of trees several hundred yards from the outer wall where he ditched Aries earlier in the day, he clambered into the saddle.

Rozita rode up on her bay mare as he swung the stallion around. "We will chase them, yes?"

He didn't ask how she knew where to find him. Nothing mattered but Rose.

Funny thing about turncoats, their evil deeds caught up to them sooner or later. As soon as he had his love somewhere safe, he planned to help Rozita's evil deeds catch up sooner.

Turning south, they ran hard and caught up to their quarry as the first rays of morning touched the tips of the cactus. The carriage wheeled into the ruins of a large stone house in a cloud of dust as Chase trotted to the front and slid from the saddle.

Removing his pistol from his saddle bag, he checked the bullets and tucked it in the back waistband of his trousers. The blood from the wound on his side dried to his shirt, making the fabric stick to his wound. Rolling his shoulders, he tightened the bandage around his upper arm and tugged his shirt free. Ripping his other sleeve into strips, he tied them together and wrapped them around his side to stem the flow of blood.

Rozita stopped her mare beside him and slid to the ground, her eyes glittering with excitement. "You will fight?"

Chase ignored her and adjusted his bandolier, adding knives to the empty spaces. When he finished, he flattened his body next to the opening in the ruins and peeked around the corner. With a knife in his hand, he crept his way inside.

Rozita gave a sigh of exasperation and marched into the center of the ruins.

Careful to keep a wall behind his back and his eyes peeled for an ambush, he followed. When he reached the woman, he glanced around. Nothing indicated another presence but the hair on his neck and the feeling in his gut told him the third person stood somewhere close.

****

"You are El Diablo?" Rising to her feet, Rose stared at him. So much made sense. Delgato deferring to the general over every decision, the massive villa, the servants, the auction, and the hatred in the general's eyes.

He bowed, mocking her with his gaze. "I am."

She searched his face. "How are you not dead?"

The general's eyes glittered. "I have your ranger to thank for the death of my Maria. I have Rozita to thank for my life."

A horse whinnied close by, and his eyes narrowed. "It is time. The bastard shall pay his dues."

Jerking her toward him, he marched her through the tumbled-down ruins and held her behind the wall to his right. Turning, with her out of sight, he faced the front of the building and waited.

Rose froze the second she heard Chase's deep voice. Her heart did double-time and leaped into her throat.

"Come out, coward, and face me like a man. You have nowhere to run." His nearness made her go weak in the knees.

The general held Rose pinned behind the wall with a death grip around her neck. Withdrawing a pistol from his waistband, he cocked it. "I have been waiting for you. We have much to catch up on."

Rose swallowed to ease the constriction in her throat.

Her captor forced her around the corner, where she faced the love of her life with a gun to her head.

"El Diablo." Rage flashed across Chase's face as he stared at her captor.

"Are you surprised? You didn't count on me being alive when you entered my compound earlier today. How does it feel to know you failed, Calhan?" The bitterness and venom in the general's voice engulfed her in a black mist.

Rose kept her gaze on her ranger's face and refused to think about the gun pressed into her temple. Now El Diablo had them both. She knew what would happen next.

"So many things make sense now. I thought you were dead. Rozita assured me Delgato took over your…business, but now I see she lied. We found a body beside Maria's at Eagle's Pass. If you didn't die, who did?" Chase's gaze remained fixed on the man holding her captive.

The general shrugged. "The son of my enemy. We

needed a body to convince you I died, and his happened to be handy."

"How did you escape? We had the villa surrounded." Chase's voice sent shivers of longing through her body. She wanted him to gaze into her eyes and smile so she knew everything would be all right.

Then Rozita's laughter tinkled across the space between them. "Haven't you guessed, *Senor* Chase? I helped him, like now." She appeared behind the ranger and sauntered over to lean on a broken stone wall.

Swallowing, Rose wished the general would allow her to turn her head.

He granted her wish. And two seconds later, he jerked her into his side. "I have something of yours and you have something of mine. Come forward and we will trade."

Rose stiffened. El Diablo wanted Chase in the open so Rozita could shoot him. Calling out with what limited air she possessed, she choked when the general nudged her temple with the pistol.

"Shhhh." He whispered in her ear, blowing hot breath across her cheek.

Freezing, her gaze sought her fiancé's where he stood twenty feet in front of her, grinning at her captor.

"Chase!" She called, but he didn't respond.

He focused on the man with the gun to her head.

She thought he didn't hear, but the tick of muscle along his jaw told her he knew of her fear and planned to unleash his fury on her captor.

Rozita sauntered a few feet closer to El Diablo. "It didn't end the way we hoped, but I did have the ranger and his woman in your villa at the same time. Am I forgiven?"

For the first time, Rose witnessed fear in the other woman's gaze.

El Diablo didn't blink. "We will discuss your loyalty after I have my revenge." He motioned for her to stand back and stared at Chase. "What are you going to do, ranger? I had such a delightful evening planned before you ruined it all by attacking my villa. I have your woman, *Senor* Calhan, as you had mine. I will kill her while you watch like you killed my Maria."

Rose held her breath, waiting to see what her fiancé would do next. Her heart thumped wildly in her chest as she stared at him.

El Diablo's hand slid under her arm to caress her breast.

Rose couldn't breathe.

The muscle tick in Chase's jaw grew more pronounced.

"You want to know how I escaped? The week before my Maria died, she came to my bed and begged to stay at my home in Eagle's Pass. Her cousin from Spain arrived to visit her and desired to see the beauty of Texas. You were getting too close, and I allowed her to go to my Texas stronghold for safety." He licked the side of Rose's face.

Shuddering with disgust, she stared at Chase, begging him with her eyes to do something.

Chase's gaze turned mercurial. "And?" He leaned against the wall beside him as if he had all the time in the world.

She knew he feigned disinterest from the fire in his eyes.

Rose took a deep breath as she stared at the love of her life. She would be ready when he gave the signal.

The general chuckled in her ear. "I planned to lead you into an ambush, but Delgato brought word of Maria's unfaithfulness to me."

He sniffed the side of Rose's neck. "My rival had a son who rode into my territory and raided my towns. I sent Delgato to report on the son's involvement. He caught Maria and the man together at Eagle Pass and sent word to me." Anger tightened his voice.

"I gathered my men, and we rode for Texas to find out the truth. I discovered Maria and her lover in the living area, where I confronted them, and they pleaded their innocence. Maria fell to her knees and begged for her life, claiming the son begged an audience with her to end the feud between our families." He pressed the barrel of his pistol tight against her scalp.

"I made the decision to spare Maria but kill the son of my enemy. He should have come to me with his offer, not one of my women. I shot him in front of Maria to ensure she never entertained a man in my home again. I turned to forgive her when the first shots struck my home. You and your ranger friends were outside. You destroyed my home and killed my men."

His voice dropped silky soft as if he relived the moment, and Rose shivered with fear.

"A bullet hit Maria, and she fell before I could forgive her. I could not figure out how you knew my location when I eluded you for months. And then Rozita confessed to leading you to me. She found a way for me to escape and suggested we place Maria under the body of my rival's son and leave my ring on his finger. An explosion broke a column loose. It fell across their bodies, crushing them and ensuring my escape." He chuckled. "I killed your ranger friends because you killed my men. I burned your farm because you burned my house. Now, I will kill your woman because you killed mine."

"No. You won't." And then the hero of all her dreams plucked a revolver from his waistband and took aim at her.

The muzzle flashed as fire burned her shoulder, knocking her backward and throwing the general off balance.

Dazed, she blinked up at the sky in horror! *Chase shot her!* Disbelief, pain, and shock rocked her to her core. How could he? None of the heroes in Mama's stories ever aimed a weapon at the princess. She stumbled to her feet to ask him what the hell he shot her for when Rozita let out a scream of outrage and withdrew a gun from her waistband.

"The least you could do is kill her." The other woman's voice rang out in the early morning air.

Everything happened at once.

Rozita aimed at Rose.

She dropped to the ground the second the woman took aim. Two more shots split the air, followed by a rifle report a second later.

Rose blinked. Rising to her feet in slow motion, she gazed around.

The general lay dead to her right, and Rozita lay in an unnatural position ten feet to her left.

Turning, she gulped as heartbreak crashed into her with the force of a tidal wave. Her darling ranger and the love of her life lay unmoving in a pool of blood fifteen paces in front of her. Her heart split into a million razor-sharp pieces and sank like a stone in her belly.

Dizzy with loss of blood and the unreality of what

just happened, Rose stumbled across the barren ground and dropped to her knees beside him. He couldn't die. Heroes never did. Somehow, they withstood dragons, poison, and witchcraft to live happily ever after. She choked on a sob. He promised to grow old with her, to have children, and to share her life. Not shoot her. Not die in front of her. Not to leave her so utterly alone. They had so much living to do. This couldn't be the end.

Tears rolled down her cheeks as she touched the side of his neck, hoping to feel the steady beat of his heart, but found nothing.

"Please, God, no." Her shoulder burned as she rocked forward to kiss his dear face. Grief and heartache tightened around her chest like a steel band while her distress dripped onto his blood-soaked shirt. How could this go so wrong?

"We must go." Consuela stood beside her and placed a hand on her shoulder. "El Diablo sent for more men when the fighting started back at the villa. They will come soon, and we must be gone."

Rose shook her head. "How can he be dead? He shot me, and then Rozita screamed…"

Her friend sighed. "Rozita aimed at you, and your ranger shot her. The general took advantage of the opportunity and shot *Senor* Calhan. So, I shot the general. Please, Miss Rose. We must go."

"I don't want to leave him here, Consuela. What if—" The earth tipped before her.

The other woman's voice came from a distance. She felt along Chase's neck with her finger and shook her head. "There is nothing we can do for him now. We will come back later. I will get you somewhere safe and then make arrangements for your ranger. Come."

Chase shot her! And died! Dimly aware of her surroundings, she allowed Consuela to help her to her feet. The loss of blood between the wound in her side, coupled with the gunshot, left her dizzy. Wilting back against the wall, she put a hand to her head as nausea rose in her throat. Her eyes refused to focus, and her limbs threatened to drop her to the ground.

Consuela tugged her around the corner and urged her forward. With an arm around Rose's waist, she half-dragged her across the hard ground. "I drove the carriage around here for a quick escape." Helping her into the carriage, she whipped the horses into a run. "I can see the dust from the *bandidos'* horses. We must hurry."

Rose fell against the cushion and curled up, holding her side. *Chase!* Blood seeped from her shoulder, making her gown sticky. She weaved in and out of consciousness as Consuela drove the carriage north and then east. Hours and hours passed.

Darkness covered the countryside when Consuela drew the horses to stop.

Lifting her head, Rose glanced around. "Where are we?" Blurry vision made it difficult to see. Rubbing her eyes, she stared at the little adobe house in front of her.

Consuela yelled, "*Madre!*" as she hurried around the carriage to Rose's side.

A gray-haired woman stumbled from the house, disbelief etched into her wrinkled face. "Consuela?" Wiping her hands on the rough woven towel in her hands, she threw it over her shoulder. "Is it really you?" Catching her daughter to her in a hug, she laughed and cried at the same time. A torrent of Spanish fell from her lips in a tidal wave of emotion.

Consuela hugged the woman back, her lips flowing

with Spanish as easily and quick as her mother. Somehow the two understood each other despite the rapid, non-stop way they spoke to one another.

Rose allowed them to help her from the carriage into the little house. “We must go back for Chase. He needs me.” Frantic to plead his case, she caught the other woman’s hands. “Please.”

“He is beyond our help, *mi amiga*.” Warm brown eyes gazed into her with compassion. “But I will go back to check on him once you are cleaned and bandaged.”

Unable to speak around the emotion in her chest, Rose nodded.

A man rose from a little table inside the cabin and stared at Consuela as they entered. Tall and handsome with dark hair and warm brown eyes, he wore plain brown clothes and held a hat in his hand.

Her companion froze for two seconds and then gripped Rose hard against her side. Uncertainty and pain chased across the woman’s face as she turned her head away.

“Mario comes every day to help me since you went away. He misses you.” Consuela’s mother glanced at her daughter, but she said nothing.

The older woman clucked her tongue over the amount of blood on Rose’s gown and indicated a curtained-off portion of the small house. “Put her in my bed, Consuela. I will tend her wounds as soon as I have heated water and gathered linen.”

The man set his hat on the small wooden table and stepped toward Consuela. “Let me help.”

After the barest hesitation, she relented, and the man swung Rose up in his arms. He carried her to the back of the house while Consuela hurried in front of them to pull the curtain aside.

A large bed stood against the wall covered with a pretty patchwork quilt. Her friend drew the blanket back for the man to set Rose on the white sheets. "*Gracias.*"

The man nodded and stared at Consuela. "You have grown more beautiful in the time you have been gone."

Blushing, she dipped her head. "I am not the same girl you knew, Mario. Much has happened."

Understanding dawned as Rose observed the two. This is the man Consuela planned to marry and who she thought forgot her.

Frowning, the man replied. "None of it is your fault."

Tilting her head, Consuela studied him. "I heard you married. You should go home to your wife and give her your compliments."

Mario stared back at her. "My wife is dead. She died in childbirth one year ago. The child died with her."

"I am sorry for your loss. You should leave." Turning away from him, her friend bent to place a blanket over her.

Catching her hand, Rose drew her down to whisper. "I know who he is to you. Let Mario have a chance. Both of you deserve to be happy." Her words were weak, but she meant them with all her heart. Consuela had a lot of love to give, and she suspected Mario knew it too.

The woman gazed at Rose and then at Mario. "Come back tomorrow. I will have more time then."

Grinning, Mario stepped aside for her mother to approach with a bowl of hot water and some cloth. "I will be here." Bowing from the waist, he turned toward the door. "I am nearby if you need anything."

Consuela smiled and pulled the curtain closed.

Her mother sat down on the bed beside Rose and picked up a knife. “Let me see how bad the wounds are.” Slitting the shoulder of her dress, she drew the fabric away, probing the wound with the tip of the knife.

Rose gritted her teeth against the pain while the room swirled around her head, and everything went black.

Chapter Eighteen

"Come out, coward, and face me like a man," Chase goaded.

His old enemy would take offense at the statement and did not disappoint him.

El Diablo stepped into view with his pistol against Rose's temple. Pretending to be surprised to see the general alive, he thought to buy some time.

His enemy lived up to everything his name implied—a devil and a devious one. Chase knew enough about the man to know if he so much as glanced at his love, she died. He wanted revenge for the death of his woman. Figuring Rozita lured him to the devil's villa with the hope she would be forgiven for her part in the attack at Eagle Pass, he knew the devil would use subterfuge and deceit to get his revenge. If the devil told her he would forgive her, he lied. El Diablo had to be the most cold-hearted killer he ever met. Sam Walker and the rangers were a testament to the fact.

Keeping his gaze on El Diablo and asking questions about the events at Eagle Pass, he tuned his senses to their surroundings. Having no idea the devil lived until he caught sight of him in the ballroom earlier in the evening, he wondered how the man slipped away and deceived him into thinking he died. While the devil talked, he took a step to the side to ensure his safety.

Somewhere the bastard had a shooter. He could feel

it in his gut.

When the general turned to speak to Rozita, he risked a glance at Rose and damn near lost his self-control. So goddamned beautiful and so terrified she could barely stand, he exercised all his self-control to not run to her side. But the situation grew tricky as hell because if he gave the slightest indication he gave a damn, she'd be dead before he cleared his knife. El Diablo invited him closer several times, confirming his suspicions about a waiting gunman.

When he refused to show any emotion, the general caressed his woman's body like a lover, and Chase saw red. He wanted to tear the devil's heart out with his bare hands and toss the body to the coyotes. Staying cool and detached while the bastard fondled Rose had to be the hardest damned thing he'd ever done.

El Diablo's sharp black eyes measured his reaction, and Chase knew he had to throw him off track. Using his cold determination to kill the bastard, he kept his gaze on his target and caught the surprise in the devil's eyes. When Rose begged him to help her, his hand shook with fury, so he shrugged to hide the tremor. As the devil finished his boasting and challenged him, Chase knew the time had come. Plucking his pistol, he shot her in the shoulder to knock her off balance. He could think of nothing else to save her life, and it worked. The shot knocked the bastard backward, making him lose his grip on the pistol. The weapon fell to the ground at his feet as Rose dropped like a sack of stones.

Rozita gave a scream of fury and took aim at Rose. So he shot her. Fire burned his chest as he pulled the trigger, and he fell like a sack of stones.

Rose. He had to help her, had to make sure she lived

and made it to safety. Panic raced through his system as he shifted position. Trying to rise, he fell back each time, too weak to move. Vaguely he remembered tears and Rose beside him. His heart twisted in his breast as he fought to speak. He struggled to open his eyes and let her know everything would be okay. But a woman's voice said something, and then his love left. Chase frowned. Who was the other woman, and where would she take his Rose? He must find her.

A vague memory tugged at his consciousness. The other woman reminded him of someone. He passed out, trying to remember who and where.

When he woke, the heat of the sun burned his face and hands. Chase pulled his body forward a few feet to the shade created by a stone wall. Relief lasted mere seconds until blackness claimed him.

When he woke again, early evening shadows covered the area around him. He lay still for several minutes gasping for air. "Rose?" God, where could she be? He must go to her and make sure she lived.

Gripping his side, he rolled to a sitting position and remembered what happened.

God, she could be bleeding out somewhere from the wound he put in her shoulder. He touched his cheek where some of her tears fell. He meant to save her life, not break her heart. The way he figured the situation, shooting her solved the problem and kept her alive. If she died, he would, too. There would never be another woman for him. Ever. He knew it to the bottom of his leather boots. He loved his Rose with all his heart and soul and prayed to God he'd have the chance to tell her.

Rising unsteadily to his feet, dizziness whitened his vision as he leaned against the stone wall. Putting a hand to his head, he waited until the stone ruins quit swirling around him.

Rose called the other woman Consuela. Rozita mentioned her sister a few times and pointed her out when they staked out El Diablo's men one day. They had a load of women, and Consuela took care of them. She worked for El Diablo, and he had no way of knowing where her loyalties lay.

Pain raced through him as he struggled toward the front of the ruins and Aries.

He hurt his love. And he had to find her to explain why he did.

With El Diablo dead for good and Rozita as well, he had no reason to fear life on the ranch as a civilian. Every real threat to Rose and their life together resided in hell as of a few hours ago, and yet he lost her. The hurt in her eyes when she realized he shot her ate at his soul. He had to explain and make her understand. Shooting her was the only way to save her. One could heal from a straight-through bullet wound. One couldn't recover from death.

Tightening the strip around his arm, he swayed and dropped his head for a minute to force the dizziness back. Ripping strips from the bottom of his shirt, he tied three of them together and wrapped them around his middle over the others before he staggered toward Aries.

It took him three tries to get into the saddle, and he swayed side to side as the pain and dizziness took control of his body. Gritting his teeth, he nudged his mount with his knees and rode him around the old shell of a house. Spying carriage tracks in the dirt, he frowned.

The tracks led away from El Diablo's strongholds and off to the east.

Chase gripped the saddle to keep upright. Consuela

must be the one El Diablo planted to kill him when he stepped into the right area, and now, she had Rose.

Urging Aries to a trot, he followed the carriage tracks for two miles on nothing but grim determination. Bleeding, wounded, and sick with dizziness, he fell from the saddle face-first into the hard-packed dirt of the road and knew no more.

Chapter Nineteen

Chase disappeared.

When Consuela returned from her search, she shook her head and sat down on the bed beside Rose. "There are many tracks made by El Diablo's men in the ruins and no evidence of your ranger. I do not know if they buried your fiancé or took him with them. Since we found no heartbeat the day of the shooting, I think they did the former."

Her heart sank. Rose nodded, too numb to answer, and turned her face to the wall. Not only had she lost her knight in shining armor, but every good thing in life. She wanted to die, too, but Consuela wouldn't let her.

"Think of your family, *mi amiga.* They will miss you. You have much to live for. If somehow your ranger lives, he will find you. Until we see a body, the possibility exists. I didn't know if I would ever see my mother or Mario again. But here we are. The sadness and heartache are real, but you can survive. Think of how he will feel if, by some fate or will of the gods, he lives and discovers you died out of grief. Be strong. If not for your sake, for his. He would not want this for you."

Rose couldn't argue with her logic and kept her heartache for the moon and stars when they had their nightly conversations. Her beautiful dream world filled with a magical wedding, a handsome groom, and an exciting honeymoon disappeared in the blink of an eye.

She would never have Chase's brown-eyed children and hold them in her arms, never fall asleep in his arms again, nor would she love another as she loved him. Her empty life stretched into the distance like an empty dirt road into the horizon. Sobbing with frustration and loneliness, she buried her face in her bent arms and cried until she had no more tears.

She had stern talks with her heart while the ache of her fiancé's death ate at her, and her shoulder healed from his bullet. The wound would forever remind her of her love and her loss. Tears filled her eyes, but she shook them away.

She cried so much she had nothing left. Not knowing where she wanted to go with her life after this, she sighed. She didn't want to think about another man, but if she ever found one, an addendum to the wedding vows concerning guns would be prudent.

Only one person alive could help her sort through loss and grief of this magnitude. Her best friend, Shanna. She would know what to say, what to do, and how to help Rose survive the wasteland she called life. Somehow, she must get through the pain until she could make it back home.

Two weeks passed before she grew well enough to travel. The bullet ripped through her shoulder and out the other side cutting a clean path with no sign of fever or infection.

She had a hard time believing Consuela and Rozita were sisters. Physically, they were similar with curvaceous bodies and long black hair. But mentally and emotionally, they were as different as two people could be. Consuela had a gentle, kind heart, and Rozita did not. Consuela enjoyed helping others and thought little of her own comfort, while her sister cared only for her own aggrandizement and despised others.

Her friend urged her to stay longer with her and her mother, but Rose wanted to get back to the United States and let Shanna know she lived. Her best friend had to be wondering what happened to her after all this time.

Rose didn't want to see any of the Calhans because they'd remind her of Chase and all she had lost. She didn't think she could even face Reese without bursting into tears. And God help her if they found her lover's body and had the funeral.

Consuela loaned her two sets of clothes for her journey, and Rose thanked her, promising to repay her as soon as she could.

Her friend refused her offer. "You are welcome to whatever you need from me. Because of you and your ranger, I am free and able to see Mama once more." A blush rose to her cheeks. "If you hadn't come along, I would still be at El Diablo's villa tending his women. I would not know Mario waited for me this past year, nor would I know of his love for me."

"Have you decided to allow him to court you then?" She smiled as Consuela blushed. The woman deserved happiness after all she'd been through, and if Mario wanted to overlook her past, Rose figured Consuela should too.

Her friend dipped her head. "I do not think I am a fit wife for such a wonderful man, but he will not accept *no* for an answer."

"Then, you should give him a chance." Tugging a colorful jacket over her sore shoulder, she tossed her braid behind her back. Not so long ago, she planned to be a wife, too. The memory made her frown.

Consuela's gaze searched Rose's face. "You will find another man and love again. You must believe this. Your ranger would want you to be happy."

She shook her head, unwilling to consider the notion. "One foray into the marriage pond is enough for me. I once thought marrying a dangerous man would be thrilling. He would protect my honor and fight dragons for me. Most girls marry farmers or ranch hands and spend very dull lives having babies and washing clothes. My father owns a mercantile and spends all his time in an apron measuring out goods. Every day I spent in Rock Creek, I dreamed of adventure and handsome men carrying me away. I wanted something more, something different and exciting. Then I met Chase and fell in love. He embodied every fantasy I ever had until he shot me."

"Then you should search for a dull man. He may not give you fantasies, but he will be there for you. There are worse things than having babies and washing clothes. You are too pretty to remain single for long." Consuela sounded so sure.

Heartache hovered beneath the surface. She couldn't bear the thought of anyone else touching her and closed her eyes for a second to gather strength. If she focused on her anger over losing him, she wouldn't feel his loss. "I don't want another man. Ever." And she meant it.

Consuela shook her head with sadness in her eyes. "You loved him very much."

Dropping her chin, she nodded. "Yes."

Consuela handed her a sombrero. "Then pray your ranger found a way to live. I do not mean to give you false hope, but without a body, death is not certain." She picked up a straw hat. "This is for your head and to hide you in plain sight. Keep the brim lowered, and from a distance, anyone searching for you will not know who you are." She paused. "I think *Senor* Calhan shot you to save your life. With El Diablo's gun to your head, his blade would not be fast enough."

Rose sighed. She'd gone over the whole scenario so many times in her head she didn't know what to believe. "If he did, the phrase *I love you to death* takes on a whole new meaning."

"I know El Diablo. If he knew Rozita double-crossed him, he wouldn't trust her word again. If she is the one who told him you were Ranger Calhan's woman, he would need proof. I think he planned to kill you both and Rozita as well. He kept his eye on your ranger the whole time he had a pistol to your head, searching for any sign of affection."

"So did I." She witnessed anger and determination.

"And yet you live. Your ranger kept his gaze on El Diablo for a reason. He shot Rozita through the heart to protect you and in doing so, lost his life. Take comfort his used his last breath for you. Someday, another man will win your heart. You deserve the same happiness you say I do."

Rose shrugged as if her heart were not shattered to dust inside her chest. "It doesn't matter. El Diablo and Delgato are both dead, and so is Rozita. They cannot hurt either of us again. I pray you have a long, happy life with Mario." Tying the sombrero on her head, she picked up the borrowed valise. "Chase Calhan was the love of my life and the keeper of my soul. There will be no one else. I will go somewhere I haven't been before and start over. Somewhere no Calhans have been, so the memories of him do not torture me." She shook her head when Consuela opened her mouth to argue. "I am serious. I cannot be close to anyone I know or the life I planned and lost. It will hurt too badly. I have thought about this a great deal while my shoulder healed, and I have made up my mind. Thank you for rescuing me at the ruins and for your kindness at El Diablo's villa. I do not know what I would have done without you." Giving Consuela a hug, she turned toward the door.

"You are a good woman with a kind heart. I will pray for you." She returned her hug and smiled.

"And I you." Walking through the door, Rose climbed onto the old cart belonging to Consuela's cousin and waved goodbye.

The cousin agreed to give Rose a ride into Texas. From there, she would be on her own. Shanna would wire her money to go home, and right now, she wanted to lie across her bed and tell her best friend everything.

Consuela's cousin and his wife were very kind. Rose rode on the back of their little cart for three days until they crossed over the border into Texas. Smiling as she stepped from the cart at the little village they stopped at, she slid to the ground and sucked in the beautiful air of her own country, happy to be back. Following her two escorts into the tavern for lunch, they ordered steaming plates of beans, rice, and shredded chicken served with flour tortillas.

Rose picked at her food, still too upset to eat more than a few mouthfuls at a time, and ended up swirling the food around her plate. Consuela's cousin and his wife insisted they pay for the meal and a night's lodging before they continued their journey, for which she thanked them with all her heart.

Later, as she climbed up the old wooden stairs to the room they purchased for her and opened the door, the full realization of her loneliness hit her. She set the small case containing her borrowed clothes from Consuela on the bench beside the door and sank down on the soft bed. Staring at the window with its yellow calico curtain, she sighed. Back in the States and on her own, alone. She needed Shanna, but a visit meant seeing Reese. The memories would tear the scab off her newly wounded heart. Until she sorted through her feelings, she required a place to stay.

Her parents would need some sort of message, or they would worry about her. She could go back to Rock Creek and live with them, but life there depressed her too much to consider. It would be as though she failed at life and ended up back where she started from. Kicking off her shoes, she lay down on the feather pillows, staring at the wooden ceiling and pondering her choices. A good job somewhere far away would keep her busy and her mind occupied.

Lying alone in the dark, she let the misery of her soul seep out until she had no more tears to cry. When she finished, she rose and splashed cold water on her face, grimacing at the puffy face in the glass. At some point, the healing must begin, and right when she thought she'd got over him, something or someone reminded her of her loss, and the tears flowed again.

She thought of Chase's older sister Madelaine. Married by sixteen and a child when she turned seventeen, she had the whole world in front of her until a tragic accident took her husband and support from her. Widowed with a son, she lived with her mother in Chicago. It had to be hard to be single with a fifteen-year-old son. Rose pitied her, but at the same time, having her lover's child kept part of him with her.

She placed her hand on her lower abdomen and sighed, unsure if she wished she were or were not pregnant. Her menses were irregular on normal days, and with all the excitement of the last few weeks, who knew what condition she might be in.

Undressing, she folded her clothes and put her night rail on. As she climbed into bed, she twisted her engagement ring subconsciously and stopped. Chase's image on bended knee as he proposed popped into her head, and she sucked in a sharp breath. She should sell the ring, and the extra money would come in handy until she found a job. And one less reminder would be an improvement.

She dreamed of Chase the way they were at the Menger when he walked in with a dinner tray. He spooned the rich stew into her mouth and buttered the biscuits for her to eat. His wicked knowing eyes smiled into hers as he waited on her. When butter dripped from the biscuit onto her hand, he bent forward and licked her fingers. Rose stiffened and tugged on her hand to remove it from his grasp, but he refused to let go.

"Let me help you, love," he whispered. His tongue dipped between her fingers, and her stomach tightened as his lean, sexy body slid onto the bed next to hers.

She shoved him away. "You shot me. Leave me alone."

Leaning toward her, his breath fanned across her cheeks as his hot lips closed over hers. His hands found the hem of her night rail, and he drew it from her body.

When she protested, his eyes darkened. "Let me see where I hurt you."

He held her still while his gaze dropped.

She shivered and grasped the blankets to draw them

over her naked chest.

But he stopped her. One long finger traced the wound on her shoulder. “I’m sorry, darlin’. I never meant to hurt you.” Tugging her into his arms as his mouth closed over hers, he kissed her the way he always did, his tongue mating with hers until she whimpered with desire.

Rose groaned.

Lifting his head, he kissed his way down her neck to her shoulder. Then his hot lips closed over the wound, creating the most sensual experience she had ever known. His lips and tongue were tender as they traced the scar.

“God, I’m sorry, love.” His hands molded her soft body into the hard planes of his. Her nipples turned to hard pebbles against his chest.

He caressed her aching breasts and lashed the tip of her nipple with his tongue. Her stomach tightened, and a rush of heat flooded over her. Her breath caught when he moved down to trail tender kisses over her flat quivering belly.

She gasped with pleasure.

“Let me love you, Rose.” One hand slid down to stroke her inner thigh while his mouth teased her lower abdomen.

Crying out, she arched into his embrace. “What about Grace?” She never did get an answer about the woman. Clamping her knees together to keep them from opening for him, she waited for his answer because her heart needed to know where she stood before she allowed him inside her again.

“You are the only woman I need or want. I love you, Rose.” His deep voice shivered through her blood and settled around her heart.

She leaned back and gazed into the heated depths of his eyes. “Do you promise?”

A wicked glint entered his eye as he moved lower. “Take them off for me, Rose.” His fingers tugged on the waistband of her pantalets. “I want to taste you, darlin’.”

She couldn’t breathe. This is what she had wanted for weeks now. With trembling hands, she tugged her pantalets from her body and dropped them on the floor.

She sucked in a breath as his fingers trailed up her thigh and stopped at the juncture of her legs, spreading them open.

He rubbed her aching core with featherlight touches until she thought she’d go crazy. And then he dropped his mouth.

At the first touch of his lips and tongue, she came off the bed. “Chase.” Her head thrashed side to side. She arched into him, wanting more.

Somehow his jeans disappeared, and his lean naked body lay next to hers while he pleasured her with his mouth.

Her climax came in an explosion of fiery, frenzied pleasure sending spasms of exquisite delight through her entire being. She couldn’t breathe and thought she would faint with ecstasy.

His hot, hard body came down on hers, and she uncurled her fingers and toes. “Chase, please. Love me.”

“I am, and I do.” His knees nudged her legs apart, and then his swollen member prodded the opening of her core. His mouth came down on hers, and he kissed with such passion he took her breath away.

He entered her with a sharp thrust of his hips and rocked into her hard and fast.

Rose groaned and shifted against him. "I missed you so much, Chase."

He trembled in her arms, groaning with pleasure while he plundered her willing body.

"Oh God, Chase." Molten lava pumped through her blood. Her head thrashed back and forth as he pulled out and plunged into her again and again. She grabbed his buttocks to urge him in deeper as she arched her back and drew her legs up to his waist.

He grabbed her hands and held them high above her head as he slowed the rhythm. "I've been waiting for this too."

She came the second time when he did and thought she'd died. She panted as ripple after ripple of delight washed over her.

Lying in the warm aftermath of their loving, she smiled until Chase rolled away from her and rose to his feet. His face darkened as he withdrew a pistol from behind him and shot her in the shoulder. He fell to her feet a second later with his chest covered in blood.

She jerked awake with a cry and sat up in confusion. Alone in the narrow bed in the hotel with her hair plastered to her head and her night rail on the floor beside her pantalets, she frowned. Her body hummed with sexual tension, and her core burned with desire. She gaped at the empty room. "Chase?"

No sound came from any direction but the hum of locusts outside in the trees. Rose shivered as the air of the empty room cooled her heated flesh. Staring at her discarded clothing on the floor, she shook her head. Chase Calhan had a grip on her heart and mind which scared her to death. He got her out of her clothes by appearing in her dreams. She shook her head over her sorry state. Trembling, she rose from the bed and tugged on her night rail.

Her hands shook as she sat on the edge of the cot. She wasn't over him. Her dream proved the point. All her crying the past couple of weeks had only kept the edge off her misery.

Padding over to the basin, she splashed cold water on her face and neck and sighed with frustration. Her body knew what she wanted, and he wasn't here. Biting her lip, Rose returned to the bed and sat. If she had dreams like this when she fell asleep thinking of Chase, she must get as far away from his family and anything familiar as she possibly could. Her chance of recovery required the sacrifice.

Tomorrow she would send Shanna a telegram and discuss her options. Wherever she ended up, she would pretend to be widowed to keep unwanted attention away. Rose sighed. Her plan would work fine if she could get her heart to quit breaking.

Chapter Twenty

Shanna met Rose in Omaha and got a room for them at an elegant hotel with their own security team on site. Reese insisted his men accompany her, and they spent their time in an adjacent room for protection.

When she stepped from the train, Shanna met her on the platform.

They didn't need to say a word. The two met in the middle for a long-overdue hug.

Rose had no idea how long they stood there while she wept into her best friend's silk jacket. She couldn't speak, and Shanna understood.

"It's all right. I'm here. Let's go back to the hotel where you can freshen up. We will have some dinner and take a walk in the gardens. We can take as much time as you like, but I want to hear everything." The soothing tone in Shanna's voice stemmed her flow of tears, and Rose agreed.

Together they strolled out to the waiting carriage while Reese's men followed two paces behind.

Two hours, two hot baths, and a wonderful dinner later, they walked arm and arm through the winding flower gardens of their hotel. Her friend verified the second telegram Chase sent when he knew he would miss the wedding. "Chief Tafford forwarded it when he discovered one of his men tampering with the telegrams. I couldn't tell you because you were gone by then."

Ranger Kaplan. Her gut twisted. She knew the culprit without being told. So, Chase didn't leave her at the altar like she supposed. If the telegram got through, they would have postponed the wedding and avoided the whole situation. Rose remained quiet. So many things wouldn't have happened either, and she would never regret the nights she spent in Chase's arms.

Over the next three days, she told Shanna everything. Her dearest friend made all the appropriate responses as she knew she would. But then came the part she hadn't told a soul. Two and a half weeks since the night her clothes fell off in her dream, and she knew for certain. She carried Chase's child.

"I don't know what to do, Shanna. For the first time in my life, I don't have a plan. I am unwed, pregnant, and don't want to live with any of the people I love. I cannot live in Chicago with you. Seeing Reese, Maggie, and Madelaine on a regular basis will crucify me with *what ifs* and *if onlys*. I cannot do it."

Silence filled the space between them as Rose stared out the hotel window at the gardens below.

Shanna sat in a satin armchair near the marble hearth with a thoughtful expression. "Where do you want to go?"

She shrugged. "To a place without Calhans."

"I don't like to think of you so far away, especially with a baby on the way, but would you consider San Francisco?" Her friend's hesitant question caught her attention.

Rose turned and walked toward the other woman. "Yes. Why?" She took a seat in the other armchair while the idea settled over her.

"Since I inherited, I receive on average two requests

a week for me to invest in some venture or other. Mr. Roger King approached me a week ago asking for me to invest in his hotels. He operates one in San Francisco and one in Tucson. He wishes to sell so he is free to travel to England and visit his family. He agreed to stay on long enough to train a general manager. I didn't consider the offer until this minute. Is this something you would consider?"

General manager. Hotel. San Francisco. An idea took root. "Does he have other positions available?" For the first time since she stepped foot across the border, she had hope.

"I'm sure he does. Tell me what you're thinking, and I will have my lawyers draw up a proposal." Shanna's smile touched all the right places in her barren world.

Rose explained about the auction in Mexico and her vow to rescue the girls. Some of them could return to their previous lives, others couldn't, depending on what the men who bought them required of them. "What if I take over as general manager in San Francisco as a recent widow? No one can prove otherwise, and I can hold my head up in society. I will have a job, security, and a place to live. My baby and I will make a new life together. I will contact Consuela, and together, we will search for these girls and offer them a job. They will have a safe place to stay and food to eat until they find other positions."

Shanna nodded. "You also have a purpose. I see the light in your eyes, and I think this is the answer to your dilemma. I won't pretend I don't wish you would come and live with me, but I understand the reason why you don't. If something happened to Reese, I couldn't bear to see his brothers every day either."

Rose dropped her head. “Have you any word from Reese?” Not sure she wanted to hear the answer, she held her breath.

Shanna’s husband went to Mexico two weeks ago to search for Chase and a possible body. Whichever he discovered.

“No. No one knows a thing, and there’s no trail. He’s as angry as you are. He hired a group of men to dig up ground in the ruins where you were both shot, but they found nothing. So, if Chase is buried somewhere, it’s not there.”

Rose let out a long slow breath. “So, there might be hope?” She didn’t mean to sound breathless, and Shanna squeezed her fingers. “With Calhans, there’s always hope. You feel however you want. If it’s easier to believe he’s alive. Do it.”

“I honestly don’t know how I feel. So much happened in the last month and a half I cannot reconcile my feelings in either direction. We spent so much time loving each other, I never expected him to shoot me. Nor did I expect him to die.” Rose met her friend’s steady gaze with one of her own. “Why would he try to kill me if he wanted to spend the rest of his life with me?”

“It doesn’t sound like something Chase would do.” Shanna sighed. “Reese believes he shot you to save you.”

Him, too. Reese and Consuela had a lot to talk about.

Silence filled the room for a few minutes until Shanna continued. “I am inclined to believe him. I may not understand the whole situation, but the one thing I *do* know is Chase loved you.”

Rose’s chin came up, and she talked fast to hide her pain. “I can think of a better way to show affection that doesn’t involve endangering someone’s life. Chocolate, for example, or any type of candy, is less lethal but an acceptable token of love and affection. Walks along the lake or in the moonlight are considered romantic and much more enjoyable than a blade in one's flesh as it fishes for a bullet. Sleigh rides or carriage rides exhilarate the soul and can be quite intimate occasions and preferable to spending time on the doctor's couch while he stitches your flesh back together." Rose took a deep breath. "Roses, daffodils, lilacs, and hyacinths, when presented to a loved one, convey the message of tenderness quite clearly with the added benefit of a delightful aroma. They smell so much better than the acrid scent of God-awful gunpowder or the herbal salves used to stave off infection from knife and bullet wounds."

Shanna smiled. "I agree, and I hope he is alive for you to tell him so. A few pointers from you, and he'll be the perfect man."

****

Two weeks later, Rose stepped from the train and sucked in the beautiful, hope-filled air of San Francisco. She imagined specs of gold floating into her body with every breath she drew, and the opportunities were endless. She gazed around with wonder. Bigger than she imagined and filled with people, she smiled as they jostled past her outside the train depot, where she stood staring at all the buildings.

"Can I help you, Miss?"

She turned. A good-looking man with dark hair and green eyes stood beside her, wearing a wide smile.

Déjà vu hit her in the stomach like a closed fist. "Not on your life or your mother's. I can find my own way." Stepping from the platform, she whistled at the line of hackney drivers picking up passengers. She glanced back at the frowning man. "Be grateful I lost my pistol, or I'd shoot you where you stand and save the world a lot of misery. Wherever you have your girls stashed, believe me, it isn't worth it. If my Texas Ranger were here, I'd have him arrest you."

The man took a step back. "My apologies, ma'am. I'm here to pick a lady up. I thought you might be her. Forgive me for bothering you."

She stopped and turned toward him. "Wait. Who are you looking for?" Shanna may have arranged for a carriage to meet her.

He pointed behind them. "Miss Rose Tanner. My carriage is there. I like to park away from the other hackneys so I don't get blocked in."

Rose refused to be embarrassed. She had experience with strange men who met her at the station and justified her reaction in her mind. She lifted her chin. "I am she."

Shuffling his cap in his hands, he glanced around them warily. "Is your Texas Ranger around? I don't want to get shot or arrested."

"No." She studied him, taking in his worn-out jeans and the patches on the elbows of his jacket. His shoes were sturdy and well-worn, and he didn't dress like Mr. Matthews at all.

A gentleman approached from the waiting carriage. "Miss Rose? My name is Roger King, and this is my carriage and driver." In his late thirties, he had wavy brown hair and hazel eyes. The man stood three inches taller than Rose with a normal businessman physique. "Welcome to San Francisco."

She glanced at him, and two words came to mind. Dull and normal.

Their ride took less than fifteen minutes.

Staring out the little windows filled with carriages and people, she acknowledged the change in her behavior. Her experience in Texas haunted her every night and a lot of the day. She lost her trust in people as well as her innocence and her heart. But her loss of Chase was the most tragic of all.

They drove for several minutes and turned down Montgomery Street. Rose sighed and clutched her small case in her lap as the salty smell of the ocean, fish, and coal smoke drifted on the breeze. Stopping in front of a large four-story building, the driver opened her door.

"This is King Hotel, miss. You won't find a better place to stay." With a slight smile, he held his hand out to help her alight.

Rose stared up at the massive stone building. "Thank you."

Mr. King stepped out beside her.

Taking a deep breath, she stepped onto the walkway and strolled inside. Tall, impressive columns and sumptuous décor took her breath away. Elegant, comfortable, and rich in detail, with breakfast rooms, supper rooms, drawing rooms, and lounges; she sighed with wonder as she walked forward on the plush, vibrant carpet. Even the air smelled delightful. Closing her eyes for a brief second, she detected the clean, crisp scent of lemon mingled with the heavy perfume of fresh-cut flowers.

This hotel, San Francisco, and freedom were the perfect remedy for her broken heart.

She thought her room well situated and delightful. Soft and airy, the bed stood against the wall to her right, where a door led her to a bath with hot and cold running water. She hadn't enjoyed such luxury since she left Chicago and her fairytale life. Rose set her case on the bed and washed the long train ride from her face and hands. Drying her face with the thick towel folded beside the sink, she stared at her reflection in the glass. Sad brown eyes gazed back at her, filled with yearning and pain.

She jumped when someone knocked on the door. "Who is it?"

Peeking through the tiny hole in the door, she spotted a hotel waiter with a basket of flowers. Frowning, she opened the door. "I think you have the wrong room. I didn't order flowers or know anyone who did."

The waiter smiled. "King Hotel would like to thank you for staying with us. Please accept the complimentary flowers and fruit tray." He indicated the table in her room. "All the guests get them. Mr. King thought you might like them, as well. Mind if I set them over there?"

Rose blushed and stepped out of the waiter's path. "Thank you." The flowers weren't from Chase. She put a hand to her heart as the thought raced across her mind. For several heart-pounding seconds, she thought he had until reality slapped her in the face. Her once lover would never buy her flowers again, kiss her lips, or hold her close—

"You're welcome." The waiter touched his cap and disappeared down the hall.

Staring back at the empty room, she closed the door. The waiter must think her crazy. Gazing into space, she wiped tears from her eyes, shaking her head at her sorry state. After all she'd been through, one waiter with complimentary flowers and fruit from the hotel made her weep. Locking the door, she walked over to inspect the fruit with a grateful heart. At least she wouldn't need to leave her room in search of dinner tonight.

The next morning, Rose ventured down the stairs to order breakfast and begin her new job.

Coming here had been one of her better ideas. Ordering coffee with her eggs, she settled back to enjoy her freedom.

Until her morning sickness took over.

Quiet, calm, and easygoing, Mr. King made the perfect boss and took her under his wing to teach her the hotel business. He never minded her frequent sudden departures for the ladies' room and on her return, continued with his advice as if she'd never left.

Though she missed Shanna and her parents more than she could say, Rose kept busy and found her new direction in life satisfying.

Letters passed between Mexico and San Francisco via stagecoaches and Consuela's numerous cousins. She married Mario a week after Rose returned to the states, and the two spent their time tracking down the women she helped funnel through El Diablo's nefarious contacts. Grateful for a chance to help the victims, she kept Rose updated on their findings.

The new manager in Tucson came from Laredo and had experience with abused women. Together with Shanna's help, they managed to rescue and relocate fifteen women within the first month. Encouraged with her success, Rose stepped into Mr. King's office to give him the good news.

He offered to take her to lunch in celebration, and she accepted.

Over the next four weeks, they rescued and

relocated fifteen more women. And with each new success story, Roger King invited Rose out to dinner, bought her flowers, or both. His emotional support and willingness to listen made her pause one day when he gifted her with a dozen red roses. Dull and normal. But kind and steady.

No news came from Mexico, and Reese eventually returned, disheartened and angry.

Shanna telegrammed Rose with the news. No one knew about the baby but Shanna until she asked permission to tell Reese and Maggie.

Afraid Chase's mother might comment on her condition with no wedding ring on her finger, she needn't have worried. Maggie took the news in stride and offered valuable advice as Rose's pregnancy progressed. Telegrams flew between the women as the days passed by.

Rose wore aprons and loose-fitting gowns to hide her swelling belly. She thought she hid her secret quite well until Mr. King invited her to a special dinner.

Dressing with care, she thought of Shanna's recent telegram expressing her surprise with Mr. King's continued presence. One of the conditions in the contract specified his desire to return to England, and her friend wondered why he delayed his departure.

Rose thought on the subject as she slipped on low-heeled slippers for her evening out. Mr. King made no secret of his interest in her. Even her impromptu excuses to avoid close encounters didn't deter his advances. He had not kissed her or touched her in an inappropriate way at all. But he did offer his arm when they walked together. Sometimes she allowed the brief contact. Other times, she did not.

Interest gleamed in his hazel eyes as he bent his head to kiss her hand. "You are beautiful, Miss Rose." His gaze swept over her pale pink high-waisted gown and rose to hers. "I shall be the envy of every man there."

She doubted it but said nothing and allowed him to escort her to a waiting carriage.

Halfway through dinner, he set his napkin beside his dinner plate. "There is a matter of some urgency I wish to discuss with you."

Rose swallowed and placed her trembling hands on her lap.

Leaning forward, he spoke in a low voice for her ears alone. "Dearest Rose, I know we have not known each other for long, and I am aware of the circumstances prompting your sudden disappearances and wardrobe choices." His gaze dropped to her rounded belly and back to hers.

She gripped her hands together and ignored her pounding heart. "How so?"

He smiled. "Your telegrams often cross my desk. So I know about the child and your unwed state. Though I would have guessed by the sadness in your eyes and the way you avoid personal discussions. I thought your decision to present as a widow clever, but truths have a way of becoming known."

When she grimaced with dismay, he rushed into speech. "I am not here to judge but to offer a solution. Your heart belongs to another. Of this, I am aware. A man who is no longer here to offer you his protection and good name. Through no fault of yours or his, you are left alone to raise his child. Though I do not suppose you are healed from the grief of his loss, I ask you to look upon my court with consideration." Taking a jewelry box from his jacket pocket, he dropped to his knee before her and presented her with a diamond engagement ring. "I care for you deeply and can offer my honor and protection. We get on well with one another, and I believe we can make a good life together. Perhaps not the life you envisioned with the father of your child, but a rewarding one with me by your side. I will give you and your child my name, my home, my life, and my wealth in exchange for the privilege to call you wife. A fair exchange in an unfair world. There is security and safety within the bonds of wedlock, which I offer to you now. I hope you will look upon me with favor and honor me with an answer. Will you marry me, Miss Rose?" Sincere hazel eyes gazed up into hers, and she swallowed the lump in her throat.

Not dangerous, not wickedly handsome, not flirtatious, not a prince. Safety and security. Normal boring life. Rose closed her eyes and asked for strength. How did she move forward with her life if she didn't know if Chase lived?

"I know you do not love me, Rose. But I am willing to offer everything I have for the sake of you and the child. Every baby needs a father and a mother. I will shield you from the cruelty of society. Will you allow me to be that for you?"

No fairytale wedding, no white charger, just a man offering to give her child a name. "Before I answer, I have a question." God, how could she be intimate with another man with Chase's baby inside her?

Kind hazel eyes smiled into hers. "It's all right, my dear. Think of this as a business arrangement until or unless you would like to make our arrangement more intimate. I shall not insist upon my marital rights until you ask me to do so. I understand being with another man might not be ideal while you are carrying a child. I will never force anything on you. You have my word."

She bit her lip with worry. Another month and everyone would know of her condition. If the truth were known, her child would be branded a bastard and be subjected to the world's harsh judgment. Mr. King offered a solution. The urge to protect the innocent life inside her surged through her veins. The practical side of her said if Chase were alive, he would have contacted Reese and Shanna. "Then, I accept." And God help her, she prayed she did the right thing.

Magical weddings, princes, and castles far away made wonderful stories for children, not for a grown woman with a baby to think of.

Mr. King slid the cool gold band on her finger with a kiss. "Thank you, my dear. You have made me very happy."

God, she hoped somebody was.

She tossed and turned for a week before sending a telegram to Shanna with the news.

Her friend accepted with surprising encouragement. "I am so happy to hear this, Rose. I did not want to urge you forward if your heart is broken, but I think this arrangement is for the best. He's not Chase, but his name will make you acceptable to society. You have the child to think about. I want you to know I will always love you no matter what man you marry."

The weight of relief Rose experienced when she opened the telegram put the spring back in her step. Everything would work out fine. Mediocrity possessed some attraction for her, after all. If for no other reason than to give her sweet baby a name.

They planned the wedding for the middle of October, and as the day drew near, Rose grew anxious. Unsure if she experienced post-wedding trauma from the last time or nerves because she didn't plan this part of her life at all, she paced at night. Dread of making a mistake filled her with unease as the day approached.

Three weeks before her wedding, Rose slipped a gown over her head and went out to the gardens to talk to the moon and stars about Chase. This marked the third time she spoke to the moon about him since she left El Diablo's compound.

Midnight darkened the hotel garden with mystery while silver moonlight created a magical, ethereal peace around her.

She poured out her heart and soul to the heavens confessing her love for Chase, her grief at his loss, and her dream to lie in his arms again. She spoke of Mr. King and his kind offer to protect and cherish her and her child. Tears spilled over and ran down her face as she unburdened her heart. She no longer believed in fairy stories and magic, but she did believe in love.

"If he is alive and out there somewhere, will you bring him to me in time?" Her soft question hung on the air and shimmered in the quiet of the garden with only the flowers as a witness. "I do not want to make a mistake. I love him and always will. If you know where he is, tell him so."

A blaze of light flashed across the midnight sky, and Rose sucked in a breath. Falling stars were a sign of promise, good luck, and good fortune. Teetering on the edge of disbelief versus fairytale and superstition, she swallowed the lump in her throat.

Last time she believed in magic, she got shot. By

Chase. Hope flared in her breast, and she placed a hand over her belly. "If he's alive. He'll come."

Hurrying into the hotel, she went to her room and undressed with shaking fingers. What if he were alive? She hadn't allowed the thought to enter her mind since she agreed to marry Mr. King.

On impulse, she knocked on his office door the next day and asked for a private word.

"What is wrong, my dear?" his brow wrinkled with concern as he took a seat beside her. "Are you having second thoughts? A lot of brides do, I am told."

"Not exactly. I wanted to ask you a question. You are wealthy, attractive, and kind. Why haven't you married before this? Any woman would be happy to have you." And she meant every word. If one didn't compare him to Chase, Mr. King was quite a catch.

He gave her a sad smile. "I have loved and lost, as well. Two years ago, on the morning of my wedding to Miss Evangeline Fairchild, I discovered she had left the country to escape becoming my wife. I have not considered the merits of marriage again until I met you."

Rose digested the information for a moment or two. So much made sense. "She is the reason you left England and the reason you planned to return. Do you still love her?"

A deep sigh escaped him. "I am afraid I do. Although I have given up on such a dream."

She understood too well, sagging with relief over his confession. She resisted the urge to laugh aloud. "We make a fine pair, don't we?"

An answering smile touched his lips. "We do. Is there anything else?"

"Just this." Leaning forward, she brushed her lips

against his. "Thank you for your kindness and understanding to me. I've grown quite fond of you in the last few weeks. I will leave you now to run some errands."

His startled expression made her pause. "You gave me a kiss. By accident or on purpose?"

"On gratitude. Nothing more. Do not worry. I shall not insist upon my marital rights." She grinned as she rose to her feet.

His chuckle remained in her thoughts for the rest of the day.

Shanna arrived a week before the blessed day to help with the arrangements.

Rose offered her the grandest suite in the hotel and ate dinner with her in the hotel restaurant following a tour of the property.

Her friend flitted around offering advice and smiling so much Rose began to worry.

"Why are you so happy?"

Shanna frowned. "Weddings are happy occasions. Shouldn't I be over the moon when my best friend gets married?"

"Most people cry." Her parents had a room down the hall, and her mother never stopped sniffing. She couldn't get over the surprise of finding out she would be a grandmother and hinted around about who the father might be.

"The baby is Chase's." Rose's chin lifted as she made the announcement, waiting for her mother's condemnation.

"And mine." Roger walked in at the same time and took her hand in his. Smiling at her parents, he asked if they were comfortable in their room.

"Of course. Thank you." Her mother nodded and said nothing more.

"Thank you," she whispered as she followed him into the corridor.

"Of course. What are friends for if not to have each other's backs?" His kindness and understanding proved there could be contentment in dull and normal. One didn't have to be a prince to be gallant.

The dressmaker delivered her gown the night before the ceremony. As Rose shook the white silk gown from paper, she sighed, remembering her excitement the last time she wed. Or tried to.

One would not believe her to be the same bride. Last time, she paced with nervous energy anticipating her wedding night with her handsome new husband. This time she sat in quiet repose, enjoying her solitude, knowing there wouldn't be a wedding night.

"You don't look nervous. Are you? Last time I thought you would wear the carpet out with your pacing. You don't even stutter around Mr. King. If you're having second thoughts, it's not too late to call the wedding off." Shanna sat in her armchair, sipping a glass of wine while she made her observations. "I want you to be happy. Not just married."

Rose turned from the window, where she stared out into the darkness. "They are no longer the same thing. I shall be married, and my baby will have a proper place in life. Nothing else matters."

"I cannot say I agree, but I approve. I would do the same in your place." Shanna's words played in her mind through the long sleepless night.

Her wedding day arrived with a glorious sunrise and a crisp ocean breeze. Shanna and her mother came to her suite two hours before the ceremony to help her prepare. The high-waisted silk gown hid her blossoming stomach beneath folds of fabric. They piled her brown hair high on her head and added a string of diamonds. White satin slippers and a pinch on her pale cheeks completed her preparations.

And then the carriage arrived to take her to the chapel. All along the way, memories of her previous wedding filled her thoughts. Her lace wedding gown, her magnolia bouquet, the canopy, the guests, the grandfather clock, and the rain. But most of all, the pain of uncertainty and doubt.

None of those things were present today, and she discovered none of them mattered. She would rather have the man than the magical wedding. But he would never stand beside her again.

She shoved the thought aside as her father took her hand. The first strains of the wedding march filled the early morning air of the chapel. The seam of her sleeve rasped the scar on her shoulder where Chase shot her.

Rose frowned. She hadn't noticed the rough edges during any of her numerous fittings and shifted her shoulder as they walked down the aisle. Her heart sped up, and her stomach twisted. *You're making the biggest mistake of your life.* The heavy feeling grew in the pit of her stomach as she took each slow step.

Mr. King gazed down at her from his position in front of the priest, and the panic in his gaze made her pause. Did *he* have second thoughts, too?

Then she stood beside him, and he took her hand in his. "Dearest Rose—" His face paled as he gazed into her eyes.

"Dearly beloved, we are gathered here today…" The

priest's voice droned on in the background, and panic filled her chest with each word.

Mr. King's face turned ashen gray when the preacher asked if anyone had just cause why they shouldn't be joined in holy matrimony.

She meant to ask the priest to stop when the doors to the cathedral flung open.

Chapter Twenty-One

He came to on a piece of hide stretched across two poles hitched to a horse. Every jolt of sagebrush, clump of dirt, and hard-as-hell rock jostled his wounds and made him swear. God, he hurt. Prying open his other eye, he glanced down at his blood-soaked clothes. He thought he died and remembered Rose crying over his body. Turning his head took every ounce of strength he possessed. "Rose."

His throat burned too badly to get the word out.

The horse stopped, and a brown face appeared above his with a skin of water. "Drink."

He tasted manna from heaven in the sweet cool liquid sliding down his parched throat and poured more into his mouth.

The man took the skin, and he protested. "More."

"No. Later. Go home." The face disappeared along with the water skin, and Chase cursed.

When he woke again, he lay on a small cot before a fire. His hands and ankles were tied to the bed with strips of rawhide while the man with the water skin probed his wounds and grunted.

"What the…hell? Where am I? Let…me go." He didn't have the strength to cuss like he wanted to and groaned instead. God, he hurt worse than a pig in a bear fight. "Rose…needs…me."

"You lucky. Almost die." The man slid a knife into

the fire and mixed herbs in a dish. "One more bullet next to heart. This time maybe die."

Chase moaned. "Not die. Live for Rose." He meant every word and lost consciousness a moment later.

Blurry images of a naked, chanting man fanning smoke across his face filled his dreams.

He glimpsed Rose in some sort of wooden hut, crying, and he ached to go to her. "Don't cry, darlin'. I'm here." Hovering above her head, he struggled to find a way to her. She cried over him. He knew it in his gut.

Someone held God-awful tea to his mouth and commanded him to drink. In Apache. Must be the old man, or he found a demon friend to help him with his torture.

Chase turned his head to see his tormentor and couldn't open his eyes. The weight of the world kept them closed, and he didn't have the energy to fight.

"Rose."

This time she cried from a hotel in Omaha, and partial relief calmed him. She would go to Shanna and Reese. His brother would keep her safe until he could get back to Chicago. The pain caught him unaware, and he cursed when a hot knife cut into his flesh.

"I thought you said one more bullet. What happened?" He focused on opening his eyes and met the interested stare of the medicine man. "You died. So, I didn't fix you. Now you alive, I'll fix."

Chase frowned; his Apache could be a little rusty. "Did you say I died?" He didn't have time to pay the Great Spirit a visit. He had to get to Rose.

"Yes, but the Great Spirit sent you back. Again. Be still." Leaning forward, he lifted a red-hot knife in the air and speared Chase in the heart.

He dreamed the same naked chanting medicine man leaned over him with glittering black eyes and laughed. "You are still alive. The Great Spirit doesn't want you."

Chase didn't give a damn whether he did or not. He wanted Rose.

He spent more time in the darkness than he did awake and dreamed he floated over a flower garden in the dark of night to Rose. She stood in the garden with her head thrown back gazing at the moon and stars.

"If he is alive and out there somewhere, will you bring him to me in time?" His beautiful Rose's soft question hung on the air and shimmered in the quiet of the garden with only the flowers as a witness.

"I'm coming, darlin'. Don't you give up on me." Turning, he witnessed a falling star and nodded with satisfaction. He'd be there as soon as he opened his eyes again, and nothing would stop him from going to her.

Ages of darkness, pain, and the musky, earthy scent of herbs passed before he woke again. When he did, he discovered he lay on the same small cot staring up at rough wooden boards. This time he wasn't tied. The room smelled of smoke, beans, and…bread?

Rolling to his side, he repented of moving the second he started because pain shot up his arm and tightened his chest. Wincing, he flexed and gazed down. His arms were sore as hell. His ribs were the same, and some God-awful aroma wafted up from his chest. The fight. Rose, and El Diablo. The medicine man. Memories flooded his mind in an avalanche. Chase squinted as he surveyed his ribs and arms. He'd been here for a while for the wounds to be healed. He gazed around. Nothing looked familiar, and he wondered who patched him up with something smelling like pig manure.

"*Senor*, you are awake."

Turning his head toward the female voice, he discovered where the smoke originated. An elderly woman with white hair and a big nose sat beside a fire tossing tortillas on a stone next to the blaze.

Not bread, tortillas.

She wore a coarse brown dress with a brightly colored apron tied around her ample waist. Beans bubbled in a pot suspended from a metal hook above the blaze.

Chase gazed around. A small wooden table stood in the center of the room with four wooden chairs. Bright yellow curtains hung over a tiny window on the opposite wall beside a row of rough boards loaded with tins and dishes. The door to the hut stood ajar to allow the smoke of the fire to escape.

Frowning, he glanced at the woman. "Where am I?"

Turning, she smiled and then glanced at the door as a hunched old man walked into the room.

The Apache medicine man, if he had to guess.

Glancing at Chase, the old man spoke to the woman in rapid Spanish.

"Kuruk wants to know where you come from and where you go." The old woman translated as she continued flipping tortillas on the stone and stirring the beans every so often.

Frowning, he asked his question again. This time in Apache.

"Neuvo Laredo."

She handed the old man a hot tortilla and a bowl of beans.

"Kuruk found you in the field and carted you home. You were wounded." The old woman flipped another tortilla.

"How long have I been here?" Anxiety twisted his insides as he waited for the answer. Rose needed medical attention and a whole lot of explaining. Memories of her tears ate at his insides.

"Long time. You were almost dead when Kuruk found you." Gesturing at his middle, she shook her head. "For some time, we not sure you live."

So he'd been told.

The old man approached and touched his forehead. He spoke in Apache. "Three times you die. Three times the Great Spirit send you back."

And three times he saw Rose. "I remember you saying something about it before you cut into me with your knife. How long have I been asleep?" Anxiety twisted his gut. He had to find out if the love of his life got medical help and made it back to Chicago like in his dreams.

Kuruk stared at him. "You remember me cutting you?"

"Yes. You told me you didn't finish taking out the bullet by my heart because you thought I died. But since I lived, you planned to help me. I need an answer. How long have I been here? I must find Rose."

The old woman made the sign of the cross. "You have not spoken a word since Kurak brought you home. You slept the sleep of the dead, and I begged him to bury you."

"Did you see any more? Talk with anyone besides me?" The medicine man ignored his question and focused on their conversation.

Chase sighed. "I saw Rose. The last time she stood in some garden talking to the moon. Thank you for taking the bullets out and helping me heal. But I must go and need to know how long I've been asleep. I must find Rose."

Kuruk nodded. "You are a dream walker. She is the reason you live. There is much explaining to do."

Dream walker? Chase leaned back and closed his eyes. Weak as a newborn kitten, he couldn't go to her until he got his strength back. Rose could be anywhere by now. "I have answered your question. Will you answer mine? Have I been here two days? Three?"

"Eight weeks." The old man held out a cup of tea. "Drink this."

Chase drank. "*Eight weeks*?" Frowning, he remembered Consuela carrying a rifle and leading her away. He knew his shot went through her shoulder because he aimed high on purpose. Untreated, the wound could be a serious threat, something he never intended. He hoped Consuela offered help. "How the hell could I be asleep for so long?" He gazed from one to the other and dropped to the empty cup in his hand. "You gave me herbs to make me sleep." The stone in his belly grew heavier. "You cannot do this to me. I *must* go!"

"Yes, I keep you asleep. The urgency of your spirit told me you would leave before you healed. You cannot rescue your flower if you are dead." Kuruk took a seat before the fire and lit a pipe.

Anxiety twisted his insides. "Then why give me more? I am well enough to go!" Throwing back the covers, he couldn't get his legs to move. Dizziness tilted the room, and he dropped back to the cot with a groan. He must ask all his questions before the herbs finished their job. "A beautiful woman with dark brown hair and soft brown eyes left the area where I received my wounds. She is Rose. Have you seen her? Or do you know where she went?" The edges of the room darkened and shifted as Chase fought to remain alert.

The old woman turned to gaze at him. "*Senor*, you just described most of the women in Mexico."

He sighed. "This one is as tall as you with a heart of gold. She had a bullet wound in the shoulder and would require a doctor. Another older woman accompanied her." Forcing his eyes to stay open, he speared the old woman with a glance. "Have you seen her?"

Smiling, she turned back to her fire. "I know nothing of a girl. Only you."

Dropping his chin to his chest, he fought for control. "She will be in danger without me to protect her."

"You must get well, *Senor*, before you can rescue anyone."

Struggling to speak, he shook his head. "She called to me, and I promised to come."

He must have passed out, for the next thing he knew, the morning sun shone through the window. He lay on his side beneath the blankets of the cot inside an empty hut. Gingerly, he sat up and waited. His head swam a little, but he could think past it. Tossing the blanket back, he discovered he wore nothing but skin. A pile of clean clothing lay on a chair next to the cot, left there by the old woman, he surmised. The shirt they found him in had been sliced into strips to tie up the wounds made by El Diablo's men. Delgato hadn't done him a whole hell of a lot of good, either.

Dressing as quickly as his addled head would allow, he tugged the jeans on and smiled. They were his and freshly laundered. A loose cotton shirt lay folded under the jeans. Slipping his arms into the sleeves with care, he buttoned it up. When he rose to his feet, the room spun around for a few minutes. Snapping up his jeans, he waited until the room quit spinning before making his way toward the door.

Flat and barren, dotted with nothing but cactus and scrub brush for miles, the countryside stretched before him. Walking around behind the house, he spotted a small stable. When he opened the door, Aries gave a whinny of recognition. His saddle and bridle were clean and close at hand. Chase saddled his horse and checked his saddle bags. Everything remained the way he left them, and he nodded with satisfaction. Pausing before he mounted his horse, he considered the people who owned the place. The old woman took good care of him, and the old man found and cared for Aries. Taking some coins from the pouch inside his saddlebag, he retraced his steps to the hut. Dropping Arie's reins, he stepped inside and stacked the coins on the table in plain sight.

Traveling northeast, with no idea where Rose might be, he figured Shanna would. When he crossed the border into the United States, he rode to the nearest telegraph office and wired her. He got an immediate response.

Happy you are alive-stop

Come to Chicago-stop

Chase stared at the paper. A stone dropped in his stomach. Something must have happened to Rose, or Shanna would give more information. He didn't like the situation at all and the ominous tones of the telegram even less. Tucking the message into his shirt pocket, he paid the operator.

As he left the little office, he glanced across the street toward a small hotel and a tavern. He needed a drink while he thought about Rose and where she'd go.

Tying Aries out front, he stepped into the dimly lit tavern. Ordering a whiskey, he took a chair at the table in the corner and put his back to the wall. Taking a sip of the watered-down drink, he frowned. He needed Rose like he needed air, and God knew she needed him. The girl possessed the biggest heart he'd ever met, trusting too much and giving too much. Without him to protect her, who knew what kind of trouble she could be in. Tossing the contents of his glass back, he swallowed the fiery golden liquid, enjoying the burn. The truth is, he needed her more. Her smile gave him a reason to breathe, her laughter gave him a reason to make her happy, and her love gave him everything else. He wouldn't breathe easy until he held her in his arms again and gazed into her soft chocolate-brown eyes.

The waitress stopped by to see if he wanted another drink, and his gaze caught on the sparkling ring on her third finger.

His gaze jumped to hers while his hand rose to the handle of his nearest knife. "Where the hell did you get the ring?" Fury roared to life in seconds and raced through his veins.

The woman froze. "He gave it to me." She pointed at the barkeeper.

He crossed the room and had the barkeeper by the throat before the man had time to grab the pistol he kept under the bar for emergencies.

"Where did you get the ring?" Chase wouldn't accept anything but the truth. Shaking the beefy barkeeper, he stared into his eyes.

The man must have read the violence of his thoughts, for he swallowed and begged for mercy.

"A man and a woman brought a girl in to eat a month or two ago. They paid for one night at the hotel for the girl and left. The next morning the girl came to the bar and offered to sell me the ring. So sad and desperate, she begged me to buy it, saying the man who gave her the ring shot her and died. I didn't have the heart to turn her away. I gave her a hundred dollars for the ring, and she left."

Chase's heart sank. If she sold his ring, she must believe he actually died, or worse. They picked it out together. Glaring at the man, he shook him again. "What else did she say? Did she mention where she planned to go?"

The frightened barkeeper shook his head. "No."

A sudden thought had him frowning. "Did she have someone with her?" If she had a new man, he'd kill them both. Rose couldn't do this to him. He waited centuries for her to come into his life, and now she did. He wouldn't give her up without a fight.

"No."

The man's reply provided a moment of relief before the urgency to find her took over again. Convinced the man knew nothing more, he strode from the bar and hurried out to Aries. Counting out a hundred and twenty dollars in coins, he strode back into the tavern.

Slamming the coins down on the bar, he stared at the man. "I bought the ring for Rose. It belongs to me, and I want it back." He scooted the coins closer to the trembling barkeeper. "There is more there than you paid. Give me my ring."

The barkeeper nodded to the waitress.

Chase left a minute later with Rose's engagement ring tucked safely in his vest pocket until he could replace it where it belonged.

Shaking his head with frustration and anger, he rode for Houston and the train depot. How could he know when he started out after El Diablo his life would come to this? He wouldn't accept anything less than her in his life. No matter what she thought or what she'd done since he shot her, she belonged with him.

Rose didn't know how much he needed her in his life or the depths of his love for her, but she would. As soon as he found her, he'd love her until she cried his name. He would love her in so many ways she would be unable to fathom a life without him. He would be the smile on her face, the lilt in her beautiful voice, and the reason her heart beat.

Encouraged, Chase nudged Aries to go faster.

Memories of their time together flashed through his mind as he rode. With El Diablo, Delgato, and Rozita dead, nothing could keep them apart.

A conversation they had one day as they walked around Delaney Estates after dark popped into his head. "Where would you go if you could go anywhere?" Her soft voice held a dreamy quality.

Staring into her soft brown eyes, he said the first thing he thought. "With you. It wouldn't matter if you were there with me."

Blushing, she squeezed his hand as they walked. "I would go to London, Paris, and San Francisco."

He'd chuckled. "Okay. Why there?" He liked listening to her logic because she had a unique way of looking at life. Her answer made him smile.

"Well, I would go to London to see the Queen, to Paris to get a new gown, and to San Francisco because I've always wanted to pan for gold. I've read all about

Sutter's Mill."

He didn't have the heart to tell her the mill was miles from San Francisco. "We could go there on our honeymoon, get a nice room to make love in, and then go dip our feet in the ocean." His offer filled her eyes with stars more dazzling than the ones in the heavens.

"Could we?" Throwing her arms around his neck, she kissed him soundly.

Chase relived the memory in detail and groaned. God, he missed her. A woman with her soft heart wouldn't understand why he fired at her. He had to find her and convince her he did so because he loved her and couldn't live without her. Judging from Shanna's lack of information, Rose made it to the States. He didn't want to think about the dangers of her traveling alone, nor the kind of male attention she would attract with her beautiful smile and gentle heart. She should be more cautious. Especially after her escapade in San Antonio with Mr. Matthews. What did she plan to do if she got into more trouble without him there to rescue her? Nudging Aries into a gallop, he leaned forward, anxious to find his girl and make things right. He had a serious need to hold her in his arms and love her senseless.

Chapter Twenty-Two

His meeting with Shanna didn't go as expected.

In fact, he didn't meet Shanna at all or Reese.

Giles answered the door and invited him into the sitting room. "I'm afraid Miss Shanna is not at home, and neither is Master Reese. If you catch a ride back to the station in the next ten minutes, you can catch the eleven o'clock train to San Francisco. By my estimation, you will arrive in time."

He rode too hard and too long to let a butler get in his way, even Giles. "I sent a telegram, and Shanna said to come here. Where are they? Why go to San Francisco? And in time to stop what?"

Giles's nose rose two inches. "Miss Shanna didn't reply to your telegram. I did. She is in San Francisco to attend Miss Rose's wedding. Master Reese is in New York helping Master Connor with a family problem, and I would imagine you are anxious to stop Miss Rose from making the biggest mistake of her life."

Chase damn near dropped to the ground. "She's *where*? Rose is *what*?" Nothing Giles said made any sense, and yet his gut said it was true. "How could she marry someone else when she loves *me*?"

Giles gave him a small smile. "You did leave her standing at the altar, sir. And if I may offer my advice, *hurry!*"

He did.

All the way to San Francisco, the clack of the train wheels echoed the searing words in his head. *She's marrying someone else! She's marrying someone else!*

Chase stepped from the train in San Francisco two weeks later, tired, sore, and anxious as hell. He relived every moment he had with Rose until he thought he'd go mad. How could she do this to him? He'd been on so many manhunts over the years as a ranger he lost count of how many times he boarded trains and packed his case. But catching Rose, stopping her wedding, and convincing her they belonged together would be the most important mission he'd undertaken to date. And he couldn't fail.

Stepping out onto the boardwalk in front of the depot a few minutes later, he assessed the line of hackney carriages and the milling crowd. Giles gave him one destination. King Hotel. Turning to gaze both ways up and down the street for an empty carriage, the sun hit the silver star on his vest and flashed in the morning light. Setting his case down, he put his fingers to his lips and whistled.

"Excuse me, sir?"

Chase turned his head to see a dark-haired hackney driver approaching from his left. "Yes?"

"Are you a Texas Ranger?" The man stopped beside him and pointed at his badge.

Studying the man, he responded. "I am."

"You look like the man Miss Rose described when she first came to San Francisco, but I thought she said you were dead."

She *did* believe he died. That took the edge off the pain he felt over her wedding so soon after Mexico. Chase narrowed his gaze. "You know, Miss Rose. Do you know what church they're at? Or how to get to King Hotel?" Grasping the handle of a knife in his bandolier, he waited.

The man took a step back, bringing both hands up in defense. "I work for Mr. King. I'll take you there." As they walked, the man cleared his throat. "Miss Rose is a nice person. She'll make Mr. King a good wife."

He grunted, not at all impressed.

"I recognized you from her description of your knives." The man held the door open and waved Chase inside.

He eyed the man. "Do you know where she is right now? When they plan to get married?"

The driver cleared his throat and avoided eye contact. "The ceremony began at eleven."

Chase glanced at the sky and didn't like the position of the sun. "Get me there, *now!*"

He doubted the driver ran through San Francisco so fast in his life and thanked the gods he found someone who knew which cathedral and how to get there. If he'd gone to the hotel first, he might be too late.

Tossing gold coins at the hackney driver, Chase didn't wait for the carriage to slow down and jumped to the curb, running for the door. He had to be in time. The Great Spirit couldn't send him back three times to have him arrive too late.

He threw open the door of the church and charged inside as the priest asked if anyone had just cause why the two people before him should not be joined in holy matrimony.

"I do. She loves me, and I love her. She agreed to be mine, and I've come to collect." His voice echoed in the silence as he stared at the back of his beloved, willing her to turn around.

The priest stopped talking and stared.

The entire congregation turned around in their seats to stare, but Chase didn't care. His gaze rested on the small woman in the white silk dress standing at the altar.

The man beside her turned and waited. Taking a kerchief from his pocket, he wiped his face and neck.

Chase frowned. Normal and nice. What the hell did she see in him?

He shifted his attention back to the love of his life. "Rose. I came as fast as I could. I know I have a lot of explaining to do, and I'm willing if you are. Please, darlin'. Come to me." Dropping to his knees, he placed both hands over his heart. "I swear before God and these witnesses I love you and cannot live without you. You are the other half of my heart, the other half of my soul, and I am lost without you. Your big heart lures me like the moonlight across the prairie, and the beauty of your smile guides me through the storm. Your love grounds my soul and brings me home to you. And you alone. No other woman will ever do. Only you. Please tell me I am not too late. Please tell me I didn't love in vain. I love you, darlin', more than my life."

His heartbeat was loud in his ears while he waited for her response.

When she turned, his gut twisted. Tears ran down her cheeks unheeded as she stared at him for long minutes. "You came. I thought you were dead." Her soft voice floated on the beams of sunlight through the ancient stained-glass windows.

"Yes. A quarter inch to the left and El Diablo would have succeeded. I'm sorry I didn't come for you sooner. I've been down for a bit healing." He must have said the wrong thing, for fire flashed in her beautiful eyes.

She moved with surprising speed and stopped a foot in front of him. She rubbed her left shoulder. "You shot me." Folding her arms over her chest, she glared. "Why?" Her foot tapped against the stone floor, and Chase had the feeling this question determined the outcome of his life.

"Because I love you. I always have, and I always will." He rose to his feet, so in awe of her beauty, he choked.

Rose snorted. "So, you shot me. What could be more romantic?" She held a hand toward the interested guests. "Does anyone have a gun? I'd like to return the favor."

The crowd twittered with mirth.

She didn't. A dangerous gleam flashed in her eyes. "I didn't think you knew how to shoot. What if you killed me?"

Chase shook his head, feeling a lot like he faced judgment day and his salvation hung in the balance. "I prefer to use knives, but I never said I didn't know how to shoot. Think about it, darlin'. With brothers like mine, do you think they would let me join the rangers and ride off alone unless I knew how to shoot, ride, and fight?"

Her shoulders relaxed as she stared at him. "But you shot at my heart." Her sad words squeezed his so hard he felt the pain all the way down to his boots.

"No. I shot at your shoulder to throw you off balance. I hit what I aim at. I would die if you did. That's the simple truth." Taking her cold, trembling fingers in his, he stared into her soul. "Please tell me it's not too late."

****

Rose couldn't believe her eyes and ears when he

appeared at the last minute. The moon and stars did their part and sent him to her in time. She wanted to throw her arms around his neck and kiss him senseless, but she required answers first.

The love and devotion shining from his wicked amber eyes hit her like the pony express. She stared at him, unable to believe he stood here with her after all this time.

Roger cleared his throat from the front of the cathedral. "If you will excuse us, ladies and gentlemen. It appears we have some sorting out to do. Thank you for coming. If you will all take your leave, we would appreciate some privacy while we work this, um, situation out."

Shanna reached her first. She gave Rose a kiss on the cheek and squeezed her hand. "I'll be at the hotel if you need me."

Her gaze swiveled to Chase. "Thank God you're alive. If you hurt my dearest friend again, I will cut your heart out whether you are Reese's brother or not."

He nodded. "I missed you, too."

She sailed away, taking Mama and Papa with her. Her soothing words to Mama's many questions floated behind her as they left the cathedral.

And then the three of them remained.

Chase turned to Roger and assessed him from head to foot. The men took each other's measure before the ranger offered his hand. "Chase Calhan."

"I gathered as much from Rose's reaction. Roger King." The two men shook hands, and Rose tapped her foot.

"Roger, I—" She meant to apologize for all the trouble he went through and for leaving him at the altar, but he put a hand on her arm.

"Do not apologize, my dear. I had a message from Miss Evangeline Fairchild this morning and didn't know how to broach the subject. She explained that her father abducted her and sent her to France to prevent our marriage. Her situation has changed, and she spent a good deal of time and money to find me. She loves me, Rose, and wishes to marry."

Her mouth gaped open. "Then why didn't you tell me? I would have understood. I cannot believe you meant to follow through with the wedding when you love someone else."

"As you do?" One eyebrow quirked at her. "You know my reasons. I gave my word to help with the, er, situation, and I planned to honor my word. Now your ranger is here, there is no need, and I admit I am relieved. I go to the wharf to purchase fare for England. I wish you a loving, healthy, bounteous life together. You may telegram me with any questions." Turning on his heel, he all but danced to the door in delight.

They stood together in the empty cathedral as the door swung shut, leaving them alone.

"So, he's my would-be replacement?" A smile twitched at the corner of Chase's mouth.

"He's been very kind." Her chin lifted in defense.

"I see. I can be kind." A gleam entered his eye as he gazed down at her. "Want to see?"

She glanced at Chase, thankful he didn't catch Roger's reference to the situation, and bit her lip. "Before this goes any further, I require some explanations."

"Fine by me. Where would you like to go?" He gazed down at her white silk dress and gave her a wicked smile. "You cannot go out in your wedding gown. How about we go back to your room to talk."

Her stomach fluttered with excitement, and she dipped her head so he wouldn't see the desire in her eyes. God, she missed him, but there were things they needed to sort out before they fell in bed together.

"We can talk here." Crossing the aisle, she took her seat in a pew and folded her hands in her lap.

Disappointment flashed in his eyes as he took a seat beside her. "I assume you do not love Mr. King, or his departure would have caused you grief." He turned in the pew so he could gaze into her eyes.

"No. I do not. I agreed to marry him for a specific reason that had nothing to do with either of our feelings." She paused. "If I did love him, what would you do?"

His gaze turned mercurial. "Fight for you. Prove to you we belong together. To not be so goes against all the laws of nature. There is peace, joy, and so much love when we are together. I am sure the sun shines brighter. My world is better with you in it, and there is nothing I wouldn't do for you. I almost died three times, and each time, I came back to be with you. And I'm happy to do so again. I meant every word I said. You are the other half of my soul and the other half of my heart. Without you, life is not worth living." The heat and sincerity of his words soothed the cracks in her heart.

She believed he meant them. "Then there's something you need to know." Taking his hand, she placed his palm over her rounded belly. "You're going to be a papa. We thought you were dead, and Roger offered to marry me to give the child a proper name and place in society. I have no feelings for him other than gratitude for his kindness."

"Then I'll allow him to live."

She thought he jested until she caught the glint in his gaze. "Yes, please do. As you heard him say, he has a true love waiting for him." When he remained silent, she leaned forward. "He did not touch me. In the two months I've known him, we shared one chaste kiss. One I gave to him in gratitude."

Chase may or may not have heard, for he bent toward her rounded stomach and caressed her as if she were made of delicate porcelain. "God, I'm happy. This is the best wedding present any man could hope to receive." Kissing her silk-covered belly, he lifted her onto his lap and whispered to his child. "I love you."

She didn't know how to react and wound an arm around his neck for balance. "Who says we're getting married? I require an explanation, as I said earlier." She had two weddings planned, two wedding gowns, two grooms, and one walk down the aisle. Despite all of this, she remained single.

"Me and our child. What is the question? I have a serious need to show you how much I missed you. And our baby needs his papa to hold him." He took her trembling hand in his and stroked her fingers, sending shivers of delight through her.

She stared at him. "I wondered for weeks if you aimed at my heart and missed. I couldn't get over the fact you shot me."

"I'm sorry I left you to wonder about my actions for so long. My wounds were more serious than I thought." He told her about his time with the Apache medicine man. "He told me I had much to live for, and I agree. I love you. I want to marry you, to make more babies with you, and to grow old together." He caressed circles on her ramrod-stiff back. "I took you to my bed because you are the most desirable woman I ever met. I've thought about bedding you since the first moment I set eyes on you, too. And you didn't disappoint. I've thought of you and our time together in San Antonio every minute since. I plan to spend a lifetime holding you in my arms at night and loving you every way it's possible to love a woman. But I disagree with your assessment. You are special, and you do have talents. If I wanted a woman who could shoot, fight, and ride like I do, I would've married years ago. I waited because I wanted something different, *someone* different. Then I met you. You are so soft, so sweet, and so Goddamn beautiful with a heart as big as the sky. You laugh at my jokes and listen when I talk. You're my lover and my friend rolled into a sexy-as-hell body. And everything I dream about in a woman. There's only one you, Rose, and you're mine."

"And Rozita?" Clasping her hand over her chest, her broken heart lifted its shattered pieces from the floor into one jagged pile as the glue of his love put her back together again. Much like humpty-dumpty at the bottom of the wall.

Chase shrugged. "I kept thinking about what you said, and it didn't take me long to see you had her pegged. There were a couple of things she did which didn't make any sense. I kept her close because I needed her to lead me to Delgato, and to you. The way I figured the situation, he abducted you from your original captors."

"You said you hit what you aim at. If you're so good, why use knives?" She truly wanted to believe his explanation for shooting her.

He dropped his hand to her arm and caressed her up

and down in lazy strokes.

Her breath hitched in her throat, but she said nothing, wanting him to tell her everything.

"When I turned sixteen, I spent my time following Reese everywhere until I got as good as him. At eighteen, I traded a man for a pistol with a hair trigger. I pretended to be a famous gunslinger and practiced out back of the barn every day. I got surprisingly good at drawing and firing, fast too. I could shoot anything in front of me dead center without thinking. I drew, fired, and hit my target every time. My older sister, Madelaine, arrived for a visit one day with her son, Jeremy. The boy just turned ten and liked to follow me around like I followed my brothers. I lined a target up in my sights when he surprised me. I had my pistol out and pointed at his head before I thought twice. With the hair trigger on my pistol, only the good Lord's mercy kept me from killing him. The experience scared the living hell out of me. So, I put my gun away and learned to throw knives. I haven't used a gun with any regularity until El Diablo had his pointed at your head." He squeezed her. "I figured if I dropped you, it would throw him off balance and save your life. I couldn't think of anything else to buy you time."

"You still shot me." Her words sounded pathetic even to her own ears, but she didn't care.

Tilting her chin up, he stared into her eyes. "You must know El Diablo is one of the most ruthless sons-of-bitches around. He would have killed you if I had shown any emotion for you at all. I *had* to pretend I didn't care or watch you die. A situation I never care to be in again. I didn't make it to our wedding in Chicago to avoid this sort of thing. You will never know how much it hurt to find you missing or how desperately I searched for you.

When I discovered you at the general's, I wanted to tear everyone apart to get to you. But I had to wait for the right time, and it nearly drove me crazy. Then, when I spotted El Diablo alive through the doors of the auction room, I realized who orchestrated the whole affair and how much Rozita played me. I've never come so close to losing my self-control as when the devil touched you in front of me. But if I had so much as flinched, he would have killed you. I knew he had someone close by, out-of-sight to shoot me when I got close. He wouldn't come out in the open unless he made sure he would walk away unharmed. Everything I said and did bought you more time until I could figure out how to get you away from him."

"Rozita told him about me. He could have killed me anytime."

"True." Chase nodded. "But like you said, Rozita betrayed him, and he had to see if she spoke the truth about you. My reactions were all he cared about." Kissing her forehead, he smoothed her hair. "I'm sorry I had to shoot you. I knew if I did, I'd have a chance to save you. Will you forgive me, darlin'? Hurting you is the last thing I ever wanted to do."

"If you ever shoot me again, I'll shoot you back," she warned. "I'm not the kind of woman who enjoys bullets. So next time you want to give me a gift, try roses or chocolates. It'll be easier for me to consider as a token of your affection."

"Does this mean I'm forgiven? Because I'm anxious to get to the kissing part."

Chapter Twenty-Three

They made it back to the hotel in record time.

Shanna took one look at their faces and persuaded the Tanners to have dinner with her in the dining room.

The second her door closed behind them, Rose's blood caught fire. She found the buttons on the front of his shirt. "Show me how much you missed me." Slipping the buttons through the holes with trembling fingers, she drew his shirt from his glorious chest. Her breath hitched as she gazed at his warm hard flesh and ran her hands over the ridges and bands. God, how could he be so beautiful? Did she sin to lust after a man to this extent? If she did, she didn't care. For desire surged through her blood with such all-consuming force, she thought of little else.

Swallowing, she traced lines on his bronzed chest with her lips, and Chase groaned out loud.

His hands fumbled with the laces at the back of her gown. "How the hell do you get this thing off? I have half a mind to cut it. It's taking too damn long to come loose." Thrusting a knee between her quivering thighs, he struggled with her strings.

Biting her lip as her body hummed with anticipation, she reached behind her and tugged until the strings gave way. Her gown fell to the floor, and then her corset.

His gaze darkened as he stared at her straining breasts. "They're bigger." Tugging her chemise down, he lathed one hard nipple and then the other with his tongue.

She shuddered and leaned back, quaking with need. “It’s been so long.”

“I agree.” With reverent hands, he slid her chemise off over her head and stared. He drew featherlight caresses over her belly and bent his head to kiss her trembling body. “Papa is here now, and everything will be all right. I’m going to take care of you and make sure you and Mama are loved and safe.”

She couldn’t speak past the tightness in her throat. He did everything right, and love flooded her body and soul. “God, I missed you.” She couldn’t believe he hadn’t died and that he stood here in her room undressing her.

He picked her up in his arms and set her on the bed. Taking hold of her garter, he rolled her silk stocking down her leg, stroking and caressing her pale flesh as he went. His lips followed. Blazing a heated trail up the inside of one leg along her calf to the edge of her pantalets. Rose sucked in a breath and swallowed. She didn’t expect to have a man touch her for some time, if ever, and Chase’s lips made her quiver with longing.

He removed her other stocking in the exact same way and stopped when he reached her knee. “I don’t think we need these any longer, do you?” Catching the waistband of her pantalets, he drew them from her body and dropped them on the floor.

“No…o…o…” Her breath came fast as she stared up at him, wanting to taste and touch every inch of his glorious, bronzed skin.

For long seconds, he gazed at her nude body with hooded eyes. “You make me so hard for you.” Dropping his breeches and his underclothes with one swipe down his body, he lay there beside her.

"Love m-me." She gazed deep into his eyes and opened her knees to let him in.

His gaze darkened. "I am, and I do." Moving between her thighs, he kneeled and caught her bottom with both hands. "Don't let me hurt you. I've never made love to a pregnant woman before." He caught one rosy nipple between his thumb and forefinger and, leaning forward, caught the other with his lips. He suckled hard.

Rose bucked against the bed. Heat flooded the space between her legs as he worked her nipple between his fingers and suckled its twin. The friction drove her crazy, making her stomach jump and her breath hitch. His other hand moved from her bottom to her belly with featherlight strokes. His lips followed, licking, sucking, and nipping at her trembling body. He made his way down her stomach to the juncture between her legs and caught her hips with both hands.

She writhed against him. "What—" The core of her femininity throbbed with heated tension, and she ached for his fullness deep inside her.

His hot mouth closed over her nub and sucked her with gentle, delicate movements while she panted with desire. "Oh God, Chase—"

He understood despite her inability to speak. "I'm here, darlin'." His tongue flicked her next, sending ripples of pleasure through her.

She twisted beneath him, impatient for his possession. "More—"

One long finger penetrated her slick aching sheath as he flicked her with his tongue.

Rose thought for sure she would die of pleasure. Her

climax shimmered before her as she threw her head back and gave her body over to his expert lips and tongue.

And then he penetrated her with his tongue.

Her eyes flew open as her body shuddered against him. “I—”

He thrust faster and stroked her bud with his fingers. She died in a million flashes of brilliant color and fell apart in his arms. Shudder after shudder of satisfaction shook her body while he led her along the cliffs of ecstasy and into the sea of blissful oblivion.

Rocking back on his heels, he lifted her trembling hips up onto his and slid his aching rod into her heated tightness with one thrust. He gazed deep into her eyes. “I’ve thought about this moment for weeks. Hell, for months. Let me love you, Rose.”

Squeezing her eyes shut as memories of her dream flashed through her mind, she opened her thighs wider. Shaking with recent satisfaction, she gazed up at him, panting for air.

Chase stared at her glorious naked body and sucked in a breath. “God, you do things to me no other woman can.”

Rose cried out as he drove in deep, and he stilled. “Did I hurt you?”

“Nnnoo…you feel—”

Sliding his fingers between her silky folds while he rocked back and forth, she whimpered and shuddered in his arms. Her breath came fast, and her lips parted as he gazed at her face. Her eyes were squeezed shut, and her face flushed with pleasure. Moving her hands from his neck to his back, she caressed him.

“Your soft hands drive me crazy, and your heat grips me like a second skin.” Rocking faster and harder, he moaned with pleasure. "I'll never get enough of you, darlin'."

Wrapping her legs high around his waist, she rode the wave of blissful delight he created with increasing satisfaction. "Oh God, Oh God, Oh God."

He pumped harder and faster. Rose writhed in agony as the wave built higher and higher. The headboard hit the wall with a fast staccato. Bending down, he drew her nipple into his mouth and tugged while he rode her fast and deep. She drowned in a sea of pleasure so intense it consumed her with its ferocity. And then it happened. Her world split apart the second time and fell around her in jagged pieces of exquisite delight. Crying out, she arched against him as wave after wave washed over her. And he followed her over the edge. His release shook the foundation of his world, roaring through him with explosive force and soul-satisfying gratification. Groaning aloud, he plunged forward one more time before he fell against her, glistening with sweat.

They held each other close until their breathing returned to normal. Then Chase rolled to his side and tugged Rose into his arms. "You have no idea how much I wanted to love you again."

A smile curved her lips. "And you have no idea how much I wanted you to." She told him about her dream and how she woke with her clothes on the floor. "I dreamed you told me to take them off, and I must have done it in my sleep without knowing it."

Chase chuckled. "And here you thought you had no special talents."

She punched him.

Chapter Twenty-Four

They arrived in Chicago on September twentieth, five and a half months after Rose left in the wee hours of the morning to go find Chase.

Giles scheduled their second wedding to take place on Sunday, the twenty-ninth. They had nine days to get ready.

Shanna and her parents beat them home by a week. "I'm so happy you two worked things out and that you're both here. This time, there will be no backing out. You will be Mrs. Chase Calhan if I have to tie you both to the altar."

Rose hugged her back. "I've planned two weddings so far, and I don't care if I never get married as long as I have Chase." And she meant it. Magical weddings were wonderful but given the choice, she'd take the man any day. For with him came everything she ever dreamed of and more. She had more weddings than most women, and none of them compared to lying in her lover's arms.

Thinking of her other wedding reminded her. "Speaking of which…" She turned to Chase with a frown. "*Who is Grace?* You never did tell me."

His grin made her weak in the knees. "If you didn't read other people's messages, you wouldn't have to wonder."

"And I wouldn't have gone to Houston and helped Chief Tafford figure out he had a spy who leaked information to Delgato." Grinning in return, she couldn't help teasing him. "Which, in turn, led you to El Diablo. Both of whom are now dead because I committed a sin. You may thank me later."

"What is all this?" Shanna turned from one to the other. "I'm anxious to hear this story." Linking her arm with Rose, she walked with her to the drawing room. "I imagine Giles has a list to go over. Your wedding is in a few days, and we have so much to do. Your new gown arrived this morning. And don't ask me how he knows. He's Giles. We looked over the seating chart and got it in order. We do need you and Chase to settle on a cake. Then there's the matter of your honeymoon." She turned and studied Rose. "You look pale. Let's have tea, and you can fill me in." Leading her over to a settee, she sat beside her and ordered tea.

Chase followed and took a seat in an overstuffed chair.

Rose smiled. "It's complicated. Chase thought he killed El Diablo and sent the first telegram mentioning his arrival for the wedding. The one mentioning Grace." Her gaze swiveled to him, and her eyebrow rose in question.

Chuckling, he leaned back in his seat. "I will explain about Grace when you get done telling her about our adventures."

So, she did.

Shanna listened intently. "What happened to Ranger Kaplan?" She glanced at Chase and then back at Rose.

"The chief investigated a break-in at the hotel Kaplan took Rose to. And after the incident with Sam and the others, he discovered the man had intercepted a telegram meant for him alone. The traitor used the information to tell El Diablo's men which route Sam planned to take. I believe you know he sabotaged my second telegram so Rose would come to Houston searching for me. Kaplan hung for seditious conspiracy and murder while we were in San Francisco." Chase shook his head. "It's a damn shame he allowed his greed to overcome his principles."

Rose didn't know he died and shivered with remembered terror. Taking a deep breath, she finished her story and sat back with a sigh.

"Who told Rozita about you?" Her friend squeezed her fingers and waited.

Relating her talk with Chief Tafford and Ranger Kaplan's odd behavior, she shrugged. "Ranger Kaplan made the mistake of mentioning me to a fellow officer the day *before* I arrived. Since none of the Rangers knew about me but the chief, we knew where the leak came from. Kaplan sent a message to Delgato, which Rozita found."

Shanna's eyebrow rose, but she didn't comment. Rising to her feet, she gave Chase a hug. "Thank you for making my dearest friend so happy."

He chuckled. "In a week, she'll belong to me, and you'll have to get in line."

Shanna sniffed. "We'll see."

"And Grace?" Taking a slice of cake and a cup of tea from a servant, Rose leaned back and waited for Chase to begin.

"During the Civil War, my dad had command of the second regiment New York rifles. Toward the end of the war, he led his troops into the Mississippi River Valley. During one of their patrols, they found a woman outside camp asking to speak to their commander. She told Dad about a handful of militias burning her home and killing her servants. Claiming she hid her children to keep them safe, she begged Dad to help her, which he did.

Having no reason to doubt the woman's story, he led his men to the place she described and into an ambush, escaping by the hair of his head. The woman had no children, as it turned out, but led a bloodthirsty band of rebels determined to kill every Yankee they could find. More than half his men died that night, and he received massive wounds. During his illness, he sent letters to all his compatriots warning them of the woman's cunning to avoid any further slaughter. Then he wrote a letter to Mom expressing his sorrow for leaving her alone to raise their children. Expressing his love in eloquent words, he lost consciousness with the quill in his hand and died a week later.

His death almost destroyed my mother and became the reason behind our need to be lawmen.

Union soldiers caught and killed Grace Bennet the day they buried my dad. Her name became a code we use among us to convey the seriousness of a situation. *Saving grace* means ambush and possible death. *Tell Mom I love her* means, if you don't hear from me in a week, come find me. A week because Dad held on for five days after the slaughter while writing his love letter to Mom."

Silence filled the room as the two women digested the tragedy.

"I'm so sorry." Rising, Rose threw her arms around her wonderful lover and wept on his shoulder.

He held her close. "We take care of our own, darlin'. And you are part of us now, as is Shanna. You'll never be alone again. Not with this family watching your back."

Rose smiled. She loved being part of his world.

Shanna rose to her feet. "Time for a change of topic. We have a lot to be thankful for. With the wedding coming up and your safe return, I want to think happy thoughts. Reese had to run to New York to straighten out a situation with Madelaine and will be back tonight. You won't believe how big the girls got while you were gone. Maggie is on her way, and your parents are out for a walk in the park. I promised to send a messenger if you arrived while they were out."

"I'll do it." Chase offered. "I imagine you two have a lot to talk about, and I'll just be in the way." He chuckled. "After next Sunday, she'll be all mine, and we'll have to schedule any talks you two have around my need for my wife." He wiggled his eyebrows suggestively.

Rose blushed, and Shanna laughed. "Okay."

"I will see you later." Kissing her cheek, he strolled toward the door and disappeared."

The two friends climbed the stairs to the nursery. "The babies are in here." Shanna blew a breath out as she sat. "I wished your parents would have agreed to move to Chicago. I worry about them so far away, and the store I wanted to buy for them is just down the road. I would be able to keep an eye on them, and you would have a double reason to come to Chicago to visit."

"Your offer is very kind and generous. I wish they would have too, but I understand why they didn't. Papa is too proud to accept something he didn't earn with his own two hands." Rose shook her head. "Between you and me. I think he likes it in Rock Creek."

Shanna glanced up. "Why? What is there to like about Rock Creek?"

Rose smiled widely. "No competition."

Her friend laughed. "You make a good point. No one else would move so far into the middle of nowhere to open a store just to outsell Mr. Tanner."

She smiled as Rose picked one of the girls up. "Did you suppose a year ago we'd end up here, two old married women with babies?"

"No, I did not." She took a seat in a rocking chair.

Shanna grinned. "Giles has a cradle waiting in storage. He commissioned it three months ago."

Setting the baby down, she gazed at her friend in alarm. "Three months? How did he know?"

Shanna chuckled. "The man is a wonder, and I don't know what I'd do without him."

Rose smiled. "If he weren't so straightforward and kind, his intuition would be creepy."

Her friend did laugh then. "Not really. I take one look at your face and I know all about the wicked things you do with Chase when you two are alone together. From the glow you have, I'm guessing you two practice daily."

Rose had no comment and figured the heat in her face answered Shanna's question. She spent the afternoon with her and the twins enjoying the pure bliss of being here with them. Almost a year, they were both little butter balls and more advanced than other infants their age. Both the girls pulled themselves up to the furniture and stood on their own. Margret took a step the day before.

Shanna held Mary's chubby fingers and laughed as the baby took a step. "You are the smartest girl! Look at you. Daddy will be so surprised when he sees you walking around on your own." She caught the baby in her arms and kissed her rosy cheeks.

Rose smiled. She loved seeing her friend so happy. Shanna deserved it after the hard life she had. Margret crawled over and held her hands up. Laughing, Rose scooped her up. "What about you, Maggie? You cannot let Mary walk around without you." Setting the baby on her feet, she took her hands. "Let's go for a little stroll."

She led the baby across the nursery to the door and back.

Nanny appeared to settle the children for their naps before she made it all the way back to her seat.

Rose kissed both the babies and followed her friend from the room.

Her eyes grew moist as she considered all the ways she could have died and not made it back to Shanna or her parents. "Thank you for doing all of this for me."

Her friend offered Delaney Estates for the wedding when Chase announced their engagement. When they protested, she brushed their argument aside. "You're my best friend and Reese's brother. Where else are you going to get married?"

Stopping, Shanna gave her a hug. "I'm so happy you're back. I missed you and our little talks. Are you still worried Chase will find someone else? He had an opportunity with Rozita and didn't take it."

Rose shook her head. "If there's one thing I learned in all of this, Chase loves me like I am. He doesn't want anyone else. He says my heart is beautiful, and for once, I don't feel like I'm lacking. I'm whole, and I'm me. It's a wonderful feeling."

"We should go find Giles and see if he needs help with wedding plans. I'm sure he has a few things to go over with you."

"I've no doubt." Rose laughed and followed Shanna down the stairs.

An invaluable butler with their best intentions at heart, the man whipped up miracles on a regular basis.

Chase returned an hour later with the news. Maggie would arrive in the morning, and the Tanners were on their way back.

After dinner, Giles led Chase and Rose into the kitchen, where several cakes were lined up. He handed them slices of each one until they made their choice.

When they finished, her lover took her by the hand and led her out into the moonlight, stopping beside the fountain.

She turned to him as his arms closed around her. "I don't know how I will sleep without you." Trailing her fingers in the cool water, she shivered at the nip in the air.

He rubbed her arms to warm her. "I thought the same thing. But it's only a week, and afterward, we will be together for always."

"For always," Rose repeated. "I like the sound of those words." She leaned away. "Where are we going to live? El Diablo boasted about burning your ranch to the ground, and I have my work in San Francisco."

"I had word from my overseer in Houston before I left for San Antonio. The ranch house caught fire, but my hands were able to put it out before it did too much damage. We will stop by there after we return from our honeymoon and fix it up for us and our life together. In the meantime, we'll go to San Francisco and hire a different manager so we can go where we like."

"I love you, Chase Calhan, and I want you to know I'd live anywhere as long as it is with you."

"I'm glad they saved my ranch house, so we don't have to put your statement to the test." He kissed her hard. "It's going to be a long cold night without you in my bed, darlin'."

She couldn't agree more.

Chapter Twenty-Five

The wedding turned out fabulous.

Chase stood beside the altar and gazed at Rose as she glided toward him in her wedding gown. Sucking in a breath, he stared at her slim body and graceful posture. Her rounded belly added to the picture and made her more beautiful than ever. With her silky hair pinned in curls on her head and strung with pearls, she could pass for a princess. Her hands held a dainty bouquet of pink roses and baby breath, complimenting the delicate flush of excitement on her cheeks. Her soft chocolate eyes shone with love and devotion as she approached, and her entire body glowed with happiness.

Chase stared at the love of his life and couldn't breathe. He didn't deserve such a treasure as her. Not so long ago, he considered staying a bachelor. With danger lurking around every corner and the life he led, he didn't want to repeat his father's fate. But then he met Rose and hadn't been the same man since. Her sweet, gentle nature seeped under his skin and captured his heart.

He couldn't wait to spend the rest of his life loving her. Smiling when she drew near, he took her hand when her father offered it to him. Squeezing her fingers as she stood beside him, they faced the priest. Nine long days and nights without his Rose in his arms and in his bed were torture. He made the appropriate responses for the priest, but his mind focused on loving Rose. Halfway through the ceremony, he leaned over and made a suggestion on what to expect when they were alone.

His wife flushed bright red, and her hand trembled in his.

Chase chuckled.

Reese coughed behind him, and Shanna choked.

Maybe he whispered a little louder than he thought. An evil grin lifted the corners of his mouth. It served his brother right for eavesdropping.

Drawing his woman into his arms for a soul-shattering kiss after they were pronounced man and wife, finally, Chase turned to face his friends and family with Rose on his arm. He gazed at Max and Conner standing shoulder to shoulder on his left. Both his older brothers were self-confirmed bachelors and had no idea what the right woman would do to their lives when they found her. Boy, were they in for the time of their lives. He accepted their slaps on the back and congratulations with a grin and stepped back so they could hug Rose and welcome her to the family.

He turned to greet Maggie, his mother, beaming at him from the first row. She had to be the toughest, strongest woman he knew, and he owed her everything. Damn proud be her son, he accepted her hug with one of his own and prayed he'd be as good of a parent as she. Rose hugged her next with a murmur of contentment. His mother already accepted his wife as her daughter, and he couldn't be more pleased with their friendship.

He hugged Madelaine next and nodded at Jeremy standing stiffly by her side. Somewhere a good man waited for her too. She thought her life ended the day James Butler died, but Chase thought differently. His older sister still had a lot of life to live and a lot of love to give. Young Jeremy needed supervision, and the right man would keep him from falling in with the wrong crowd.

Chase accepted Reese's congratulations with a hug. "Thank you, brother, for taking care of my girl after I took my leave. You've always been there for me, and if you ever need anything, just holler."

Rose and Shanna hugged and cried, both talking at once, and he had no idea how they kept their conversation straight. When they broke apart, they hugged again and wiped the tears from their faces. Both smiled and turned to their men, satisfied with their talk. Chase glanced at Reese and shrugged. He grinned back and caught his wife by the hand.

They all returned to Delaney Estates for dinner, dancing, and cake.

When Rose changed into her traveling dress for their honeymoon abroad, she stood at the top of the curved staircase to toss her bouquet.

The guests gathered beneath her, laughing and calling suggestions on whom to throw it to. The bride turned her back, closed her eyes, and tossed it.

His brother Max caught the dainty flowers with a look of surprise. He took a quick step back and gazed up at Rose in confusion. "How did I get them? I stood to the side on purpose" Gazing at them for a second, he tossed them up in the air. "Someone else can have them. I will never marry."

The women in the crowd jumped to catch the offending bouquet.

Chase grinned. "Never say never, brother. The right woman will weasel her way into your life when you least expect it, and you'll be caught dead to rights."

Max grimaced and wandered off to find a glass of whiskey. “I wish you the best, Chase, but marriage is not for me.”

Taking his wife by the arm, Chase led her out the front door to the waiting carriage. With Rose in his life, he could do anything. Glancing at the sea of faces, he waved goodbye as they threw rice and well-wishes. Catching Rose and making her his had been the greatest adventure of his life and he’d do it all over again if the rewards were as sweet as they were this day and this minute.

Contentment and satisfaction settled around his wild, reckless heart. His solo days of riding hell-for-leather into trouble were over, and he was just fine with that. Together, he and Rose would do it all.

A word about the author…

I love to read and used to sneak romance books from my mom's room when she was gone. I cut my teeth on regency romance which grew to contemporary and on to fantasy. As an adult, I like the paranormal and occasionally dip my toe into dystopian.

I knit, crochet, and quilt. I love roses and the smell of gardenias makes me giddy with delight. My constant companions are my two large dogs. Beethoven is an Aussie/ Great Pyrenees mix and Mozart is a Mastiff/Collie mix.

I occasionally bake when the mood strikes me. Which isn't often because I consider cooking and baking necessary evils.

My husband of forty-one years is my greatest fan/critic and I don't know what I would do without him. My family is my greatest support and I love every minute I spend with them.

Thank you for purchasing
this publication of The Wild Rose Press, Inc.

For questions or more information
contact us at
info@thewildrosepress.com.

The Wild Rose Press, Inc.
www.thewildrosepress.com

www.ingramcontent.com/pod-product-compliance
Lightning Source LLC
Chambersburg PA
CBHW070058030726
47506CB00002B/513
* 9 7 8 1 5 0 9 2 5 2 6 4 0 *